You were born with potential.
You were born with goodness and trust.
You were born with ideals and dreams.
You were born with greatness.
You were born with wings.
You are not meant for crawling, so don't.
You have wings,
Learn to use them and fly.

What in your life is calling you?
When all the noise is silenced,
the meetings adjourned,
the lists laid aside,
and the wild iris blooms by itself
in the dark forest.
What still pulls on your soul?

Rumi

To the memory of my beloved mother, Ruth Margaret Urbanek. You were the inspiration for this novel, and I miss you every day. You showed me how to live an authentic life with courage and grace. I'm doing my best to pay it forward.

THE
BENNETT
WOMEN

By Roberta R. Carr

Cover art by Debora Strand. Cover design by ritawoodcreative. com. Back cover image by Andrew C. Carr.

ISBN: 978-0-692-44979-0

Printed in the United States

Other books by this author

Fiction
The Vernazza Effect
The Foundation

Non-fiction
The 8th Field Hospital

ONE

Oregon

Muriel Bennett loved her daughter, Susanne, but adored her granddaughter, Lilia. She sat at her kitchen table sipping coffee as her girls packed their belongings. Within the hour, the two of them would drive to the airport and fly in opposite directions, and she would have this big house to herself once again.

Muriel and her late husband had designed and built their dream home by the lake, and her favorite feature was its many windows. No matter where she sat, a spectacular view of nature welcomed her. From the kitchen table, she also could see down a long hallway that led to three bedrooms. She chuckled to herself as her granddaughter tiptoed out of one of them toward the front door. Muriel knew exactly where she was headed.

Lilia spotted her grandmother, pressed a finger to her lips and whispered, "I'll be right back." She had one foot out the door when Susanne caught up with her.

"Where are you going? You know we're leaving soon."

Lilia turned and groaned. "We have an *hour*, Mom. I want to say goodbye to Ben."

"Didn't you do that last night?"

Lilia rolled her eyes and walked away while Susanne sighed and returned to her bedroom to finish packing.

Muriel shook her head and wondered if the two of them would ever get along. A small flock of chickadees settled on a bird feeder, diverting her attention outside. The sun sprayed golden rays between towering pine trees as morning mist hovered over the lake's calm surface.

A week ago, Lilia had persuaded her to go canoeing, and navigating down the steps to her private dock had proved challenging. Muriel had experienced a moment of dizziness, but Lilia hadn't noticed, thankfully. Muriel stepped carefully into the canoe as she held her granddaughter's hand. Lilia hopped in and pushed off as Muriel dropped her head back, welcoming the sun's warmth on her face. It felt heavenly being on the lake once again.

"Wish I didn't have to leave so soon, Gran. I'm sure going to miss you."

"And I'll miss you, my sweet girl."

"Can you believe this is my last year of college?" Lilia moved the paddle through the water, first one side then the other, in a slow and steady rhythm. "I probably won't be home for the winter holidays. Busy concert schedule."

"Yes, but we had a wonderful summer, didn't we?"

Susanne entered the kitchen and dropped two brochures on the table, jarring Muriel from her pleasant memory.

She pulled a mug from a shelf and filled it with coffee before sitting opposite Muriel at the table. "Thanks for letting Lilia spend the summer, Mom."

"No need for thanks. She's a pleasure to have around."

Susanne's eyes shifted between Muriel and the brochures. "She and I are both worried about you living here alone. This place is too big and isolated."

Muriel braced herself for the onslaught as her daughter's eyes bore down on her. Susanne had arrived three days ago and had disappeared one afternoon. Muriel had overheard her talking to someone on the phone about residential care, but hadn't said a word, not wanting to stir trouble.

"Do you really need so much room? Four bedrooms? Three baths? It's way too much for one person to manage."

Muriel picked up the glossy flyer entitled "East River Retirement Living." The cover had a picture of a young woman sitting next to a gray-haired lady in a fancy gazebo. Both models wore broad smiles revealing unnaturally white teeth, reminding her of mini glaciers. A picture-perfect background of blue sky, fluffy clouds, manicured grass and blooming lilac rounded out the scene. "And you think I'd be better off living here?" She waved the marketing material in the air.

"All I'm asking is for you to have an open mind. Take a tour. I think you'll be impressed with the place."

Muriel had an open mind, but not one Susanne valued. "I'm comfortable living here for now. But I'll let you know if things change."

Susanne's face grew flush, just like when she was a teenager and didn't get her way. "What will it take for you to—"

Muriel set the brochure on the table and pushed it toward Susanne. "Would you like a sandwich to take on the plane? Maybe ham and Swiss?"

"Avoiding this conversation doesn't help. If something happens to you, I have to pick up the pieces. Let's be proactive for both our sakes."

Susanne's buzzwords irked Muriel down to her core, making her feel like a corporate minion who must follow orders or lose a job. "I'm going to be *proactive* and pack a lunch for Lilia." She pushed away from the table and moved toward the refrigerator as Susanne rubbed her temples.

Next door, Lilia and Ben sat comfortably in two chairs on his backyard deck, facing the lake. "Thanks for teaching me backgammon this summer. It's a fun game," Lilia said.

He balanced a cane between his knees, resting both hands on top. "We sure had some close ones."

"I still don't get—"

Lilia's phone vibrated, so she pulled it from her back pocket and glanced at the screen. "It's a friend from school. Do you mind?" She began talking without waiting for a reply.

"Hey, Joel! Miss me?"

"I always miss you. When's your flight?"

"This morning at eleven-thirty. I texted Peter."

"Did you practice?"

"Of course! Why would you even ask?"

"No reason. It's just…we're eager, you know, to get our group practice started."

Lilia spoke with him for a few more minutes before ending the call, sighing loudly. Had he called to make her feel guilty for spending time with Gran instead of attending a music program? She had practiced the cello every day, probably more hours than the rest of them combined. She knew the quartet had a busy—

"Is everything all right?" Ben asked, interrupting her thoughts.

"Sorry about that." Lilia lifted her chin toward Muriel's house next door. "Mom's waiting so I better get back." She leaned over and hugged him. "I don't know when I'll see you again."

"I'll be here." He smiled warmly. "Who knows? I might even go to your graduation with Muriel."

"I'd really like that, Ben." She gestured toward the house again. "I need to run. Take good care of yourself." After a final hug, she dashed off.

Lilia returned to Muriel's house and found her mother

standing in the living room talking harshly to someone on her cell phone. Susanne tapped her wristwatch as Lilia raced past to gather their suitcases and pile them into a rental car.

Susanne came outside after finishing her conversation, tossed a briefcase into the trunk, and slammed it shut. Lilia had seen her mother's distant, annoyed look many times and knew a problem was brewing.

"Everything OK, Mom?"

"Business that couldn't wait. Nothing for you to worry about." Susanne gestured toward the house. "Let's say our goodbyes so we can leave."

Lilia sighed with frustration over her mother's easy dismissal, but what else could she do? She had learned long ago that silence was the best defense when it came to Susanne Bennett. Further questioning would only make things worse, so she followed her mom into the house without saying another word.

Susanne entered the living room and looked around, but Muriel was nowhere in sight. She called out, "Mom? Where are you?"

"Photo hallway," Muriel shouted back.

Susanne waited for her to appear, but when it didn't happen she sighed and walked toward her mother's voice with Lilia in tow.

Muriel looked up from a long wall of family photos. "Do you know I don't have a single picture with the three of us together? I have individual photos, some of the two of you, many of Lilia and me, but none of the three of us." She glanced at the photos again before asking, "Can we pose for a formal portrait next time we're together?"

"Of course, Gran. Whatever you want." Lilia hugged her tenderly. "Ben said he might come with you to my graduation. Wouldn't that be something?"

Muriel nodded and touched Lilia's face, wanting to savor its beauty. "Take care of yourself, sweetheart. I'll sure miss having you here with me."

Susanne tapped her watch again. "We need to leave, Lil."

Lilia used her phone's camera to take a selfie with her grandmother. "I'll send this to you later. Don't forget to check your email."

Susanne leaned over and gave Muriel a quick hug. "Please think about East River, Mom. It'll be so much less for you to worry about. You'll make new friends."

Muriel nodded to save the peace. She had survived her daughter's visit without a serious blowup and wanted Lilia to leave with only happy memories, not one of she and Susanne arguing at the last minute. Besides, a nod didn't mean agreement.

The Bennett women walked outside and said their farewells. Muriel stood at the end of the driveway and waved until the car disappeared down the gravel road, leaving a dust wake. Susanne would fly home to California, Lilia would return to college in Boston, and life would continue for her on Lake Woahink. She brushed away a tear while thinking about how difficult goodbyes were starting to become for her.

She loved Lilia so much and would miss their evening talks, cooking together, playing music and painting. She loved Susanne, too, but not in the same way. She and her daughter had performed a quiet dance of pretense for years now, and it was too late for them, but not for Lilia. Muriel had passed all of her hopes and dreams onto her granddaughter, and if prayers could carry her toward a happy future, she would never have a disappointing day in her life.

A profound sadness squeezed Muriel's heart as she ambled toward the house. She liked to pretend that carefree summers with her granddaughter would last forever, but she needed to face a grim reality: eighty-two years and declining health numbered her days on this earth.

She slowly climbed the steps leading to her redwood deck and sat on a chair, gazing at the lake. This place—the trees, birds, water, serenity—had been her sanctuary for more years than she could remember. Muriel knew there was a time for everything: a time to be born, a time to die, a time to plant, a time to uproot, a time to laugh and a time to weep.

The one thing she didn't know was how to reconcile all parts of her life, so when that final curtain came plunging down, she would die with no regrets.

Two

Oregon, Four Months Later

Catherine had been Muriel Bennett's closest friend and next-door neighbor for over thirty years, and she sensed that something wasn't quite right this evening. She sat in her living room next to a cozy fire, watching an old Bette Davis movie to distract herself from a growing uneasiness.

The two women prided themselves on being stubbornly independent as they navigated their eighties, and often joked about living the good life on Lake Woahink's geriatric row. For several years now, they had an agreement. Every night before Muriel turned in, she would lock her door then flash her porch light twice. Catherine, a night owl, never went to bed until she saw the signal, and once spotted, she would return it. The ritual provided a moment of peace inside days burdened with unspoken worry over the fragility of their lives.

Neither Catherine nor Muriel had any intention of ending up in a nursing home like Ben's wife, Esther. That couple had been Muriel's other next-door neighbors for two decades, and her Alzheimer's had devastated all of them. They lost their fourth bridge player, Ben's best friend gradually vanished, and an aching sorrow hovered like fog over their lives. Fate had dealt Esther a cruel blow, but she was oblivious, lost in a world that no one understood. Ben, Muriel and Catherine, however, lived every day in the currents of her tragedy.

A window in Catherine's living room faced Muriel's front porch, and after the cuckoo clock struck nine-thirty without a flash from Muriel, Catherine phoned her. Five rings resulted in voice mail, so she pushed out of the recliner, put on a coat, and headed over to check on her friend.

The moonless night made the lake look like a huge black hole in the earth, a no man's land. Water lapped on the shore, and Catherine's breath lingered in the chilly air like puffs of cigar smoke. She pulled her coat tighter while stepping carefully on the flagstone path that linked the two homes, using a flashlight to guide her way. After ringing Muriel's bell and getting no response, she opened the door and walked inside.

"Muriel? It's Catherine. You all right?"

No response.

Muriel never went out at night without telling her or Ben, a promise between friends who looked after each other. Catherine raised her voice. "Muriel? Is everything OK?"

Still nothing.

Catherine closed the door and looked around. Lights were on, soothing music from a Vivaldi string sonata played softly in the background, and everything seemed in order. She passed through the living and dining rooms on her way to the art studio. Muriel had often lost herself in painting, occasionally ignoring time completely. Catherine hoped to find her dear friend sitting at the easel.

She flipped on the light and looked around. Muriel's late husband had built the studio to include everything on his wife's wish list: large space, student easels and ample storage. During the day, a wall of windows brightened the vast room and provided Muriel with an unrestricted view of the lake. Her impressive paintings hung on the towering walls, but she was nowhere in sight.

A portrait-in-progress rested on Muriel's easel, making Catherine smile. One evening last August, Ben saw Muriel's granddaughter, Lilia, walk alone to the backyard deck carrying her cello. She had stood and gazed at the lake, lost in melancholy for the longest time. Ben had almost turned away, feeling like an intruder on a private moment. Instead, he had picked up his Nikon camera.

Lilia's long golden hair blew in the breeze as she sat on a bench and positioned the instrument between her knees. She held the bow, closed her eyes, and started playing for an audience of frogs and fish. She lost herself in the music; the cello became her partner in a mellow conversation. As the soulful notes floated on rays of sunshine, Ben immortalized the scene with his Nikon's telephoto lens.

After Lilia had returned to school, Ben had given

the pictures to Muriel, who cried tears of pure joy over what he had captured: her beloved granddaughter in her essence. Those images had inspired her current painting, which would become Lilia's college graduation gift.

Catherine left the studio, her fear growing with each failed sighting. "Muriel, where are you?" She turned down a short hall leading to the kitchen and gasped, covering her mouth with both hands to suppress a scream. Muriel lay sprawled on the floor between a large kitchen island and the stove with her eyes closed, an area rug crumpled at her feet.

She hurried to her side. "Oh, Muri…" Catherine's heart pounded in her ears—*thump, thump, thump*—as she hovered over her friend, shaking her shoulder. "Muriel! Wake up!" Her mind froze in a moment of disbelief. She finally stood and searched frantically for a telephone. She dialed nine-one-one and begged a dispatcher to send help right away.

Next she called Ben for support. He answered with a sleepy voice.

Catherine cried, "Muriel's in trouble! Come quick!"

The line disconnected without Ben replying, but Catherine knew he would arrive soon. She settled next to Muriel, holding her hand and saying every prayer she knew. Seconds became minutes; minutes seemed like hours as Muriel's chest rose and fell with each breath. Catherine glanced at pieces of a broken dinner plate that had launched spaghetti and salad everywhere. Silverware lay scattered on the floor, and one of Muriel's shoes had come off. Her dear friend must have fallen hard to cause this chaos.

Ben arrived and struggled to bend down on one knee to get a closer look. "How is she?" He cupped Muriel's hand, assessing her condition and murmuring words of comfort.

"Oh, Ben, how'd this happen?" Catherine's brain raced with questions that didn't have clear answers. "Should we call Susanne? Or Lilia?"

He shook his head. "Muriel wouldn't want that. Not yet, anyway." When a siren sounded in the distance, Ben looked up. "Let's wait and see what happens." It took a Herculean effort, but he pulled himself upright using his cane and the kitchen counter. "You stay with her. I'll go meet them." He shuffled toward the front door and found two neighbors standing on the porch.

"I saw the lights from across the street and got worried," Robin said as she held her ten-year-old daughter's hand. "Is Muriel OK?"

Ben ruffled young Jasmine's hair, a surrogate grandfather's kind act. He spoke to Robin while rubbing his neck. "No, she's not. Catherine found her passed out on the kitchen floor." He squinted toward the siren. "It might be best to take Jasmine home. I'll call after we learn more."

Robin glanced at the ambulance's flashing red light

as it pulled into the driveway. She reluctantly nodded and said, "I'll be waiting to hear from you," before stepping away.

The first responders rushed up the driveway with a wheeled stretcher. "She's in there," Ben said, pointing toward the kitchen. "Please take good care of her."

The ambulance raced to Oregon General Hospital as Catherine and Ben sat in Muriel's living room to gather their wits. Catherine broke the silence. "Susanne needs to know about this. Lilia can wait, but not Susanne. We should call her."

As Muriel's best friend, Catherine had a unique perspective on the Bennett women, having witnessed their family drama play out in various ways over the years. She knew firsthand how much they loved one another, but there was a dark side. When Muriel's son died in the Vietnam War, a part of her died, too. Poor Susanne took second place to Muriel's grief. The girl longed for her mother's affection until the day she left for college. Even after all these years, they still had a strained, complicated relationship.

Notifying Susanne about Muriel's accident seemed like the obvious next step, but it wasn't that clear cut. Once involved, Susanne would insert herself into the decision-making process, making Muriel's life more complicated. Catherine had seen it happen many times.

But things were different for Lilia, Susanne's daughter. Muriel had loved her only grandchild unconditionally since birth, and twenty-two summers together at the lake house had only strengthened their bond. They connected through art, music, love and acceptance, and Muriel was fiercely protective of her. She would never disrupt Lilia's music studies unless it was absolutely necessary.

"Let's go to the hospital. Maybe she's awake," Ben suggested.

Catherine nodded. "If she's still unconscious, we'll call Susanne. Agreed?"

"Sounds about right." Ben slowly stood and sighed. "Will you drive? I don't see too well at night anymore."

The two friends tidied the kitchen, not wanting Muriel to come home to a messy reminder of the accident. They turned off the lights and music, and on the way out, Catherine flipped the porch's light switch up, down, up, down, up.

Ben squinted at the brightness and read Catherine's mind. "I hope she'll be here tomorrow to do that for herself."

THREE
ಬಂಡಿ

Oregon

Catherine and Ben arrived at the hospital's emergency department and introduced themselves to a woman sitting behind a reception desk. When they asked about Muriel, the woman punched a few keys on a computer and said, "Mrs. Bennett arrived forty-five minutes ago."

"May we see her?"

The lady shook her head no. "She's having x-rays right now." She glanced at the computer again. "How well do you know her?"

"We're close friends and neighbors. Why?"

"We have her records, but I need to verify some of the information."

Catherine answered questions about Muriel's medical insurance, social security number, birthday, home address, next of kin, medications, and allergies without hesitation. Afterward, the receptionist directed them to a waiting area where they joined several other people who looked as tired as they felt. The room's decor included a flat-screen television that was broadcasting the national news, rigid chairs, and a rack of reading material placed next to a bottled water dispenser.

Ben selected a magazine and sat down to read, but his chin soon dipped, causing the *Field & Stream* to slip through his fingers and land on the floor. Catherine retrieved it and thumbed through the pages to pass the time, wishing she could silence the TV.

Sometime after midnight, a woman dressed in a white coat and blue scrubs stepped into the waiting room. "Is anyone waiting for Muriel Bennett?"

Catherine tossed her magazine aside and said, "We are," while shaking Ben awake and making introductions.

The woman smiled and extended her hand. "I'm Collette Anderson, her doctor. It's nice to meet you. Mrs. Bennett thought you might be here. She asked me to speak with you about her condition."

"How's she doing?" Ben said, rubbing the sleep from his eyes.

"She's awake but has a concussion and two fractured ribs."

Ben gripped Catherine's arm like a life preserver. "What does that mean?"

The doctor sat next to them and explained. "Mrs. Bennett hit the back of her head hard enough to cause a bump. She woke with a headache and some dizziness but doesn't remember much about the accident."

Catherine and Ben were speechless.

"As her brain heals from the trauma, she may experience short-term difficulty with concentration and balance. Time will tell."

Catherine covered her mouth to suppress a gasp.

Brain trauma? After regaining her composure, she inquired about Muriel's ribs.

"X-rays revealed two middle rib fractures that we're
treating with ice packs and pain meds. She's very lucky
the fall didn't cause a hip or arm fracture."

Catherine found difficulty in accepting the word
lucky to describe any aspect of Muriel's condition. She
asked the doctor if she could bring Muriel home, already knowing the answer, but needing to ask anyway.

"Not tonight. I want to monitor her closely for the
next twenty-four hours to make sure she doesn't have
complications."

Catherine knew Muriel wouldn't like being admitted to the hospital, but what could any of them say or
do about it now? "May we see her?"

"Yes, but just a short visit. She needs to rest." Dr.
Anderson pulled a paper from her pocket and glanced
at it. "Records indicate that her closest relative is a
daughter who lives in Northern California. Does she
know about her mother's accident?"

Catherine and Ben glanced at each other. "The
three of us look after one another." Catherine pointed
at the receptionist. "I answered all her questions."

The doctor played with her stethoscope while
studying Ben and Catherine closely. "You're obviously
good friends, but the daughter should be notified. Her
mother sustained serious injuries, and she's not out of the
woods yet." She paused. "Would you like me to call her?"

Ben rubbed the back of his neck. "We know Susanne well. May we call her in the morning?" He held up his watch. "It's pretty late."

Dr. Anderson took a moment before responding, looking back and forth between Catherine and Ben. "That should be fine." She stood and motioned for them to do likewise. "Shall we go and check on Mrs. Bennett? I bet she'll be happy to see the two of you."

Muriel lay in a bed connected to machines that monitored her heart and respiration rates as an IV delivered fluids to her body. She looked deathly pale as Catherine and Ben stood next to her, shaking their heads.

After a few minutes, she slowly lifted her eyelids. A weak voice emerged. "Guess my disco days are over."

Catherine's eyes moistened as she held Muriel's hand. "I hope you never quit dancing, disco or otherwise."

"You sure gave us a scare, old girl," Ben said. "You feeling better?"

"Got a little headache, but I'll survive."

Catherine leaned close and whispered, "Doctor Anderson wants us to call Susanne. Is that OK with you, Muri?"

"Please don't. I'll be fine." Muriel closed her eyes while taking a painful, shallow breath. "And *please* don't bother Lilia. She doesn't need to worry about this."

After a halfhearted nod, Catherine said, "It's late,

and your doctor wants you to rest. You need anything before we go?"

Muriel considered the question. "There's a package for Lilia on the kitchen counter. Would you mail it?" She closed her eyes and took another difficult breath.

"Sure thing," Ben said. "Anything else?"

"No. Just that."

Ben kissed her forehead. "Sleep well, old girl. We'll see you tomorrow."

"Promise that you'll follow orders, Muri," Catherine begged. "We need you back home with us."

Muriel gently clasped each friend's hand. "I love"—she yawned, then pushed out the words—"I love you both so much." She closed her eyes and drifted off to sleep.

Catherine drove home and parked in Ben's driveway. She let the car idle as she gathered her thoughts. "What time shall I pick you up tomorrow?"

"How does ten sound? We need our sleep, and I promised to give Robin an update." Ben glanced toward Muriel's home. "We'll mail Lilia's package on the way to the hospital. And I know Muriel said not to call Susanne, but maybe we should. You know how—"

Catherine gently covered his hand with hers to comfort him. "Try not to worry, Ben. We'll figure things out like we always do. Right now, let's focus on keeping Muriel's spirits up."

He rubbed his forehead and sighed loudly. "I never imagined saying this, but maybe a home caregiver isn't such a bad idea. Muriel may not recover as quickly this time."

"Let's not go there just yet. Remember our pact? It's her choice, no one else's."

"You're right, of course. Please ignore the ramblings of a tired old man." A chilly wind blew into the car as Ben opened the door. "G'night, Catherine. Thanks again for the lift."

He shuffled up the walkway then turned and waved before entering the house. After the front door closed, the porch light flashed twice. Ben had never done that before, and the gesture unleashed emotions in Catherine that had been accumulating all evening.

Their world was rapidly changing, and none of the rules were clear. No one had given them instructions on how to grow old gracefully. Catherine, Ben and Muriel wanted to end life on their terms, but what did that actually mean? Was stashing pills the answer? Or praying for a fatal heart attack during sleep? Maybe falling on a kitchen floor and not being discovered until it was too late? Death was nipping at their heels, and they couldn't run any faster.

She glanced at Muriel's house while drying her eyes, telling herself that everything would turn out fine, but this time felt different, more ominous. The accident had stirred a sense of foreboding inside of her that couldn't be explained, like an invisible threat. She bowed her head and prayed for a miracle, desperately willing a speedy recovery for Muriel so life could return to normal on Lake Woahink's geriatric row.

FOUR

ଽୢେଓଞ

Northern California

Susanne Bennett woke before dawn in her Los Altos Hills mansion. She rarely needed more than six hours of sleep, and it had always been that way. Her high energy level had riled her family on more than one occasion, but it served her well in college, graduate school, and corporate America.

The unguarded moments before dawn were often the most unsettling as her mind leaped all over the place. Even though she had been divorced for two years, she still slept on her side of the bed, leaving Jim's space untouched. Twenty-six years of togetherness had created certain habits that weren't easily broken. His abrupt departure three years ago had knocked her off balance, but she never let on for their daughter's sake.

Her marriage to Jim Parker had seemed rock solid; he was the yin to her yang. His reasons for leaving were such a midlife cliché: "We don't have anything in common anymore."—"I want to live my life authentically." —"You're married to your job instead of me."

The truth was more painful than the excuses. He had traded her in for a younger model: youth instead of wisdom, beauty instead of brains. So much for loyalty. At least he had the decency not to leave before Lilia left for college, sparing her their drama.

A pinkish orange light broke through the dark eastern sky, as Susanne retrieved her phone from the nightstand. As CEO of her company, she needed to keep her finger on the pulse of the world's economy. Since work never stopped in the six time zones that impacted her business, even Saturdays required monitoring. She scanned *The Wall Street Journal* and the headlines from *The New York Times*. Everything from mergers, legislative changes, and political races to the price of fuel and terrorist activities affected her organization.

Susanne checked the weather in Boston where her daughter, Lilia, attended school—forty-nine degrees and partly cloudy—then slid out of bed, dressed in running gear and headed out the front door. She had asked Lilia to join her on these early morning runs many times, but she had always refused, saying "Running is your thing, Mom, not mine."

Susanne followed a series of connecting paths, crisscrossing her way through town until she reached miles of open space trails. She did some of her best thinking during these early morning jaunts. She posed a problem at the beginning, and a solution would often emerge by the end. Today the subject was Vietnam. Her technology company needed a larger manufacturing plant, and Southeast Asia provided the perfect location to build one. As an emerging nation on the international business scene, Vietnam offered favorable taxes and had a low-cost workforce. Both features would reduce expenditures, adding millions to her company's bottom line. Her VP of manufacturing, Dave Simms, and his team had been in Ho Chi Minh City for weeks working with their Vietnamese counterparts to finalize the deal. Negotiations were getting tense, and even though a letter of intent had been signed, the final contract had not.

By mile seven, Susanne's elderly mother had replaced Vietnam on her worry list. Muriel lived alone in Oregon, and her health was slowly deteriorating. Last May, a chest cold turned into pneumonia, requiring hospitalization. Osteoporosis and arthritis had begun chipping away at her mother's body, yet Muriel pretended nothing was wrong. A month ago, she fired the second caretaker Susanne had hired. Why couldn't she see the risk of living alone? Normal people acknowledge problems and accept help, but not Muriel Bennett. She had an inverse reaction to all things practical, using irritating humor to sidetrack every conversation Susanne tried having with her. "I want to live my next life backward," she would say, quoting George Carlin. "I'd wake up in a nursing home feeling better each day, and then get kicked out for being too healthy." Her mother could be such a stubborn and unrealistic woman at times.

After she returned home, Susanne's body thanked her for the workout, but an imp had invaded her brain, continuing to taunt her about Muriel and Vietnam. Her live-in housekeeper greeted her with a cool glass of water and inquired about breakfast.

She took a long drink then returned the glass. "Fruit, yogurt and your homemade granola, please. Give me twenty minutes to shower."

After breakfast, Susanne worked in her home office for the next few hours pouring over financial sheets, reading a board of directors report, and contemplating the Vietnam venture. Her phone's ringtone jarred her from the corporate cloud.

"Hello, Dave. I've been thinking about you."

He laughed nervously. "Should I be flattered or worried?"

Susanne got to the point. "What's happening over there?"

"The Vietnamese stepped away from the table. They're holding out for a shorter land-lease option, which pisses me off. We've been very clear about our position. And don't get me started about our numerous concessions. It's time to call their bluff."

Susanne closed her eyes as her neck tensed. This wasn't the news she wanted to hear. "What needs to happen to get them back talking?"

"Their chairman wants to meet with you. In person next week. I'm told it's a sign of respect, but who knows? These people are hard to read."

These people? Pissed off? Susanne let Dave's inappropriate comments slide knowing he faced a lot of pressure to close the deal. She scanned her calendar: product website launch on Monday, budget meeting on Tuesday, fly to New York on Wednesday to meet with product development, strategic meetings with marketing about February's trade show.

Seeing no opening for the next several weeks, she weighed the pros and cons of sending her CFO or another high-ranking executive in her place. She rubbed her temples, intuitively knowing what needed to be done, but her mind kept whirling.

"Susanne? You there?"

"I'll get working on my flight arrangements."

Dave released a loud, happy sigh that he didn't try to hide. "Great! Is there anything you need from me before you arrive here?"

"Just keep all communications open, Dave. This is a big one; we can't lose it."

Susanne opened the French doors in her office and breathed in fresh air. She stared at her backyard oasis, mindlessly focusing on a stone waterfall that cascaded into a Caribbean-blue pool. The gentle, rhythmic splashing had a soothing effect on her.

Although she'd never traveled to Vietnam, she had visited the country many times in her mind—and not just for business. The country had cast a shadow over her life like a solar eclipse. The eerie twilight created by the natural phenomenon lasted only minutes, but for Susanne and her mother, the darkness had never ended.

Susanne continued to rub her temples as her body began to quiver. For a moment, she was no longer a successful CEO leading a multibillion-dollar technology company, nor a person named in *Forbes'* "World's 100 Most Powerful Women" list. Instead, she became a terrified nine-year-old child, reliving the day that changed her life.

FIVE
ഇരുങ്ങ

Oregon

Catherine woke early from a restless night's sleep and prepared coffee, toast, and a soft-boiled egg for breakfast. She tried reading the newspaper but flitted from article to article, not finishing a single one. By nine-fifteen, she couldn't wait any longer, so she phoned Ben.

"Good morning, Catherine. How'd you sleep?"

"Not well. You?"

"About the same." He paused. "I talked to Robin. She wants to clean Muriel's house today. A welcome home gift."

"That's thoughtful. Does she know where to find the hidden key?"

"I showed it to her this morning before I picked up Lilia's package." Ben cleared his throat. "I'm ready whenever you are."

After leaving the UPS store, Catherine and Ben drove to the hospital. "When should we call Susanne?" Ben asked as he twisted his wedding band back and forth.

Catherine tapped her finger on the steering wheel, mulling the question. Finally she said, "Let's check on Muriel first. You know how Susanne likes facts." She glanced at Ben. "You agree?"

He turned away and stared out the passenger window. "Sounds about right."

Catherine turned into the hospital's parking lot. "Maybe Muriel will come home today and we won't have to call anyone."

Ben sighed as he pointed to an empty parking space close to the front entrance. "Wouldn't that be something?"

Catherine and Ben entered Muriel's room and found her gazing out a window. "You're looking better," Ben said, causing Muriel to turn their way. "Those nurses must be taking good care of you."

Muriel's eyes brightened. "Oh, what a nice surprise."

Catherine gave her a big hug. "How are you? That headache gone?"

"Not quite, but it's better."

"Any news about coming home?" Ben asked after hugging her, too.

Muriel scrunched her face. "My doctor won't say, but I'm pretty sure"—she held her chest while pushing up in bed—"I'll be here another night." She wore a teasing smile. "I don't know if I'm more worried about losing my money, mobility, or marbles. All three seem to be disappearing before my eyes."

Ben chuckled as he motioned toward her chest. "Painful to breathe?"

"A little."

Catherine sat down in a chair next to the bed. "Doctor Anderson asked us to call Susanne last night. We didn't, but maybe we should do that now."

Muriel glared at her. "You sound like a social worker who visited me earlier this morning. She screeched like a parrot, 'Call Susanne, call Susanne, call Susanne.' I told her to fly away and leave me in peace."

Catherine and Ben glanced at one another but didn't say anything.

Muriel continued, "If I called, all Susanne would do is harp about me living alone." She pressed her hand to her chest and closed her eyes while taking a difficult breath. "Why put myself through that aggravation?"

Ben idly tapped the floor with his cane. "Susanne and Lilia love you, Muriel. They'd want to know about this so they could help you."

"Lilia's busy with her music, and Susanne…well, you know her story." Muriel closed her eyes, taking another shallow breath. "I just don't want…" She squeezed her eyes shut and held her chest, gasping for air. "Something's not right…can't breathe."

Catherine and Ben exchanged panicked looks before Catherine charged out of the room, returning with a nurse.

"What's wrong, Mrs. Bennett?"

"Hard to…breathe…chest hurts," Muriel cried.

"On a scale of one to ten, how severe is the pain?"

"Twelve."

"The nurse yanked the call button and yelled, "Page Doctor Anderson now!" She placed a blood pressure cuff around Muriel's arm, then took her pulse and temperature.

Within minutes, the room teemed with medical personnel. Ben and Catherine stepped into the hallway, feeling frightened and useless. A man in scrubs pushed a gurney past them and turned into Muriel's room. A short time later he exited, whisking her away down the long hallway.

Catherine and Ben approached Dr. Anderson, who was typing on a computer at the nurse's station. "Hello. Remember us? We're Muriel's friends."

The doctor looked up and nodded, but didn't smile.

"What happened to Muriel?" Ben asked.

"I'm guessing she has a collapsed lung. I've sent her to radiology for a CT scan to confirm it."

"A collapsed lung?" Catherine asked, not understanding what that meant.

"A fractured rib probably punctured a lung during yesterday's fall. We'll know more after the test."

Catherine and Ben looked at each other, wondering what to do next. Dr. Anderson broke the silence. "Have you spoken to her daughter?"

"No. Not yet. Muriel didn't want—"

"I understand there are issues between them, but this is serious. Mrs. Bennett isn't thinking clearly right now. She needs you to do that for her." Dr. Anderson glanced at her watch. "I'm leaving to check on her soon. Now is a good time to make that call."

The doctor finished typing, then rushed down the corridor in Muriel's direction.

Ben watched Dr. Anderson until she vanished around a corner then spoke to Catherine. "She's right, you know. We should call Susanne."

Catherine found a chair and placed her face in her hands, trying to reconcile the right thing to do for Susanne *and* Muriel. More than anything, she wanted to pretend that none of this was happening. She closed her eyes and imagined the three of them back home together, enjoying their comfortable routines.

Catherine reached into her purse, took out a cell phone, and stared into space. She eventually turned the device on, twirled it in her hands a few times then finally dropped it back in her purse. "I'll call after Muriel's test and we know more. Susanne likes facts."

Several hours later, an orderly wheeled Muriel past the waiting area, and Catherine and Ben followed him to the room. After transferring Muriel from the gurney to a bed, the orderly left as a nurse adjusted her monitors. Catherine and Ben inched closer for a better look, and both gasped at the same time when they saw fluid draining from her chest into a glass container through a clear plastic tube.

"What happened?" Catherine whispered.

A nurse gently touched her arm after swapping out an IV bag. "Her doctor will explain. I'll page her."

The two friends couldn't stop staring at Muriel. Catherine held her hand and called out her name, but she didn't respond except for a weak groan. She had never seen Muriel so pale and lifeless, not once in thirty years.

Dr. Anderson soon arrived and explained what had happened. Yesterday when Muriel had fallen, a rib had pierced a small hole in her right lung, which allowed air to accumulate in her chest cavity. That extra air had put pressure on the lung, causing it to collapse.

The doctor glanced at Muriel's chest. "We inserted this tube next to her rib cage to remove excess air and fluids so her lung can inflate again." She motioned toward a large glass bottle filled with pinkish fluid. "That canister collects drainage from her chest cavity."

"Will she be all right?" Catherine asked, her pulse racing with worry.

"Right now, she's groggy from the medication. She'll continue to have pain for a week or so, but should recover." Dr. Anderson held up a finger. "I'll be right back."

The doctor returned carrying a plastic device that had a mouthpiece connected to three chambers, each housing a ball. "This is called a tri-flow. It's used to strengthen the lungs. Mrs. Bennett must blow into it every hour when she's awake." The doctor handed it to Catherine. "You can nudge her into doing the exercises.

It's important for her recovery."

Catherine briefly examined the device then set it on a table next to Muriel.

"She can't stay in bed or she'll lose more strength. The nurses will get her up soon, plus I've ordered a physical therapy consult."

Catherine reached into her purse, pulled out a tissue, and patted her eyes. "This is going to be a long recovery, isn't it?"

"She has some work ahead of her." Dr. Anderson softened her voice. "Mrs. Bennett is fortunate to have friends like you, but she needs her family to help make some important medical decisions."

Ben lifted his chin toward the plastic tube in Muriel's chest. "Because of that?"

The doctor nodded.

"I understand." Catherine lowered her head.

Dr. Anderson excused herself and left the room, closing the door behind her. Catherine and Ben sat next to Muriel, carefully guarding her last minutes of privacy. They had tried their best to honor her wishes, but the situation was now out of their control. Muriel's life was about to change in ways that would devastate her, but they couldn't protect her any longer.

"It's time to call Susanne," Ben said.

Catherine sighed, thinking about the big picture. "Can we wait until Muri wakes up? I bet Susanne would like to speak with her."

Ben ran a hand through his hair and didn't respond right away. He gently cupped Muriel's hand as his eyes reddened. "That sounds about right."

SIX
❧❧❧

Northern California

Now that she had committed to traveling to Vietnam, Susanne experienced a surge of excitement. She liked playing in the gray areas of business where the past didn't dictate the future. People who thought outside the box transformed the world, and this type of thinking would secure the Vietnam deal. Its success equaled her success, and she had no intention of failing.

She asked her executive assistant to clear her calendar for the week and to coordinate all travel arrangements. She ignored his sigh, an innocuous rebellion from a talented employee. His job required him to turn on a dime to keep pace with her schedule, and his salary and bonuses reflected that responsibility.

Ho Chi Minh City was fourteen hours and a date line ahead of the Bay Area. Susanne decided to leave Monday evening on the corporate jet. If all plans went smoothly, she would land in Vietnam on Wednesday morning, giving her ample time to strategize with Dave and his team before Thursday's meeting with their Vietnamese counterparts.

She discussed wardrobe needs with her housekeeper, who got busy packing. The last item on Susanne's list involved calling Lilia to tell her about the trip. She glanced at her watch: a little after five in the afternoon on the east coast.

Lilia answered on the second ring. "Hey, Mom. Good timing. I just got home."

"How's my talented daughter?"

"She's exhausted. Peter's pushing us like crazy."

"He's the quartet leader. That's his job. How are things with Louis?"

Lilia sighed loudly. "I *know* he's the leader, Mom. No need to remind me every time we talk."

Susanne opted for restraint and ignored the attitude. "Music coach?"

"You're getting your money's worth. Louis is running me through the Bach solos. I'm on number five. No worries. You hired the best tutor in Boston. Maybe in the world."

"Is the sarcasm really necessary?"

"What can I say? Louis is a Rottweiler."

"Lilia, why are you acting so flip?"

Lilia sighed even louder. "You rarely call on Saturday night. What's up?"

Susanne could tell her daughter was in no mood to talk, so she got to the point. "I'm traveling overseas on business and wanted you to know."

"Where to this time?"

"Asia. I'll be back by next weekend if all goes well."

"Things always go well for you, Mom."

"Are you feeling OK? You sound"—*testy, childish*—

"off kilter."

"School's great. Peter's leading. Louis tutors. Competition's heating up. I'm practicing every waking hour. Did I cover all the bases?"

"I don't appreciate your tone, Lil. There's no need to get hostile."

"Sorry. It's been a long day."

"Remember to eat a healthy dinner to help sustain your energy."

"Yes, Mom. I'll be sure to eat my veggies."

Time to end this call before I say something I'll regret. "Do you need anything before I leave?"

"Nope. Enjoy your trip."

After ending the conversation with Lilia, Susanne wandered to the backyard with a glass of Chardonnay and sat on a cushioned wicker chair. She closed her eyes and breathed slowly, letting cool air massage her face. It took all her patience these days to cope with her daughter's ever-changing moods. Susanne respected Lilia's hard work but didn't understand her surly attitude. Lilia had been born with a musical gift, and she and Jim had maximized every opportunity for their only child. A bright future awaited her if she continued to focus and work hard.

Susanne and Lilia hadn't seen each other since August. Plus, Lilia wouldn't be coming home over the winter holidays due to a busy concert schedule. Susanne wondered if they needed to spend some time together. She decided to coordinate a stopover in Boston the next time she flew to New York on business. Feeling hopeful about the idea, she returned to her office to continue working.

Four neatly stacked piles lay on Susanne's desk: the original proposal for the manufacturing plant, financial spreadsheets, an unsigned contract, and a country profile. Her research team had compiled a comprehensive packet of information concerning the project, leaving nothing to chance. She picked up the country profile and scanned it.

Working with other cultures required different protocols, and Vietnam had some unique ones. Unlike Western business where relationships usually remained professional and occasionally became social, the Vietnamese nurtured and valued friendships. Their formula was simple: the more one shared personal data, the stronger the business relationship. Susanne was contemplating how to manage this expectation when her phone rang. She didn't recognize the number.

"Susanne Bennett."

"Hello, Ms. Bennett. My name's Cheryl Hill. I'm a social worker at Oregon General Hospital calling about your mother. Do you have a minute?"

Susanne's body immediately tensed with fear. A call like this could mean only one thing: crisis. She stood and began pacing around the room. "What happened to her this time?"

"Mrs. Bennett fell at home last evening. She was admitted to the hospital with a minor concussion and two rib fractures. Today her lung collapsed, and a chest tube was inserted. She's doing fine, but her doctor asked me to notify you."

Susanne dropped into a chair as her heart started pounding, a gallop rhythm she felt all the way to her ears. She knew something like this would happen. Muriel Bennett had been an accident waiting to happen, and now it had arrived at the worse possible time. "Why wasn't I called last night?"

"I'm not sure. Mrs. Bennett's doctor asked me to speak with her this morning. That's why I'm calling now. She'll need help after leaving the hospital, and I'd like to discuss options with you."

"Does she know you're calling me?"

"Um, she knows how serious her condition is."

"I bet she told you not to bother me, didn't she?"

"She mentioned your busy schedule."

Susanne rubbed her neck to soothe the discomfort, wondering how much information to reveal.

"Two of her friends have been looking after her."

Susanne had a few choice phrases on the tip of her tongue but held back. "Let's be clear about one thing, Ms. Hill. I'm responsible for my mother. Not her friends. Is that understood?"

"I hear what you're saying."

Susanne needed to have another chat with Catherine and Ben who were undoubtedly whispering in Muriel's ear right now. She loved her mother and wanted to take care of her, but Muriel and her friends made that impossible when they kept her in the dark.

"Your mother is a lovely woman, Ms. Bennett. She has a wonderful sense of humor."

"Yes, she does." *But she's not using it this time to escape from reality.* "Earlier you mentioned exploring options. What are your thoughts?"

"Well, after your mother leaves the hospital, she'll need help. She is…how can I put this…not very realistic about her condition."

Susanne took a long, deep breath. This social worker had no idea just how unrealistic Muriel could be. *What to do? Think, Susanne, think. Every problem has a solution. It's out there; you just have to find it. Think…*

All of a sudden an idea surfaced, a golden opportunity. Susanne sat up straight, planting her feet firmly on the ground. "You mentioned my mother needing extra assistance. What kind?"

"Mostly with walking and pain management. But she'll also need help with cooking, cleaning, shopping, and things like bathing and hair washing. A physical therapist will start working with her tomorrow to build strength. That effort needs to continue after she leaves the hospital."

"It sounds like she needs a higher level of care."

"A week or so of rehab would do wonders for her. The goal, of course, is for her to return home when she's stronger."

"Clearly, my mother requires specialized care. Have you worked with the staff at East River Progressive Care?"

"Of course. We've referred many patients there."

"I spoke with the director last summer. The place offers a full range of services from rehabilitation to residential apartments. It's just what my mother needs."

"It's a well-respected facility."

Susanne took another slow breath. She had tried guiding her mother toward a safer way of living for years but had been rebuffed at every turn. Now she needed to act, to leverage this situation in a way that supported Muriel's health and well-being for the long run.

"After my mother is discharged from the hospital, I want her transferred directly to East River for rehab. She may resist, but it needs to happen so she can receive the best possible care. Agreed?"

"I, umm...I think you may want to talk with her first. She has some strong opinions on this subject."

Yes, I know all about her opinions. "I'm leaving on a business trip overseas tomorrow. I'll stop in Oregon when I return to check on her. Meanwhile, let's get the paperwork started. Cost isn't an issue."

"Well, I wonder if—"

"For the record, my mother and I have already had a conversation about residential care. I'm calling my lawyer to discuss conservatorship as soon as we hang up. I need my mother safe. That won't happen if she's living alone."

"You know, she may be open to hiring help. She seems to really enjoy living at home. I can provide a list of resources for you."

"Ms. Hill, I know your intentions are good, but let's focus on finding a permanent solution. One that'll ensure her ongoing safety. East River can provide that, but I need you to work with me to make it happen. Can I count on you?"

After a moment of hesitation, Cheryl responded in a low voice, "I'll relay your wishes to her doctor."

Susanne closed her eyes and considered delaying her trip for a few days so she could fly to Oregon now to deal with this situation. But Dave had moved mountains to coordinate meetings, and any change would disrupt the tense negotiations. She needed to honor her work commitment.

"Please fax the paperwork to me right away. I want the transfer to happen without any glitches."

"I understand, Ms. Bennett. I'll speak with Doctor Anderson today."

"And one last thing. I don't want my daughter, Lilia Bennett-Parker, called for *any* reason. She's under a lot of pressure at school and doesn't need this distraction. I'll handle all communication."

Susanne walked into the kitchen and poured another glass of wine with shaking hands. This whole incident could have been avoided if Muriel hadn't fired those two home care workers. She had created this problem herself, and Susanne wouldn't be made to feel guilty, *especially* after Muriel had told them not to call her. Susanne had tried to be reasonable, tried to respect her mother's wishes, but now she needed to act, a daughter's duty.

She sipped wine and closed her eyes, picturing Muriel living in an East River apartment after a stint in rehab. She would have meals prepared for her, someone to clean the place and nursing care would be available twenty-four/seven on the premises. Muriel would have a ready group of bridge players, and the East River landscape matched Lake Woahink's scenery so she would feel right at home. She could even give art lessons to other residents, which should make her happy.

Change was never easy. Susanne had watched it flow thick and fast in the technology industry. Holding on to familiar or old ways could destroy an organization. She had led many change initiatives at her company and had successfully guided employees through the turbulent times.

Now, she would use those same skills to help her

mother navigate the next phase of her life. She knew how difficult moving to an assisted living facility would be for Muriel, and she committed herself to helping her adjust to a safer way of living.

Susanne drank more wine, then picked up the phone to call Tara Collins, her lawyer, even though it was a Saturday evening. They had already discussed conservatorship on two prior occasions, but Tara had discouraged her from pursuing it. Susanne doubted that would happen tonight.

SEVEN
ഇറ

Lilia Bennett-Parker pressed her phone's off button after ending another frustrating conversation with her mother. So…the CEO was off to Asia. Big deal. She flew on business all the time. Lilia guessed she had been reduced to a task on the busy executive's to-do list. Call daughter before jet takes off. Check.

Lilia studied her phone's features. Even in silence, Susanne Bennett taunted her. The smartphone, another success story for her mom's technology company, had a five-inch display, a two and a half gigahertz quad-core processor, a sixteen-megapixel camera with video and sixteen gigabytes of internal storage. The device was supposed to "enhance your life in surprising new ways," according to the marketing gurus. Lilia had a story or two about the woman behind the hype.

Susanne Bennett owned a rosy-cheeked marionette puppet named Lilia, and she had mastered the two-hand control bar, making Lilia dance and perform at her whim. *Oppressive.* Now there's a word that captured her mom's essence. To be fair, Susanne did pay for all her worldly possessions: the phone, apartment, utilities, food, clothing, education, and music lessons. Lilia picked up her Emile Gillet handcrafted cello and touched the fingerboard. Her mom had paid for it, too.

When Lilia was seven, she and her parents had attended a performance by the San Francisco Symphony, and her mother had coordinated a private backstage tour following the show. A cellist smiled at Lilia and asked if she wanted to play her instrument. Without waiting for an answer, she scooted back on her chair, creating enough space for the two of them. She placed Lilia's small hand on the bow, covered it with hers and began playing "Twinkle, Twinkle, Little Star."

Several weeks later, a child's cello and chair appeared in their home music room, sitting next to her father's baby grand piano. Music lessons began right away, and soon the instrument consumed her life: hours of daily practice, music camps, concerts, and competitions. Her mom liked to say it "enriched" Lilia's life and her dad didn't disagree. No one had asked what she wanted.

Lilia strummed a few chords, wondering if that cello lady knew she'd been used. After returning the instrument to its case, she picked up a gold music box on the coffee table and lifted its lid. A tinny rendition of "Over the Rainbow" played, making her smile. Her father had given it to her as a tender reminder of their first duet.

When her mom traveled, which was often, she and her dad enjoyed upping a song's tempo for fun. Pachelbel's "Canon" became Rockebel's "Canon," and their lively rendition of The Turtles "Happy Together" could have won a Grammy. She closed the music box, feeling a rush of excitement. Her dad flew to Boston every other month to see her, and tomorrow was the day.

Lilia glanced at a clock. Peter was hosting a dinner party for the quartet in forty minutes, and he expected punctuality. She took a quick shower, dressed, and headed out the door for the half-mile walk.

Peter Tremblay had won first place in the young artist division of the Canadian International Violin Competition at age thirteen. He had rejected several recording offers, citing the need to mature as an instrumentalist. Somewhere along the way, he developed a passion for chamber music, which had turned into an obsession to form a string quartet with players of equal talent.

He and Lilia had met in their freshman year at the New England Conservatory of Music during an orchestral ensemble class. After several weeks, he had asked her to join his quartet. She couldn't believe her good fortune, and now she, Peter, Joel, and Viktor had been playing together for three years. They were the envy of the campus.

Lilia arrived at Peter's apartment, knocked and then entered. "Anybody home?"

"Make yourself comfortable," Peter yelled from the kitchen as he tossed fettuccine into boiling water with one hand and stirred Bolognese sauce with the other.

"Will you open the Cabernet to let it breathe?"

"Of course. Anything else?"

He lifted his chin toward a green salad and French bread on the counter. "Those can go on the table." Peter removed a piece of fettuccine with a fork, allowing it to cool for a few seconds before taking a bite. "Ahhh. Perfect al dente." He drained the pan and placed the steaming noodles on a large platter just as Viktor and Joel arrived. "Good timing," Peter said as he poured sauce over the pasta and garnished the top with fresh basil leaves.

After finishing dinner and clearing the table, the musicians gathered in the living room. "There's no such thing as a free meal," Viktor kidded as he flopped down on an old beanbag chair. "How come we're here, boss?"

Peter offered a closed-lip grin and refilled his wine glass. "Can I pour for anyone else?" After topping off everyone, he settled on the couch, rolling the red liquid around. "We had a solid practice today, and we're making excellent progress." He paused and set his glass on a table. "But we can do better. That's why you're here tonight."

Joel, Viktor and Lilia shot glances at one another, trying to decipher the mixed message. Peter filled the silence with a familiar lecture. "We're on the homestretch and can't let anything derail us." He stood in front of them like a university professor on the first day of class, all-knowing and all-powerful. "In three weeks we'll be the guest quartet at the Boston Symphony, the residence competition is heating up, and the Naumburg is right in front of us."

Joel sipped his wine. "We all know the path, Peter. Why bring it up now? Isn't this supposed to be a relaxing evening?"

"How about this?" Peter faced Viktor with a cold stare. "Last week I overheard you telling an attractive redhead that the quartet would be a lonesome trio without your viola."

"*What?*" Viktor's eyes widened as he released a nervous laugh.

"You heard me. You were bragging at our expense." Peter glared at Viktor. "The behavior was unprofessional and needs to stop."

"I...I was joking, you know, just having a little fun."

Peter ignored the rationale and turned toward Lilia. "And your head hasn't been in the game for months."

All eyes were on Lilia, whose cheeks grew almost as red as her wine.

Joel leaned forward and stared at Peter. "Now wait a minute! Lilia adds a depth of sound like no cellist I've ever heard. You're way off base."

Peter picked up his violin bow and caressed its string. "Maybe so, but her tempo was off today, and that's not acceptable." He faced Lilia. "Each of us must be fully committed. No distractions, no excuses."

Joel stood and opened his arms wide to expose his chest. "Guess it's my turn now." He faced Peter. "Have at it."

"Stop being melodramatic. It's my job to call out dysfunction."

"You're talking in code," Joel accused. "Just tell it straight."

All eyes were on Peter as he laid the bow down and picked up his violin, studying its spruce soundboard. "The great Pablo Casals said, 'The most perfect technique is that which is not noticed at all.'"

He paused to let the sacred words soak in.

"That's what I expect from each of you. I want others to hear the *music*—not your technique. For that to happen, we have to *become* the music—not just play notes."

No one moved or said a word.

Peter continued, "We're entering the big league, people. We need to play with relentless precision and passion. *Every* time."

Joel glared at Peter. "I don't know what's going on with you, but we've never sounded better." He grabbed his coat. "Thanks for dinner, but I need fresh air." He walked over to Lilia and dropped an arm around her shoulder. "Can I give you a lift home?"

"Umm, no thanks." She glanced at their host. "I better stay and talk with Peter."

Viktor donned his coat and said, "Guess we'll see

each other at Monday's practice?" He quickly wrapped a scarf around his neck and nervously looked at Joel. "Ready?"

Peter spoke. "Don't forget about the private dinner party next Saturday. We're playing Beethoven, and I want it perfect."

Viktor nodded as Joel rolled his eyes, but neither man said a word. Joel caught Lilia's eye one more time to see if she had changed her mind, but she shook her head no. The two men left the apartment, leaving Peter and Lilia alone.

Peter began closing blinds, clearing wine glasses, and clanging dishes. Lilia caught up with him in the kitchen and gently touched his forearm, reminding him of her presence, but he pulled away. "Don't go there."

Lilia stepped back and stared, stunned by his coldness. His harsh words and behavior had triggered some uncomfortable memories.

A month after Peter had recruited her for the quartet, she had found herself in his arms. Theirs wasn't a Romeo and Juliet romance, but the relationship was practical and worked for them. Plus, Peter did have a tender side, and she cared for him. His mentoring had also launched her music into the stratosphere.

Several months after their relationship had started, Peter ended it abruptly. He had offered excuses such as "We've run our course" and "It's getting too complicated," but she never quite understood his reasoning. At least they had managed to salvage a professional relationship—or so she thought.

"What's going on, Peter? I mean, my tempo may have been off during practice, but not that much."

Peter absentmindedly wiped the counter with a dishtowel before saying, "Joel, Viktor, and I pursued music programs this summer, but you went home. Today's practice wasn't an isolated event, Lil. Last week your Razumovsky was raspy, and you played like a soloist. I'm worried about your commitment to the quartet."

Lilia stepped back in disbelief, knowing she had done nothing but dedicate herself to music her entire life. His words raced through her body like a snake's venom, making her nauseous and sweaty. Peter watched her with piercing eyes that chilled her. He had used his considerable talent to breathe life into the quartet, but he acted indifferent to things nonmusical like an aging grandmother who needed help.

"I'm honored to be in your quartet, Peter. My commitment hasn't changed. I want our success, too."

His scrutinizing stare continued. "We have a lot riding on the next six months, Lil. I need to know if I can depend on you." He inched closer. "Can I?"

Lilia stepped back and touched the locket that never left her neck, a symbol of perseverance. "I won't disappoint you or the quartet," she whispered.

After Peter dismissed her offer to help with the

dishes, she quietly gathered her things and slipped out the door to go home. She wrapped her arms around her body, feeling cold inside and out. As she increased her pace, two questions came to mind: What had caused Peter to erupt tonight and how could she *become* the music when she was already playing her very best?

Both questions remained unanswered as she entered her apartment and locked the door behind her, knowing she faced a long, sleepless night.

EIGHT

Oregon

On Sunday morning, Catherine and Ben opened Muriel's door slowly and peeked inside her hospital room, unsure of what they would find given yesterday's crisis. "Don't worry. I'm still alive," Muriel said, smiling as they entered the room.

Catherine observed her closely. She lay in bed with the chest tube securely in place as fluid dripped into the glass container. Her hair had been combed, and her eyes sparkled like blue topaz.

"You sure had us worried, old girl," Ben said as he made his way over.

Muriel fingered her chest tube. "This thing is sucking the life right out of me."

"But you're feeling better, right? Catherine wondered if Muriel was being serious or joking.

"I certainly am. And I'll teach you a big new word. *Pneumothorax.*" Muriel struggled through its pronunciation. "It means my lung popped. Like a giant balloon."

Catherine smiled as she settled into a chair next to the bed. "Any news about a release date?"

"No. But they're getting me up to walk today. I guess that's a good sign."

Catherine watched Muriel's chest rise and fall.

"You're breathing easier, too. You sure gave us a scare."

Muriel nodded but said nothing. She had no intention of revealing just how truly frightened she had been yesterday, seeing no need to burden her friends now that she was better.

Ben rubbed his forehead. "I can't stay long. Esther is expecting me, and I can't disappoint her." He raised his chin toward Catherine. "We drove separately."

Muriel and Catherine both nodded, knowing how much he loved his wife.

Ben touched the bed rail, idly moving his finger across the shiny bar. "Speaking of my better half, the strangest thing happened." He paused and sat down, using the rail for balance. Once settled, he piled his hands on top of his cane and looked off into space. Muriel started to speak, but Catherine touched her arm to stop her. She wanted to give Ben a moment to himself. Dark circles under his eyes hinted at exhaustion, and Catherine didn't want to rush him.

After a minute or two, Ben regained focus. "What was I saying?" He placed a hand on his chin, and suddenly his eyes brightened. "Oh yeah, I remember." He continued, "Last night while watching TV, I glanced at Esther's chair and saw her. I swear she sat right beside me. In the flesh, not an image or ghost. She smiled but didn't speak then suddenly disappeared." He slowly shook his head. "I know she wasn't really there, but it sure felt real."

"She's always in here." Muriel patted the place over her heart. "Please go see her, Ben. I'm fine. Catherine will stay with me."

He inhaled deeply while rubbing his brow. "It's caving in on us, you know. Old age. Things aren't as straightforward anymore." Ben paused, then playfully pinched Muriel's toe through the blanket. "You need to return home to finish Lilia's portrait." He pushed out of the chair. "Oh, by the way, we mailed her package. It should arrive by Tuesday."

"What would I do without you?" Muriel blew him a kiss. "Please give my love to Esther."

"I'll check in with you later," Catherine told Ben. "And give Esther my love, too."

"Will do." Ben smiled at Muriel. "I'll return tomorrow." He raised his chin toward a walker pushed up against a wall. "We'll have a race. The loser has to cook dinner." He winked at her before shuffling out of the room.

"Do you think he'll be all right?" Muriel asked Catherine once they were alone.

"I tried telling him that ninety-nine percent of his worries will never materialize, but you know Ben. He frets about everything. He'll feel better after visiting Esther."

An hour later, the social worker, Cheryl Hill, stuck her head in Muriel's room. "Hello again, Mrs. Bennett.

May I come in?"

"Sure. You can meet my good friend, Catherine."

After introductions, Cheryl inquired about Muriel's health.

"I'm having PT this afternoon, and my neighbor Ben just challenged me to a race tomorrow." Muriel tilted her head toward the walker. "He doesn't stand a chance."

Cheryl smiled. "It's nice to see you in such good spirits." She glanced at Catherine. "May Muriel and I have a moment alone, please?"

Muriel spoke up. "Catherine can hear anything you have to say. We tell each other everything."

Cheryl nodded, then reached into a briefcase and pulled out a file, dropping several papers on the floor. "Sorry." She quickly recovered the escapees. "Guess I'm all thumbs today."

Muriel and Catherine gave each other a "what's with her" look, but remained silent.

Cheryl settled into a chair and cleared her throat. "I called your daughter yesterday and told her about your accident and surgery."

Muriel frowned. "And why would you do that? *Especially* after I asked you not to."

Catherine closed her eyes and released a worried sigh.

"Since you listed Susanne as next of kin on legal documents, Doctor Anderson wanted her notified."

Cheryl's eyes darted between the chest tube and drainage canister. "You have a serious health condition, Mrs. Bennett. You need family support right now."

Muriel reached over and tugged on Catherine's hand, causing her to look up. "This special lady gives me all the support I need."

The social worker shifted in her chair, trying to get comfortable. "A good friend can certainly be of comfort during difficult times"—she paused—"but so is family. You have some important medical decisions to make. That's why I called your daughter."

Muriel let five seconds pass before asking, "Well? What did Susanne have to say?"

"She…she expressed concern about your health."

Muriel briefly closed her eyes, feeling a storm brewing. She could still make her own decisions, and didn't understand why people had to meddle in her affairs. She knew Susanne would press for assisted living. Now this social worker had unnecessarily inserted herself in the middle of their private family matters.

"And what did you two decide on my behalf?"

"Decide? We didn't decide anything…specific. We talked about recovery options after you're discharged from this hospital."

"Uh-huh." Muriel paused to let her squirm a little. "Well, since Susanne hasn't called, I guess you're here to deliver the bad news."

Cheryl shifted in her chair. "Bad news?"

"Ms. Hill, my daughter always has an agenda. Just lay it out for me." Muriel crossed her arms and waited.

"Well, as I said, Susanne is quite worried about you." She glanced at her notes. "She wants you to get proper care so you can heal. And be safe."

"And what does 'heal' and 'safe' look like to you and Susanne?"

Cheryl avoided the question. "Your daughter is leaving on a business trip, but will visit you after she returns." She glanced at her notes. "She knows you'll be here for the next few days, and then wants you to continue your recovery at East River Progressive Care. It's a well respected—"

"Oh, I'm quite aware of its reputation, Ms. Hill. That facility also has lovely residential apartments where seniors can"—Muriel tapped her head—"hmm, let's see if I remember the script, 'East River is a place where residents can enjoy an active lifestyle in a safe and beautiful community while leaving the details to others.'" Muriel goaded her. "How'd I do?"

Cheryl sighed and offered a conciliatory smile. "Pretty well, actually." She returned the file to her briefcase, shaking her head. "You're a bright, charismatic woman, Mrs. Bennett. It's my job to connect the dots between people and their needs. Right now, I'm here to support you however I can."

Cheryl gathered her things and stood. "I enjoyed meeting you, Catherine. Muriel's fortunate to have such a trusted friend." She turned to Muriel. "I'll check on you tomorrow and we'll talk again."

"We can chat until we both run out of breath, but nothing will change."

Cheryl said her goodbyes and left the room.

Catherine walked over and closed the door. "You sure don't make things easy."

"I'd already be in an apartment if I did that."

"She's only doing her job."

Muriel faced the window, watching trees being shoved around by the wind. "You'd think she would call. Susanne, I mean." She fingered the chest tube and sighed softly. "But I don't blame her. I wasn't the best mother."

"Oh, Muri. Don't do that to yourself."

"I wasn't there for her when she needed me. I think they call it karma."

Suddenly, Muriel seemed to age ten years. Catherine had witnessed Susanne's and Muriel's struggle throughout the years. An emotional distance existed between them, and it was usually ignored, but this time was different. Muriel needed help from family but was too proud to ask, while Susanne refused to listen to anything her mother had to say. Someone had to break the impasse.

"Do you want to talk with Susanne before she leaves on that trip?" Catherine fished out a phone from her purse and held it up. "We can call right now."

Muriel toiled with a loose thread on her blanket, wrapping and unwrapping it around her finger. "No. I don't think so." Her eyes drifted to the window again. "Lately, I've been thinking about our treasure chest." She paused. "I'm not saying I'd do anything, but I don't want to lose my options. And I certainly don't want to be stuck in an apartment for the rest of my days."

"Susanne just wants you safe, Muri."

Muriel turned and faced Catherine. "You're wrong, Cat. It isn't about me being safe. It's about her not wanting to be bothered. I wasn't there for her, so now I'm treated as a disruption to her carefully planned life, a puzzle piece that doesn't quite fit."

Catherine listened to Muriel, then gazed out the window at a row of birch trees that arched over a stream and lined a brick pathway around the hospital. *How appropriate*, she thought, knowing the birch was sometimes called "The Watchful Tree" because of eyelike impressions on the bark. The trees guarded patients like Muriel, who were at crossroads in their lives.

Muriel's reference to the treasure chest echoed in Catherine's head, making her stomach churn. In 1997, Oregon voters enacted the Death with Dignity Act, which allows a terminally ill individual to end his or her life. What the legislation didn't do was offer end-of-life options for people with non-terminal disorders such as crippling arthritis, advanced diabetes, congestive heart failure, or Alzheimer's—conditions that often rendered life unbearable.

Several years ago, Ben, Muriel, and Catherine had addressed that gap. They had conducted a three-person vote and unanimously amended the law, creating the Treasure Chest Act. They had bought a small replica of a jeweled pirate's chest, and whenever they received a pain prescription, half of the pills ended up in the chest. Muriel kept it hidden in her bedroom closet under lock and key. It contained enough narcotics to kill all three of them.

During dinner conversations, they sometimes mused about whether or not they could actually take their own life if things got bad. No one said for sure, but just knowing the pills were an option gave them peace of mind, especially after watching Ben's wife, Esther, slowly fade into—

"Earth to Catherine," Muriel teased, jarring Catherine back to reality. "Where'd you fly off to?"

Catherine gently pushed Muriel's feet over and sat on the corner of her bed. "I was thinking about our treasure chest." She played with her necklace, moving a pearl back and forth on its silver chain. "You're not serious, are you? About taking pills."

Muriel released a long sigh. "No. Not really. But I also can't go to East River. It's not for me, Cat. And it's *not* going to happen."

Catherine stroked Muriel's leg through the blanket, trying to soothe away her worries. "You know I'll always be here for you, right?"

Muriel nodded and scooted up in bed.

"And there's nothing I wouldn't do for you."

Muriel smiled, causing her face to wrinkle like clothes left in a dryer for a week. "You are, without a doubt, the best friend a woman could ever have."

"Ben's right about Lilia's portrait," Catherine said. "Let's focus on getting you healthy so you can go home to finish it. No more talking about that silly treasure chest, OK?"

Muriel's eyes reddened, and she turned away. She didn't weep easily but had never felt this vulnerable. She didn't want to die and leave those she loved, but her body had become a thief, stealing strength and resolve. She had a long bucket list: spend more time with Catherine and Ben, finish Lilia's painting and paint a hundred more, attend Lilia's graduation, enjoy her concerts, view endless sunrises and sunsets on her lake. Maybe mend her relationship with her only daughter. The list went on and on.

"I want to get well, too, Cat. And I want to go home more than anything."

"Even if you have to spend a few days at that rehab place, so what? Susanne can't force you to stay there permanently without your consent." Catherine smiled. "You haven't completely lost your marbles as far as I can tell."

Muriel brushed tears away and sat up. "Well then, I

better get to work instead of laying here blubbering like a baby." She motioned toward the walker. "Would you help me take a few steps?"

Catherine scooted off the bed. "You bet." Her eyes glanced at the chest tube and drainage container. "Shall we call the nurse so she can help us manage all that?"

"Allow me." Muriel pressed the call button, smiling as if she had discovered the secret of the universe.

NINE

Boston

It was a rare night when Lilia's dreams didn't include music. Right now, in the shadows before dawn and ahead of consciousness, she wasn't a twenty-two-year-old cellist, but a four-year-old pianist, sitting next to her father back home in California. Jim Parker had taught her a new song, "Wheels on the Bus," and he nudged her to play the tune on his baby grand piano. She placed her tiny fingers on the white keys and pressed them as best she could. Afterward, her father clapped and shouted, "Bravo! Brilliant! Genius!"

Lilia fought to stay with the dream a little longer, enjoying the memory, but she soon opened her eyes. The cello stared grimly at her, stiff and intimidating. "Play me!" it screamed like a drill sergeant. "Sit up and give me twenty bars! Now!" She reached over and plucked a string, causing a G note to reverberate in the room.

"I could trade you for a piano, you know." Lilia placed her hand over the string to silence it. "Don't mess with me." She flung her finger across all four strings. "Take that!"

She got up and dressed, ate a bowl of Cheerios with a banana, then headed out the door for her private lesson with Louis.

Louis Ottmann had become Lilia's music coach three years ago, but it almost didn't happen. After an exhaustive search of qualified candidates, Susanne chose Louis, offering to double his usual fee to work with Lilia. "I coach talent, not money," Louis barked, dismissing Susanne with a wave of his hand. "I will hear her play, and then decide. No deals."

Born in Germany, Louis had immigrated to the United States with his parents during the Second World War. His reputation as a brilliant cellist spread quickly, and he embarked on a successful career in solo and orchestral music. He had performed with major orchestras throughout the United States, Europe, Asia and South America and had received many accolades throughout the years.

Four years ago, he developed a tremor in his right hand that ended his professional career. He often said that classical music helped explain the philosophical differences in mankind, and now, thanks to his disability, he could enlighten the next generation of musicians. He worked as a professor at Lilia's college and served as a private coach to a privileged few. Lilia never took her good fortune to be counted as one for granted.

She arrived early at their regular meeting place, a music room on campus. Given her chaotic schedule, Louis had agreed to coach her on Sunday mornings.

Both of them appreciated the uninterrupted peace and quiet of an empty building.

Lilia removed the cello from its case, settled into a chair and plucked a few strings, making a few adjustments. After running scales, she played Bach's "Suite Number 5 in C Minor." She was building to a passionate crescendo when a door squeaked and interrupted her performance.

"A great musician would never stop playing because a door opens."

Lilia relaxed in her chair. "Good morning to you, too, Louis."

"You handled the ebb and flow of the outer movement nicely, but the energy was off."

Lilia raised her bow and made an air circle. "Shall I begin again?"

He nodded, closed his eyes and listened. Lilia played, Louis interrupted to impart his wisdom, and the pattern continued until an hour had passed.

Lilia sipped some water, then looked up at Louis, "May I ask you a question?"

"Certainly."

"What does it mean to 'become' the music?"

He rested a hand on his chin and observed his young virtuosa, wondering what burdened her today. "It's what happens when you continue to play the Bach even if a door opens." He enjoyed catching her smile.

"Why do you ask?"

"Peter quoted Casals, saying something about the most perfect technique shouldn't be noticed. He wants us to 'become' the music, not just play notes. What does that mean?"

"A violinist has no business quoting a cellist."

Lilia tried unsuccessfully to stifle a chuckle.

Louis continued, "The difference between the language of music and any other language is that you cannot learn music."

She briefly pondered his response, but it didn't make sense. "I don't understand."

"It's like this. People are either born with music in their soul or not. If you have it, 'becoming the music' simply involves connecting to one's essence and allowing years of practice to unfold. When those two things merge, you become your music and will inspire millions."

Lilia sighed but didn't say anything.

"Peter is technically proficient but lacks humility. You, my dear, have both qualities plus you carry music in your heart."

He paused to let his words sink in before imparting more advice.

"In order to tap the soul's energy, you must worry less about pleasing others and focus more on nurturing yourself—mentally, emotionally and spiritually. It's about knowing and believing in your truest self, my dear Lilia."

His response still puzzled her, but she didn't want to trouble him anymore. He often spoke in riddles, and she hoped his words would eventually resonate. "Thank you, Louis."

He added, "Performing isn't only about dramatics and playing perfect notes. It's also about being in the moment, connecting with the audience in an authentic way."

He could tell by Lilia's expression that she wasn't convinced. A line often formed in the middle of her forehead when something didn't make sense to her. Today, two lines appeared.

"You must believe in yourself and strive to make the most minuscule progress every day. It's all any of us—including Peter Tremblay—can ask of ourselves." Louis glanced at his watch. "Have I answered your questions?"

Lilia nodded, feeling grateful to have Louis in her life. After he left the room, she practiced for two more hours, trying to find her truest self. She didn't know if she succeeded, but the Bach sounded amazing.

She put the cello to bed and hurried home. Her father would arrive at her apartment within the hour, and she couldn't wait to see him.

Jim Parker had earned a doctorate in American history from Harvard University and had taught at Stanford for many years. During high school, Lilia attended one of his classes just for fun. His presence had filled the lecture hall. After he started speaking, her dad disappeared and a respected professor, James S. Parker, PhD, emerged: "Since 1776, few countries have captured the imagination quite like the sweeping story of the United States of America, a superpower in the world today." He had gone on and on, delighting and captivating his students. He revealed his true passion and keen intelligence while performing on the academic stage.

Today the two of them would drive to Boston's Museum of Fine Arts to see a special exhibit of the Magna Carta. Her dad had sounded so excited over the phone: "It's the foundation of our American liberties, Lilia. And we're about to see it! Do you know how special that is?"

A knock on the door interrupted her silent reverie.

Lilia opened the door and flung her arms around his neck. "It's sooooo good to see you, Daddy! I've missed you."

"And you're getting more beautiful every time I visit."

Lilia felt her lips widen into a smile. "Let me get my coat and I'm good to go."

"Reservations at the Capital Grill aren't until one." He gestured toward the couch. "May we sit and talk for a few minutes?"

"Of course." Lilia waved him in. "Good flight?"

"Just some minor turbulence." He cleared his

throat and sat down. "May I have some water, please?"

Lilia filled a glass and handed it to him. "You excited about the exhibit?"

Jim took a long drink before responding. "I am. How about you?"

"I'm happy we're going together."

He lifted his chin toward the cello. "How's that business coming?"

"Oh, you know. Life's a little crazy right now. But I'm managing."

"Good to hear." Jim's eyes drifted toward a window.

"Dad?"

He rolled his shoulders a few times, looking anxious and uncomfortable.

"Daddy? You seem distracted. Is something wrong?"

"I have news."

Lilia sat down and watched him closely.

"It's something that may surprise you."

"Dad! Just tell me!"

"Hannah's pregnant."

"She's what?"

"Hannah and I are having a baby. In four months. We got married two weeks ago in Tahoe."

Married? A baby? Lilia felt like a speeding bus had rear-ended her as she waited at a red light. And it wasn't just because of her dad's announcement. His words had instantly awakened some painful memories.

"Lilia? Say something."

She closed her eyes and held the locket that never left her neck. Her father's newsflash had transported her back to the most difficult day of her life. She was only seventeen and had given birth to a baby girl. Lilia had only held the baby once before her parents shoved her off an adoption cliff. She had signed the papers with a broken heart, and would never see her little girl again. Now, here was her dad telling her about his baby. A child he would get to keep and raise. And love.

Jim leaned over and embraced her. "I know this news must come as a shock."

Lilia slumped like a rag doll next to her father.

He held her close, stroking her hair. "Nothing will change between us. You'll always be my little girl."

"Congratulations?" She said, not knowing what else to say or do.

"It's good, Lilia." He lifted her chin so he could look into her eyes. "I hope you'll be happy for us."

She backed away. "Why'd you wait until now to tell me? I mean, didn't you want me at the wedding?"

"I…we decided to marry on the spur of a moment. Plus, I know how busy you are."

"But you knew about the baby. Why didn't you say anything earlier?"

Jim glanced down. "We wanted…I wanted to tell you in person. I imagined it might be—"

"Difficult for me?"

"Well, yeah. I worried the news might upset you."

At least he got that right. Lilia didn't know how to respond, so she got up and walked over to her cello. The instrument stood tall and firm, predictable and trustworthy. She slowly traced its hourglass shape with her finger. "Do you know this has been the only constant in my life? Everything else comes and goes. Starts and stops. Did you—"

"It's not exactly what we planned, but I'm not running from it."

"Like you did with Mom and me?"

Jim sat back and rubbed his forehead. "That's not fair. I've *never* run from you."

Lilia took a few moments to gather her thoughts. Her dad was right. She wasn't being fair. He had been the one to comfort her after a bad dream, to pick her up from school, to drive her to music lessons. He could make her laugh like no one else, and had always been her soft place to land. And he had never missed a visit since she started college. But Lilia felt something else at play this afternoon, a disquieting awareness that lingered in the spaces between spoken words.

"So, I guess you'll have your hands full with the new wife and baby."

"Her name is Hannah, and yes, some things will change. But I'll continue to see you as often as possible." He smiled. "And after this year, well, you'll be so busy that you probably—"

"I won't need you anymore?"

"That's not what I was going to say."

"What were you going to say, Dad? You have a new family. There'll be a new daughter or son to play music with." Lilia's voice weakened. "And I'll be on my own."

"Lilia, please. Don't overreact."

Overreact? What'd he expect? He had moved out of their house the second she had relocated to Boston. Everyone pretended things were fine, but tension filled the room whenever the family got together. Holidays, recitals, and birthdays had never been the same since the divorce, and they both knew it. Now, he hadn't included her in his wedding *and* delayed telling her about his baby.

She looked up at him and held her chest, feeling winded. She suddenly knew where the conversation was headed. He was beginning to distance himself from her just like he had done with her mother. She sensed his shift toward a fresh start, a second chance at happiness.

"I'm not hungry anymore." Lilia decided not to make things easy for him. "When does your new wife expect you home?"

Jim stood and placed his hands on her shoulders. "I love you, Lilia. I always will. Hannah and the baby won't change anything. You'll still—"

She broke free. "Hannah and the baby change *everything*, Dad! You knew how this would affect me. That's why you're acting so weird, isn't it? You feel guilty."

"Some changes are inevitable, but—"

"But nothing. You get what you want. Mom does what she does. And I go with the flow like always, right?"

"I'm sorry if this news is difficult for you. I only want you to be happy."

"Happy?" Lilia raised her voice. "Seriously?"

Jim tried hugging her, but she pushed him away.

"I...I want to be alone right now. Please leave."

"But I—"

Lilia opened the door. "Now. I want you gone."

"Lilia, please. Be reasonable."

She pointed to his car. "Go home to your pregnant wife. I'm sure she needs you."

Jim sighed, slowly picked up his coat and tried to kiss her good-bye, but she moved out of reach, staring at the floor.

"If you change your mind, I'll be here until—"

"I won't." Lilia's chin began to quiver, but she remained steadfast.

He walked outside and stood on the porch as the door closed between them.

She hurried to a window and opened a mini-blind slat just wide enough to look outside without being noticed. Her father returned to the rental car and dialed a number on his phone. He spoke, but she couldn't read his lips. He rubbed his forehead and looked tense, unsmiling. He ended the call, opened the car door and started walking up her steps, but paused and ran his hand through his hair. He eventually turned around and got back into the car.

Lilia knew she was acting childish and almost rushed out to apologize, but decided she had nothing to apologize for. He had dropped the wedding and baby bombs, knowing the news would upset her. He was the one changing the rules and was clueless about her feelings. And she definitely wasn't his little girl anymore. Louis had said she needed to believe in herself, to tap into her soul's energy. Lilia decided it was time to grow up and face reality. Stand on her own. Live her life.

Then her dad drove away, and she cried like a little, lost girl.

Eventually she picked up the cello, lifted the bow and started playing to calm herself, but her heart wasn't in the music, so she stopped. She opened her locket and stared at her baby girl as raw emotion swept through her.

Her chest heaved because her dad's new family meant she'd get left behind. She cried because Peter demanded too much. She wept because her mom kept her on such a tight leash that she felt strangled. She sobbed because no one gave her a vote five years ago, and now it was too late. The entire world felt upside down, and she didn't know how to right it.

TEN

ജ∽രു

Oregon

After visiting Muriel, Ben left the hospital and drove to the Collier Memory Care Center to spend time with his wife, Esther. He visited her three times each week— more for himself than for her.

Five years earlier, he and Esther were to host the weekly dinner party and bridge game with Muriel and Catherine. Esther had asked him to shop for groceries and handed him a list. She didn't go with him because she needed to make her famous Granny Smith apple pie, everyone's favorite dessert.

Ben had driven to the market and returned home with chicken breasts, potatoes, broccoli, fresh blueberries and French bread. He and Esther had put the food away together. An hour later when she had mentioned their bridge party and asked him to go shopping, he smiled and showed her the food. They both had a good laugh, chalking up the incident to old age.

But it was more. Forgetfulness became memory loss, which led to confusion and personality changes. Even with these problems, Ben somehow managed to care for her with help from neighbors, family and home care nurses.

Then, something happened that changed everything.

A year ago, Esther had managed to leave the house and walk down the steps to their private dock without Ben knowing. She was attempting to step into their two-person sailboat when he spotted her. He rushed down the stairs and prevented her from falling into the water, but the incident had sealed her fate.

The Collier Memory Care Center provided quality medical services with dignity and respect, and even though Ben knew he had made the right decision to place her there, leaving her behind pained him deeply. They had been married sixty years, and he felt lost without her by his side.

He arrived at the hospital and parked in a disabled space. He opened the car door and slid one leg out, then the other. Once balanced, he planted his cane for support, picked up the flowers he had purchased on the way over, and made his way to the front entrance.

Ben entered the lobby and saw what he liked to call the "Alzheimer social hour." Nurses had positioned wheelchairs so patients could see and "converse" with one another. Some people spoke with disconnected phrases as others sat impassively with empty stares.

Ben greeted each person by name and handed the alert ones a daffodil; their smiles brightened his day. He saved the last three flowers for his bride.

Esther was sleeping when he shuffled into the room. He replaced dried roses with fresh daffodils after filling the vase with clean water. He was organizing the bed-side table when she opened her eyes.

"I know you," Esther said softly, smiling. "You're that nice man who visits me."

"It's nice to see you again, Mrs. Campbell." He kissed her tenderly. "How are you?"

"That nurse never comes when I call her."

Ben used to treat her sentences like they deserved proper responses, but he learned months ago that their days of coherent conversations had ended. He reluc-tantly adapted to a new way of communicating: as she blurted out random words and phrases, he would share relevant topics with her.

"I have news about Muriel."

"Who are you?" Esther spoke with a panicky voice. "And why are you here?"

Ben told her about Muriel's accident and hospital-ization even though none of it would make sense.

"Do you like sailing?"

"Matt called and sends his love."

"Who's Matt?"

"Your youngest grandson."

"Where's that nurse?"

And so the communication continued for the rest of the afternoon. For Esther, life was like cotton candy, no real substance. Ben applauded the fact that she had used words today even though they were scrambled. Last time she had disappeared into a hidden world and didn't speak during his entire visit.

He kissed Esther's forehead after she closed her eyes. "Well, I better quit yacking so you can sleep. Pleasant dreams, Mrs. Campbell."

He wrapped his hand around hers. "I'll be back on Tuesday and will try to bring happier news. Both Muriel and Catherine send their love."

Esther looked peaceful, her chest rising and falling evenly with each breath.

"I'll miss you." He kissed her again then shuffled out of the room.

Ben stopped and spoke with a nurse who reported nothing new about Esther's condition, then left to go home. He got in his car but glanced over his shoulder at the building. He counted windows until he arrived at the fifth one, knowing the room belonged to Esther. He stared at it for a minute, remembering their good times.

He started the car and began driving home. Few cars were on the highway and Ben let his mind wander.

Having Esther recognize him today sure felt good even if it lasted only a minute or so. Muriel needed to get out of bed, otherwise she'd become weak like Esther. Can't lie around and expect to improve. She wanted to race tomorrow. Ha! That was a good one. Should he let her win? Nah... If he won, she'd have to cook dinner. Maybe fix her famous chicken pot pies. Mmm, he could almost taste the flaky, buttery crust and rich gravy. Matt loved her pies, too. He called frequently and shared news; a terrific grandson, that one. And he never forgot to ask about Esther. Some people said that he and Matt were—

"Oh God! Noooooooo!"

Screeeeeech…crash!

The entire accident lasted only ten seconds from beginning to end, but to Ben it was an out-of-body experience, continuing to eternity.

Only ten seconds: a deer runs across the highway. *One thousand one.* Ben hits the brake. *One thousand two.* The car skids. *One thousand three.* The car hits the deer. *One thousand four.* An airbag deploys. *One thousand five.* The steering wheel crushes Ben's chest. *One thousand six.* The car runs into a ditch. *One thousand seven.* The car slams into a tree. *One thousand eight.* Ben's head cracks the windshield. *One thousand nine.* Ben lays unconscious. *One thousand ten.*

Another driver who witnessed the incident called for help, and an emergency crew arrived on the scene within twenty minutes. Firefighters cut through the car's steel frame and pulled Ben out of the driver's seat. A paramedic detected a weak pulse and started an IV. After placing a brace around his neck, they slid him into an ambulance and rushed to the hospital with a siren blaring.

The doctors and nurses worked feverishly for over

an hour trying to save his life, but the injuries were too severe. On Sunday, December 9th at 6:07 in the evening, eighty-four-year-old Benjamin Campbell, beloved husband, caring father, doting grandfather, devoted neighbor and dearest of friends had taken his last breath. Ben Campbell was dead.

ELEVEN

Northern California

At seven o'clock on Monday morning, Susanne's chauffeur arrived at her estate. Michael always wore a dark suit, white shirt, tie and polished black shoes. He loaded suitcases into the Lincoln's trunk, then held the door open.

"Morning, Ms. Bennett. How are you this fine day?"

"I'm fine. How's traffic?"

"No accidents to report. You should arrive at the usual time."

As Michael navigated the road, Susanne settled into the backseat. Her mind raced like an Excel spreadsheet, calculating every minute of her life to the second.

After graduating from UCLA with a degree in computer science, she enrolled in Stanford's business school, earning an MBA with an emphasis in statistical analysis. She went to work for a large IT company in Silicon Valley as a systems engineer and quickly ascended the corporate ladder, gaining both technical expertise and a reputation for achieving results.

After she had served as senior vice president of systems, the CEO tapped her to lead a corporate spin-off, creating a subsidiary that designed and manufactured electronics such as cell phones, tablets, and computers. Over the past decade, she had grown the company to Fortune 500 status.

Four things consumed her business life: setting company strategy, creating the right corporate culture, capital allocation and hiring top talent. One of her project teams had clocked many hours—including long weekends—to launch a critical new product website. They met budget and timeframe goals, and the site would go live this morning. Susanne would be there in person to congratulate them for their contribution.

Afterward, she would lead her executive team meeting. Organizations built their culture in dozens of ways and honoring this weekly tradition allowed Susanne to set the tone for hers. Even though she held the company's big picture, she depended on her inner circle of vice presidents to contribute ideas and achieve results. Each Monday, many issues were identified, discussed and resolved, which allowed operations to proceed smoothly.

A business lunch with a potential new distributor captured the next space on her calendar. The board of directors had tasked her with growing the company's revenue by five percent during the next fiscal year. Like a strong chain, all her goals were interconnected: build a larger factory, produce more product, increase distribution to consumers, achieve financial targets. This new vendor would be a crucial player to her overall success.

Following lunch, she would meet with a steady stream of staffers who required her input for project and budget issues. Finally, she would meet with her executive assistant to address last-minute issues before leaving for Vietnam.

After a productive workday that played out as expected, Michael drove Susanne to the airport, navigating through heavy commuter traffic. Flying on a corporate jet afforded perks such as easy ramp access, minimal security procedures and almost no waiting time on the tarmac. Susanne justified the expense, knowing Dave and his team would fly home with her.

"Thanks, Michael. I'll call you later about my return flight. It's up in the air right now."

He looked at her through the rear-view mirror and grinned. "Ms. Bennett, did you just make a joke?"

Susanne smiled at her driver, wondering if she did have a tiny bit of Muriel Bennett's DNA after all.

Yesterday, the social worker, Cheryl Hill, had called to confirm that Muriel's transfer to East River would occur on either Tuesday or Wednesday. Susanne planned to fly directly to Oregon from Vietnam to coordinate Muriel's final move to a residential apartment. Despite Muriel's ability to push all of her buttons, Susanne loved her and wanted to protect her. This move would accomplish that goal.

Leaving her home and friends after so many years

would be a tangible loss, but Susanne hoped her mother would eventually come to accept—even embrace—the change. Apartment living offered a comfortable way to enjoy an independent life, giving Muriel peace of mind, knowing medical and other support was readily available.

The corporate jet had space for eight passengers inside its sleek gray interior. A black leather couch faced a flat-screen television, and six luxury seats filled the back section. A small galley with a table and two chairs rounded out the front. After a brief refueling stop in Tokyo, Susanne would land in Vietnam on Wednesday, losing a day after crossing the International Date Line.

She settled into a leather seat and stared at her phone. She had delayed calling her mother, knowing Muriel really didn't want to talk with her. Dr. Anderson had kept her updated, but now that transfer plans were underway, the time seemed right to make the call. She dialed the hospital's number and reached a nurse who told her Muriel was asleep. The nurse recommended not waking her and promised to deliver well wishes. Susanne breathed a small sigh of relief as she powered down her phone and tucked it away.

As jet engines roared, the reality of her trip began to sink in. Susanne buckled her seat belt and looked out the window. A lifetime ago, her brother Stephen had boarded a troop ship in the San Francisco Bay that was destined for the shores of an escalating war. His early letters described rough seas, bad food, marathon poker games, a stop in Guam, and fear of the unknown. He returned home in a casket.

As the jet sped down the runway and raised its nose toward the twilight sky, Susanne's body began to shiver as memories of Stephen filled the cabin. She folded her arms for warmth as she gazed at the horizon, thinking about Vietnam. The country had taken an excruciating toll from her family, and now, because of a twist of fate, she was forced to relive some of her darkest hours.

She found it impossible to untangle the myriad of emotions plaguing her, so she stopped trying. Instead, she reached into her briefcase, pulled out several files, and got to work. She had a factory to build.

TWELVE

Boston

Lilia woke on Tuesday morning with her dad on her mind. The fight with him had stirred painful memories, and their conversation had frustrated her in ways that were hard to articulate without sounding like a spoiled brat. She knew they would eventually reconcile, but nothing altered the fact that he was starting a new family, and their relationship would change because of it. Leaving her mom and breaking up their family had caused enough turmoil, but he had always made her a priority. Now, his new wife and baby would come first, and she'd get the leftovers. Those were the facts.

Coursework had filled her Monday, and she tried to imagine what her mother would say if she knew that opera and voice studies padded her curriculum. She laughed, picturing Susanne snatching her out of class, locking her in a practice room with her cello, and throwing away the key.

A loud buzz returned her to the present. She slipped into a robe and opened the front door as a UPS guy turned around, smiled, and pointed to a package on her step.

"Thank you!"

The man returned her wave, then jumped into his

brown truck and sped away.

Seeing her grandmother's return address warmed her heart. She closed her eyes and imagined being back in Oregon with Muriel, enjoying a calmer life of canoeing, painting, and hiking.

Lilia opened the box and found crumbling oatmeal cookies, scenic photos of the lake, a pair of wool socks, fifty dollars, and a note telling her how much she was loved. She immediately called her grandmother to thank her but got voice mail, so she left a message.

It was early on the West Coast, plus Muriel rarely answered the phone if she was working in her art studio. She also let hours pass without listening to her answering machine—quirks that Lilia forgave easily. She glanced at her watch, set the box aside, and hopped up. She had quartet practice in an hour and needed to get ready.

Lilia hurried to the music room and found Peter, Viktor, and Joel tuning their instruments. All three looked up at her, but only Joel smiled.

"I still have five minutes," Lilia said, even though an explanation wasn't necessary.

Peter ignored her and continued warming up, Viktor focused on his viola, and Joel maintained his supportive smile while adding a friendly shrug.

Lilia removed her cello from its case and began her warm-up routine.

Ten minutes later, Peter placed his violin on his

lap, sat up straight, and waited until he had everyone's attention. "On Saturday we play Beethoven's Number 14 in C sharp at Doctor Williamson's party. The man is an influential board member of the Boston Symphony, who has the power to launch our careers. I expect perfection from everyone. Let's begin."

Peter lifted his violin into position, closed his eyes and played the first note, wrinkling his brow like a dying man in pain. Soon, Joel blended in, followed by Viktor and lastly Lilia, until no instrument stood out, the quartet becoming a single musical expression.

Two hours later, Peter rested the violin in his lap and smiled for the first time that day. "That session was outstanding. Well done."

Peter rarely doled out compliments, and the quartet basked in his praise. When Lilia played, she often listened twice, once for her part, then again for the whole. Today the quartet had exchanged tiny rhythmic motifs that were so evenly calibrated, the sound tasted like honey melting in your mouth. Sweet and satisfying.

"We'll practice this piece again on Thursday. Please be at my house by four on Saturday. I'll drive." Peter packed up his violin and left the room.

Lilia was leaving the building when Joel came up from behind and tapped her shoulder. "You have time for a cup of java?"

"Sorry, Joel. I'm on my way to speak to Professor

Chan's strings class. Rain check?"

He rested his arm across her shoulders. "You already have five of those."

She smiled and said, "One day I'll collect," as she eased away from him.

He shrugged. "Can't blame a guy for trying. Guess I'll see you around."

Lilia watched him walk away. She liked him as a friend, but nothing more. After her and Peter's failed relationship, the quartet didn't need any more drama. Plus, they had too much at stake to lose focus. Right now, the cello was her lover, and she needed to be faithful.

She glanced at her phone. No message from her grandmother. Why hadn't she called?

Lilia strolled to a cafe, ordered a bowl of turkey chili and crackers, and settled in a corner booth to eat lunch. She took a few bites, then pressed the first name on her speed dial list but got Muriel's voice mail again.

Her grandmother rarely ignored her for this long. If anything, she did the opposite. They talked on a regular basis, and she normally returned her calls in a timely manner. Lilia scrolled through her phone book and pressed Muriel's best friend's number.

"Lilia?"

"Hi, Catherine. You have a minute?"

"Well, sure. I...how are you?"

"I'm fine, but Gran isn't picking up. Have you talked with her today?"

Catherine didn't respond, almost as if she had pressed the mute button by accident.

"Catherine?"

"I'm here. Sorry. I have a lot on my mind."

"Have you seen Gran?"

"Yes…but…oh, Lilia, so much has happened."

Lilia's pulse accelerated. "Is my grandmother OK?"

"No, honey. She's not."

Catherine described Muriel's fall and told Lilia about the pneumothorax and upcoming transfer to East River for rehab. She shared Muriel's incremental progress and begged Lilia not to worry, relaying Muriel's deepest wish that she stay in school and focus on her music. Catherine assured her that she would visit Muriel every day and report back.

Lilia felt many things after Catherine finished her story but shocked and frustrated topped the list. She pushed her chili bowl aside and rubbed her forehead.

"She didn't want to bother you. She knows how hard you're working."

Lilia sat up. Her grandmother wasn't a *bother*. Why did everyone treat her like a helpless child who needed to be shielded from bad news? And who gave music a higher ranking over family? Not her.

"Mom's been pushing Gran toward East River for months. She hates that place."

"Yes, I know, but…she's going there for rehab only. Just until she gets her strength back."

"Mom's in Asia. Does she know about Gran?"

Catherine didn't answer right away, but Lilia could hear her breathing.

"Catherine?"

"Yes, Lilia. She knows."

"And she left anyway?" Lilia could barely speak as she pictured her grandmother lying in a sterile hospital bed without any family support. She mentally sorted through her week and made a spontaneous decision.

"I'm booking a flight."

"I wonder if—"

"I'm flying to Oregon, Catherine," Lilia announced. "Thanks for telling me about my grandmother. I'll call you later." She ended the call and closed her eyes as her mind raced.

She didn't blame Catherine for not telling her about Gran earlier, but this situation wasn't just mild dizziness or vague memory lapse. Lilia pounded the table, making her chili bowl jump as she pictured her mother's corporate jet taking off, flying away from responsibility. It didn't surprise her Susanne had left for Asia knowing Muriel was injured. She always chose work first. What angered her was the fact that her mother didn't have the decency to tell her about the accident. That choice was insensitive and unforgivable.

She searched for available flights and found a five

o'clock out of Logan that landed in Portland at nine-thirty at night. She would take a taxi to the house and visit Muriel first thing in the morning to assess the situation. It was a reasonable plan.

Then she thought about Peter Tremblay and her commitments to the quartet.

She hunched over her phone and pressed Peter's speed dial button, hoping to find him in an understanding mood. He answered right away, and she told him everything.

"How long will you be gone?" he asked, icily.

"I won't know until I see her."

"Will you be here for Thursday's practice?"

"Peter, she's in the *hospital*."

He sighed loudly into the phone.

Lilia pictured the vein in his forehead popping out like it always did when he got mad, temper tantrums he never outgrew. She considered justifying her actions but decided against it, not wanting to fuel his anger.

"What about Saturday night?" he asked.

"What about it?"

"Will you play at Doctor Williamson's party?"

"I'm hoping so."

"Hope doesn't make things happen. Commitment does."

Lilia wanted to press the red button to end the conversation in the worst way. "I'll call as soon as I know more. *Please* try to understand. This is my grandmother."

He ignored the emotional plea. "You're taking a big risk, Lil. Your decision tells me a lot about your priorities."

Lilia nearly exploded and decided it was time to hang-up before saying something she'd regret. "I need to go, Peter. I'll be in touch. Goodbye."

She set the phone on the table with shaky hands. She wasn't some musical machine to be played at everyone's beck and call! She took a few deep breaths to calm herself, and then picked up the phone, pressed her shoulders back and got to work. After making flight reservations and arranging transportation, she phoned Catherine with the details, and then hurried home to pack. She had a sick grandmother who needed her.

THIRTEEN
୨୦୬ଓ

Oregon

Catherine arrived at the hospital just in time to watch Muriel navigate a walker down the hallway. Her face had more color than yesterday, she stood fairly erect, and her chest tube had been removed. A hospital employee followed close behind, but Muriel did the work.

"Look at you! Such progress," Catherine said.

"Why, thank you. I'm getting ready for the race with Ben." Muriel's face grew serious. "How's he feeling?"

Two days earlier, Catherine had told Muriel that Ben had the flu and couldn't visit her in the hospital. Telling her the truth wasn't an option because the news of his death would devastate her, and she needed all of her strength to heal. Now Catherine had broken a promise not to tell Lilia about Muriel's accident. She cringed over being such a deceitful friend.

"He's not worse, is he?" Muriel reached for Catherine's arm. "You can tell me."

Catherine answered honestly. "No, he's not."

"Well, that's good to hear." Muriel smiled and placed her hand back on the walker.

Catherine switched subjects and motioned toward Muriel's chest. "No more tube?"

"They yanked it out this morning. Hurt like crazy."

"No problems, though?"

Muriel started to reply, but the therapist interrupted. "We have more work to do, Mrs. Bennett." She smiled at Catherine. "Would you mind waiting in her room until we finish? We shouldn't be more than fifteen minutes."

Morning sunlight and fragrant bouquets filled Muriel's hospital room as a Mylar balloon with a "Get Well Soon" message floated in a corner. Catherine sat in a chair and closed her eyes as another round of grief hit. Where would she find the words and strength to tell Muriel about Ben's death?

Yesterday, Catherine had spoken with his grandson, Matthew, and learned he was flying to Oregon to take care of business. She wondered why Ben's son wasn't coming but decided not to probe, figuring the family had their reasons.

Catherine's heart ached with sorrow. Even though the hospital staff had done a good job at keeping Ben's death from Muriel, Catherine knew the facts would slip out eventually. She had to tell her before anyone else did.

"I'm baaaaack," Muriel said as she entered the room, "like a bad habit."

Catherine opened her eyes and steadied herself as she admired Muriel's upbeat attitude.

"Let's get you settled, Mrs. Bennett," the therapist said as she guided Muriel toward the bed. "You've earned a good rest."

"Can I take you home with me?" Muriel asked half-seriously. "You're one of the good ones."

The therapist smiled and helped Muriel into bed. Their friendly banter continued for another few minutes before she left the room.

"So, Ben's still sick. Has he seen a doctor?" Muriel asked as she settled into bed. "Wish I could make chicken soup for him. He likes when I use big chunks of white meat and thick egg noodles."

"He certainly enjoys your cooking," Catherine said, searching for ways to redirect the conversation to protect Muriel for as long as possible. "Tell me about the chest tube."

"Well, they came in and pulled it out. Not much else to say."

"What happens now?"

Muriel lowered her gown to show Catherine a gauze dressing on the side of her chest. "That needs to stay put for a few days. If the wound heals, I'm home free."

"That's wonderful news." Catherine tried focusing on Muriel, but images of Ben slipped into her thoughts, making themselves comfortable like relatives visiting over the holidays. She looked away as her eyes started to mist.

"Cat? What's wrong?" Muriel scooted up in bed. "Is it East River? Please don't worry. It's only for a week. I'll be fine."

"Oh, Muri, I'm happy you're doing so well. But something did happen, and I've been keeping the news from you."

"It's Ben, isn't it? He's sicker than you're letting on."

Catherine wanted to soften the blow but didn't know how. Ben was dead, and no well-articulated platitude could ease the pain.

Muriel's face grew pale. "Catherine! What is it?"

She pulled a chair next to Muriel's bed and sat down, cupping Muriel's hand tenderly. "It's about Ben but not like you think."

"You're starting to worry me."

Catherine reached inside her purse to retrieve an article from the local paper and handed it to Muriel, hoping it was the best way to tell her. "Please read this."

Muriel put on her glasses and read every word. Twice. She stared at the photo of Ben's car wrapped around a tree for a long time before returning the article to Catherine with a shaking hand. She removed her glasses and laid them on a bedside table, then looked out the window with great focus like a movie had just started, and she couldn't talk or move.

"Muriel? Please. Say something."

"Have you spoken with his family?"

Catherine nodded. "Matthew is flying here today."

"Do we know about the funeral? I want to attend."

Muriel's stoic reaction surprised Catherine. She hadn't shed a single tear while Catherine had just tossed a second tissue in the waste bucket.

"Matthew said Ben will be cremated here. He's taking the ashes back to Pennsylvania to be buried in the family plot. I don't know about the service."

"What about Esther?"

"Matthew didn't mention her. I'm sure that's one reason why—"

A nurse entered the room. "Hello, Mrs. Bennett. May I check your dressing?"

Muriel followed the nurse's directions without making a single comment.

The nurse handed the tri-flow to her. "Even though the tube's out, you still need to exercise your lung every hour. Will you please take a few puffs for me?"

Muriel pushed the device away as she moved her head from side to side. "I'm speaking with my friend right now. May we have some privacy?"

"It's important for your recovery, Mrs. Bennett." The nurse returned the tri-flow to the table. "You don't want that lung to deflate again."

Muriel looked at the nurse with deadpan eyes and remained silent.

The nurse gave her an "I'll see you later" look, and then left the room.

"Did Ben suffer?" Muriel asked.

Catherine reached over and touched her arm. "Probably not, Muri. It happened so fast."

Muriel lay impassively on the bed. "I'm tired and

would like to be alone now, please."

In thirty years of friendship, Catherine had seen Muriel this despondent only one other time: after the death of her beloved husband. She knew everyone grieved differently, but Muriel's strange reaction to Ben's death concerned her. They had always leaned on each other during times of crisis, and it didn't feel right that Muriel had asked her to leave.

"Please let me stay, Muri." Catherine almost told her about Lilia coming home, thinking the news might comfort her but decided against it. Muriel had specifically told her not to tell Lilia about the hospitalization and Catherine couldn't risk upsetting her anymore tonight.

Muriel's chin started to tremble, and she mumbled something about a final curtain coming down and nothing else mattering. She politely asked Catherine to leave for the second time.

"I'll go"—she slowly stood—"but I'm returning first thing in the morning."

Muriel gave her an empty stare before closing her eyes and ceasing all conversation.

Catherine left the room, wanting to go anywhere but home. She viewed herself as an optimist, a glass-half-full type of person, but not tonight. She wanted to stay and grieve with Muriel, hoping they could support each other. But Muriel had asked her to go.

How would the two of them endure this heart-breaking sorrow? How would Ben's death affect Muriel's recovery? And where would she find the words to tell Lilia about Ben? The burden weighed heavily on her mind as she left the hospital.

FOURTEEN

Oregon

Catherine drove home and noticed a small car parked in Ben's driveway. His grandson must have arrived from Pennsylvania, and Catherine wondered if she should pay him a visit now or give him time to settle in. She pulled up next to the curb and let the car idle, trying to decide what to do.

She rubbed her hands together in front of the heating vent while staring at the empty passenger seat. Three days earlier, Ben had sat next to her on the way to the hospital to visit Muriel. She sniffed the air and detected a hint of Old Spice. Ben saw the good in all things, and now he was gone, reduced to a scent.

Part of her wanted to go home, climb into bed and sleep for a week to still her aching heart. She glanced at Ben's house and saw someone walk past the living room window. Ben would want her to treat his grandson with kindness, so Catherine turned the car off, composed herself and walked to the front door.

She barely recognized the young man who answered. He stood over six feet, perhaps by an inch, and his collar-length hair was parted down the middle and tucked behind his ears. He wore a stubble beard and had Ben's warm brown eyes.

"Hello, Catherine."

"Is that you, Matthew? My, how you've changed!"

He pointed to his head. "More hair."

"How long since your last visit?"

"Three summers." Matt opened the door wider. "Would you like to come in?"

She nodded and sat down on the couch. "How was your flight?"

"Good, thanks."

Catherine couldn't stop staring at him. "You look a lot like Ben, only taller and without gray hair."

Matt looked down and swallowed a few times before asking, "Can I get you something to drink?"

Catherine shook her head, not wanting to trouble him. "I'm sorry about your grandfather, Matthew. We loved him so much."

He sat in a chair facing Catherine, placing an ankle on his knee. "He and my grandmother sure enjoyed living next door to you and Muriel all these years."

All in the past tense, Catherine thought as she rubbed her hands together, trying to chase away the chills. "How long will you be in town?"

"A week or so." He paused and looked away. "Dad and Mom are busy with the store, so they sent me. I can work from anywhere."

"Ben said you do computer work."

"I write software."

Over the next thirty minutes, they reminisced about

past summers by the lake and Catherine told him about Muriel's accident. Matt mostly listened to Catherine's stories, asking only a handful of questions.

"Have you seen your grandmother yet?"

"No, I just got in. I'll visit her tomorrow."

"Are you aware she's lost all memory?"

"Granddad kept us posted."

An awkward silence ensued, and Catherine stood, guessing he might like to be alone. He had always been rather taciturn, and today was no exception. "I enjoyed seeing you again, Matthew." She moved toward the door and turned around. "If I can help with anything, please don't hesitate to ask."

Matt nodded as he showed her out.

"Ben bragged about you all the time. You sure made him proud."

He slid his hands in his back pockets and looked down, avoiding eye contact.

"Lilia is flying in tonight." Catherine looked at her watch. "Her plane lands in a few hours."

Matt's head popped up. "Lilia's visiting Muriel?"

"Yes, but she doesn't know about Ben yet. I'm telling her tomorrow."

"Granddad said she stayed here last summer."

"She did. And she spent a lot of time with Ben. He even taught her how to play backgammon."

"Taught me, too. He loved that game."

Catherine hugged him like her own grandson, then

stepped back and smiled. "You inherited his eyes."

"That's what people say."

"I'm here if you need me. For anything."

He offered a quick nod. "Thanks for stopping by."

Catherine left the house and finished the short drive home with Matthew Campbell on her mind. Such a polite young man. All grown up and so mature, way beyond his years. And smart, but not much of a talker. Then again, he had just lost his grandfather.

She parked in her driveway, walked to Muriel's house and turned on the porch light for Lilia. Between coping with Muriel's injuries and learning about Ben's death, tomorrow would be a long and difficult day for the dear girl. Maybe a welcome light would brighten her spirits.

Matt watched Catherine drive away then enter Muriel's house, marveling at the way the neighbors cared for one another, a kindness his parents had taken for granted. He sat in his granddad's chair, reminiscing about life with his grandparents.

Reliving aromas of his grandmother's homemade bread and apple pies baking in the oven made his mouth water. She showed her love through cooking, and she loved greatly. He could almost taste her crusty macaroni and cheese casserole, savory meat loaf, and crispy fried chicken with mashed potatoes and gravy.

He strolled into the kitchen and found an empty

glass cake dome covered with a layer of dust sitting beside two brown-speckled bananas on the counter. The refrigerator contained a half-empty quart of milk, prunes, sweet pickles, white bread, and ham that had cracked, shriveled edges. Two navel oranges rolled around in the crisper next to three American cheese singles. His granddad's life had sure changed for the worse.

Matt meandered outside and rested his hands on the deck railing. He filled his lungs with fresh air while taking in the panorama. Summers at Lake Woahink had offered an escape from the family drama back home. In Oregon, he could count on an easy life of slow mornings, few rules, and doting grandparents. He and his granddad had spent countless hours on the lake searching for trout. His parents often forced conversation, but not his grandparents. Matt appreciated that Ben had recognized silence as an acceptable mode of communication after fishing lines had been dropped into the water. He brushed away tears, regretting he hadn't visited his grandfather during the past few years. Now Ben was gone, and they would never cast lines together again.

He gazed toward Muriel's home, thinking about Lilia. They had grown up on this lake, seeing each other regularly for a week or two every summer until his junior year of college when work prevented it. His last few visits to Oregon hadn't coincided with hers, but Ben had shared bits of news about her. She had never left his thoughts, and now he would see her again.

Matt removed a photo of Lilia from his shirt pocket he had found on his grandfather's desk. She was playing the cello on Muriel's backyard deck. Her long blond hair blew in the breeze, and her lean frame sat erect as she held a bow against the strings. She had grown into an attractive woman, and Matt stared at her image for a long time.

He glanced at Muriel's overgrown lawn and decided Lilia shouldn't have to see it in that condition. He hiked over to his granddad's shed, found an ancient mower and guided it toward Muriel's lot. He pulled the power cord several times before the machine roared to life, then cut the grass, traversing back and forth as a dewy, green fragrance floated in the air.

After returning the mower to the shed, Matt laced up his running shoes and headed out on the road. He crossed the highway, running past trees and a long stretch of smooth, wet sand. He stopped to watch dune buggies climb the steep slopes and race back down, twisting and turning in the powder. He rediscovered trails between towering pine trees inside the state park, and after an hour or so, he returned home.

He showered and dressed, then heated a can of vegetable beef soup in a small saucepan and ate it with stale saltines. Afterward, he opened a book and reread the same five pages until he saw a car pull into Muriel's driveway. He tossed the book aside and moved next to the window to get a closer look, thankful that Catherine had turned on Muriel's porch light.

A graceful young woman stepped out of a yellow taxi. She walked toward Muriel's front porch, pulling a small roller bag behind her. She lifted a flowerpot and reached for something before fumbling with the lock. She entered the house and closed the door.

Lilia Bennett-Parker was even more beautiful than he remembered.

FIFTEEN

Oregon

Lilia landed in Portland at almost ten at night and wanted to rush to the hospital, but knew her grandmother would be sleeping, so she hired a taxi to take her to Muriel's home. After paying the fare, she found the hidden key in the flowerpot and entered the house, locking the door behind her.

The place was eerily quiet as she set her things on a table. Muriel's favorite swivel chair cast a long shadow over the room, and Lilia sat there to feel her grandmother's spirit as she looked around. The house appeared clean and orderly, more than normal.

Lilia loved this place—the smells, the decor, the memories—but it felt too lonely without her grandmother's presence. She rolled her suitcase down a long hall toward her bedroom, stopping to admire a wall of family photos. No one but a grandmother would nail so many holes into a wall to pay tribute to another human being. Lilia relived every year of her life through the images, a testament to love.

Feeling hungry, she walked to the kitchen in search of something to eat. She found spaghetti in the refrigerator and microwaved it while pouring a glass of milk. After supper and washing dishes, she wandered through the house toward her grandmother's art studio. She had spent countless hours in the room watching Muriel immortalize people and nature with her unique flair. Her eyes blurred with tears as she thought about Muriel lying alone in a hospital bed. It took all her strength not to drive there tonight.

After Lilia turned on a light, she spotted an unfamiliar portrait resting on Muriel's easel. She moved closer to study it, mesmerized by the work in progress. Lilia knew she was the girl in the watercolor, but couldn't reconcile her feelings with the picture her grandmother had painted. Lilia slowly traced the image with her finger, studying its nuances. The person in Gran's interpretation appeared content, confident and at peace, not filled with self-doubt and insecurity.

Lilia scrutinized several photographs of her playing the cello that were clipped on the easel's edge. The pictures were similar but had subtle differences involving posture and facial expressions. She had seen herself perform in training videos that Peter had recorded, but these images captured something more raw and honest. Who took them? When? And why?

Discovering the portrait renewed a desire to be near her grandmother that couldn't be suppressed, so Lilia left the studio, located Muriel's car keys and rushed to the front door.

"Hello—"

Lilia gasped and stepped back, holding her chest.

"Oh! Catherine, you scared me."

"I saw the light." She glanced at Lilia's purse. "Were you going somewhere?"

"To see Gran." She started to step outside, but Catherine blocked the way.

"Honey, it's late. You know she'll be sleeping."

"Yes, but I...I need to be with her."

Catherine motioned for her to return inside the house. "May we talk first?"

Lilia wanted to push past her and drive to the hospital, but could tell Catherine wasn't budging. She exhaled a frustrated sigh, then tossed her purse and keys on a table before plopping down on the sofa in a fit of exasperation.

Catherine sat next to her. "How was your flight?"

"I don't want to talk about air travel." She started to rise, but Catherine touched her arm, causing her to look down.

"I need to tell you something."

Catherine looked disheveled as if she had worn the same clothes for days. Her short gray hair appeared flat like she had just removed a snug hat, and her eyes seemed red and puffy.

"What is it?" Lilia asked as she calmed down, wondering about Catherine's appearance.

"Something happened last Sunday."

Lilia waited for an explanation.

"I don't know an easy way to tell you this."

"Is it about my grandmother?"

"No," Catherine shook her head, "it's about Ben."

Catherine described Ben's car accident as Lilia listened in stunned silence.

"He's *dead*?"

"They couldn't save him, honey. I'm sorry. I know how much you loved him."

Lilia looked beyond Catherine as a movie about Ben from last summer played in her mind: long talks, endless backgammon games, picking squash, raspberries, tomatoes and green beans from his bountiful garden. She saw them driving together to visit Esther at the nursing home and eating hot fudge sundaes together afterward. He had asked her to play the cello many times and encouraged her like a doting grandfather. What were their last words? She couldn't remember.

"Does Gran know?"

"Yes. And she's struggling with it."

Lilia sat frozen, completely numb and unable to respond.

"Matthew is here." Catherine motioned toward Ben's house. "He flew in today."

"Matt's here? With his parents?"

"He came alone."

Lilia sank into the couch and released an audible sigh. "I'm tired, Catherine. I'd like to be alone."

"Is there anything—"

"I just need some time." Lilia's chin began trem-

bling. "Don't worry. I'll wait until morning to visit Gran."
She curled up on the couch.

Catherine covered her with an afghan and rubbed
her back. "I'll stop by in the morning if that's all right."

Lilia responded by pulling the blanket tighter
around her body and closing her eyes. Her chest began
to heave, and mascara smudged her face as tears fell
from her eyes. Catherine handed her a box of tissues,
continued to rub her back for a few more minutes then
left the house, locking the door behind her.

Lilia awoke before sunrise after a restless night. Thoughts
of Ben's death combined with her grandmother's accident, her dad's new family, upcoming concerts, and
Peter's erratic behavior caused heaviness in her chest.

She looked out a window toward Ben's house. A
porch light emanated a dull yellow glow, but darkness
entombed the rest of the place. Lilia hadn't seen Matt
in several years, and now their reunion would be all
about condolence. She couldn't imagine him having to
take care of everything by himself.

He could probably use a friend, so she decided to
visit him after spending time with Muriel. That choice
calmed her and provided an odd sense of purpose as if
another person's tragedy lessened her own misery.

Lilia made coffee, dressed in a heavy coat and
wandered to the backyard deck to watch the sunrise.
The cup warmed her hands as low clouds played hide-

and-seek with the trees and water. Dark clouds floated in front of the sun, causing intermittent grayness as a flock of Canada geese flew overhead in a V-formation, flapping their wings in perfect rhythm.

A doorbell interrupted the silence, so she got up and walked inside the house.

"Hi, Lily!" Jasmine bounced up and down as Lilia opened the front door. "Momma said I could see you before school!"

Lilia's heart warmed as Jasmine, a ten-year-old bundle of energy, mispronounced her name. She and her mother, Robin, had moved into the neighborhood after Robin's divorce two years ago. Robin's parents owned the vacation home and had offered the place to them rent-free in exchange for maintaining it. They had quickly become part of the community. Lilia hugged the little girl. "Nice to see you again, Jazzy." She glanced up at Robin and Catherine. "Good morning."

"Hope you don't mind the early visit," Robin said in a lowered voice.

"It's fine." Lilia opened the door wider. "Come in."

"We can't stay. I need to get her to school"—Robin glanced at Jasmine—"but I wanted to offer my help. Sometimes I clean and run errands for Muriel. If you need anything, just ask."

"I wondered why the house looked so good," Lilia said. "Thanks for helping my grandmother."

Robin smiled and looked away.

Jasmine continued bouncing like she had springs in her shoes. "Guess what's on Saturday, Lily?"

Lilia bent down so they were eye level. "Can you give me a clue?"

"My Christmas concert! And I'm playing the piano!"

Last summer, Lilia had taught Jasmine a simple version of Beethoven's "Für Elise." She had been an enthusiastic student and had worked hard—not only on the song, but scales. They often played easy cello-piano duets to entertain the adults during the long summer evenings.

"How many songs are you playing?"

"Three! Can you believe it?" Jasmine kept bouncing, unable to contain herself.

"You sure sound excited."

"Will you come to the show? *Pleeease!*"

Lilia glanced at Robin, seeking a rescue.

Catherine spoke to Jasmine. "Honey, Lilia needs to get ready to see her grandmother right now. Can we talk about this later?"

Robin held Jasmine's hand. "Please let Muriel know we're thinking about her." The two turned and started walking back home.

"Bye, Lily!" Jasmine shouted and waved over her shoulder. "See you later!"

Lilia shut the front door after Catherine stepped inside. "That's kind of her to help Gran. She talks about them all the time."

"Robin's a godsend, and I think Jasmine reminds her of you." Catherine paused, placing an arm around Lilia's shoulders. "How are you holding up?"

"I'm OK. Long night."

Catherine removed her coat and made herself comfortable. "When would you like to leave? I'm happy to drive us."

Lilia considered the offer. Catherine was Muriel's best friend and could help her navigate the hospital and staff, but Lilia wanted private time with her grandmother. She didn't want to disappoint Catherine but needed to think of Muriel right now.

"If it's all right with you, I'd like to go alone." She picked up a ring of keys. "I'll take Gran's car."

Catherine frowned. "Will you call and let me know how she's doing?"

Lilia made all the promises Catherine needed to hear so she would return home without hurt feelings. Once Lilia was alone, she dressed, ate a piece of toast, then walked outside toward the car.

She adjusted the driver's seat and mirrors, catching her reflection. She longed to be that poised, confident woman in her grandmother's painting, not some timid girl who feared making the wrong decision. She started the car and glanced at Ben's home as another wave of sorrow swept through her.

Lilia didn't know how things would turn out once

she arrived at the hospital, but was certain of two things. She and her grandmother would grieve together over Ben's death, and Muriel would have the final say about where she recovered. Lilia took several deep breaths, pushed back her shoulders, then drove away with all the confidence she could muster.

Sixteen

ಬಂ೧

Oregon

An elderly man sitting behind a "Welcome Visitors" sign at Oregon General Hospital directed Lilia to the fourth floor after studying a patient roster. As she traversed the stark halls leading toward her grandmother's room, the smell of disinfectant made her stomach queasy. Various machines made loud beeping sounds, and bright flourescent lights nearly blinded her. She couldn't wait to rescue her grandmother from this germ-infested prison.

Lilia peeked inside Muriel's room and found her sleeping, so she tiptoed to a chair and sat beside the bed. Muriel looked frail and weak, and the morning light accentuated her paleness. Her curly gray hair had been washed but not styled, and skin hung from her arms like a baggy shirt. A greenish-yellow bruise about the size of a silver dollar appeared on her forearm, and a hissing sound passed through her chapped lips each time she exhaled.

Lilia wrestled with tears as she studied her grandmother's appearance. The person lying in front of her looked nothing like the vivacious woman she had left behind last August.

Muriel began to stir and slowly opened her clear-blue eyes, the only part of her that hadn't changed.

"Lilia?"

"Hi, Gran. I'm home."

She rubbed her eyes and did a double-take. "I don't understand."

"Catherine told me about your accident."

"But…you have school. Why are you here?"

"It's almost the holiday break."

"Doesn't the…I thought you had concerts."

"Not right now." Lilia lowered the bedrail and stroked her grandmother's arm. "How are you feeling?"

Muriel brushed the hair away from her face. She straightened the covers all around her, glancing everywhere except at Lilia.

"Gran?"

Muriel finally looked at her with a strained smile. "Oh, I'm pretty good."

Lilia tenderly held her grandmother's hand and whispered. "I know about Ben."

Muriel closed her eyes as her chin began to tremble. She tightened the grasp on Lilia's hand, then gazed at her with watery eyes.

Over the next several hours, Lilia and her grandmother shared countless stories about Ben. Lilia told her about school, the quartet, and her dad's new family. Muriel explained her collapsed lung and the plans to recover at East River.

"Is that where you want to go?" Lilia asked.

"They're transferring me today."

"That's not what I asked."

"Your mom likes the place."

"What do *you* want to do?"

"It's probably for the best."

Lilia ambled over to the window. "You know Mom's in Asia, right?" She turned and faced her grandmother. "She left knowing you were here."

"She's busy, sweetheart. East River's a decent place."

Lilia absentmindedly tugged on a balloon floating in a corner. Her grandmother clearly wasn't herself. If Muriel truly wanted to go to the rehab place, then fine. But Lilia sensed that wasn't the case. She had always talked about staying in her home, and Lilia didn't understand the sudden change of heart.

"May I speak with your doctor?" Lilia asked.

"About what?"

"I want to better understand your condition and—"

A nurse entered the room interrupting their conversation. "Good morning, Mrs. Bennett. It's time for your sponge bath." She looked at Lilia. "May we have a few minutes alone?"

"I'm her granddaughter," Lilia explained, not wanting to leave the room.

The nurse smiled. "I bet Mrs. Bennett is happy to have you here."

Lilia and Muriel shared a look. "You want me to

stay, Gran?"

"I'll be fine. Go get yourself some coffee."

Lilia pointed at the door. "I'll be right outside if you need me."

Lilia headed directly to the nursing station and asked to speak with Muriel's physician. A nurse paged Dr. Anderson, who arrived quickly and explained everything that had happened during the past five days. The doctor expressed relief that Muriel finally had a family member with her.

Armed with facts and renewed determination, Lilia returned to Muriel's room and found her alone. She wore a fresh gown, her teeth had been brushed, and she had more color in her cheeks. Lilia styled Muriel's hair as they talked.

"Feel better?"

Muriel shrugged. "I can't complain. The nurses take pretty good care of me."

"I spoke with your doctor."

"Doctor Anderson's a nice lady, isn't she?"

Lilia nodded and set the comb down. "She said you need help building your strength. She likes East River but said you could also recover at home."

Muriel looked right into her eyes. "Not with you."

"Maybe not, but you have other options."

"East River isn't so bad."

Muriel's apathy frustrated Lilia to no end. She

knew how much her grandmother disliked the place, but now she seemed resigned to go there. Lilia wanted to honor her grandmother's wishes and not cajole her into doing anything she didn't want to do, but Muriel's expressionless face and abrupt responses spoke volumes. Her concussion and lung problems, combined with Ben's death, had obviously taken a toll on her. She clearly wasn't herself. Most importantly, she hadn't cracked a single joke all morning.

"Doctor Anderson can send a nurse and physical therapist to your house. Since I'm here, why not let me help coordinate that? You being at home would save me lots of driving."

"I know what you're doing."

"Then let me help you."

"Not when it's your last year of school."

Lilia crossed her arms, not caring if she looked or sounded like a petulant child. "I'm already here and not leaving until you're better. End of discussion."

Muriel released a loud sigh.

"Besides, we both hate hospitals,"—Lilia wiggled Muriel's finger—"even rehab ones."

"You can be quite persuasive."

"If things don't work out, you can always go to East River. It's a no-lose situation."

Muriel sat up in bed and stared out the window.

"Come on, Gran. Let's try home and see what happens," Lilia pleaded.

"When do you return to school?"

"In a few days. Will you please let me take care of you while I'm here?"

Muriel grew silent, looking alternatively out the window and at Lilia. She shook her head and released a half-smile. "What'd you call a woman who has one leg shorter than the other?"

Oh, this was a good sign. "I give. Tell me."

"Eileen."

Lilia dropped her head back and laughed. Not at the lame joke, but at the joy of seeing her grandmother begin her climb out of such a dark, hopeless place. A spark of energy had returned, filling Lilia with a ray of hope.

"Your mother won't like this decision."

Lilia made no effort to respond.

Dr. Anderson canceled the transfer to the rehab facility and made arrangements for Muriel to receive care at home. A nurse entered her room holding several papers. "I hear you're leaving us today, Mrs. Bennett."

"Looks that way." Muriel turned and smiled at Lilia. The nurse glanced at Lilia, then pointed at the closet. "Your grandmother's clothes are in there if you want to help her get dressed."

Twenty minutes later, Muriel sat on the edge of the bed as a nurse explained, "A walker, commode, and cane will be delivered to your home later today. A therapist should arrive around two." The nurse examined Muriel's chest dressing. "Please keep that dry. A nurse will be out tomorrow to check on it."

She sorted through a checklist then looked up. "I think that's it, Mrs. Bennett. Do you have any questions before your granddaughter takes you home?"

Muriel looked at Lilia, deferring to her.

"No, we'll be fine," Lilia spoke in her most confident voice, appreciating that no one could read the thought bubble above her head that taunted, "You are in over your head!"

After filling two prescriptions and signing discharge papers, an orderly wheeled Muriel outside and helped her into the car while Lilia called Catherine. Lilia told her about bringing Muriel home and asked for help to get her inside the house. Catherine praised the good news and promised she would be watching for them.

Once they were on the open highway, Muriel joked, "I feel like you've busted me out of jail, and we're on the lam."

"Yeah, we're a real Thelma and Louise. Nobody better mess with us."

Lilia parked in Muriel's driveway and glanced at the front steps. A young man wearing a dark green shirt tucked into jeans sat next to Catherine and Robin. All three stood and began walking toward them as she turned off the engine.

She opened her door and looked up. "Matt?" She had known him nearly her entire life, but barely recognized him. He seemed taller and more muscular, and had longer hair and a beard.

"Hello, Lilia. It's good to see you again."

He had a deeper voice than she remembered.

Catherine bent over and smiled at Muriel as she touched Matt's arm. "You remember Ben's grandson, don't you, Muri?" Without waiting for an answer, she motioned toward Robin and continued chattering. "She cleaned the house and is preparing dinner. I bet you're excited to sleep in your own bed tonight!"

Muriel stared at everyone but didn't speak. She placed a hand on her chest as her eyes began to moisten. Lilia touched her grandmother's arm, guessing she must feel overwhelmed by all the attention. Muriel looked at her home, and Lilia knew what to do.

"Thanks for meeting us." Lilia pointed to dark clouds gathering overhead. "Shall we get Gran inside before the rain starts?"

"Of course." Catherine backed away as Matt moved to Muriel's side of the car and opened the door.

"Hello, Matthew." Muriel choked on her words, barely able to push them out. "It's been a while."

"It's nice to see you again, Mrs. Bennett." He gestured toward an old walker. "I found this in Granddad's garage. It's a little rusted but still works."

Muriel touched his arm. "I'm sorry about your

grandfather. We loved him so much. I don't know what we'll do without him."

Matt looked down. "Thank you."

He held Muriel's arm at the elbow and helped her out of the car, positioning the walker in front of her. She grabbed the handles firmly and slowly began scooting across the driveway as Matt held her arm for extra support.

Robin rushed ahead and opened the front door as Catherine entered the house and removed a throw rug from the entrance so Muriel wouldn't trip.

Lilia watched the homecoming unfold with a sense of awe. This motley group of friends acted more like family. She couldn't recall a time when she felt more grateful as she followed them inside the house and closed the door. She needed to call her mom and tell her about Muriel soon, but for now, Gran was where she wanted to be, and nothing else mattered.

Seventeen

༄༅࿇

Vietnam

After flying all night, Susanne's jet landed at Tan Son Nhut International Airport a few minutes before eleven on Wednesday morning. As she unbuckled her seat belt, she felt rested and ready for business.

A hot and muggy, eighty-two-degree day greeted her as she stepped off the jet and onto Vietnamese soil. She removed her coat and followed a man who wore a khaki shirt that had a small red star, a symbol of communism, stitched into its fabric just below the collar.

Once she entered the terminal, that red star appeared everywhere, making the place feel like a military operation. The red star men directed all foot traffic, showing zero emotion toward arriving passengers. No smiles, no warmth, no welcome. Susanne passed through immigration, had her passport and visa stamped, then quickly followed the exit signs.

Swarms of Vietnamese congregated on the other side of a window wall, waving their hands and shouting like traders from the New York Stock Exchange. Susanne's forehead beaded with sweat from the humidity as she strained to find a familiar face.

"Susanne!" Dave Simms waved his hands and smiled broadly. "Over here!" he yelled. "It's great to see you!"

"Hello, Dave. It's good to see you, too." Susanne glanced at a short Vietnamese man standing next to her VP. The man wore a powder blue shirt with rolled sleeves, jeans, tennis shoes, an Angels baseball cap, and a wide toothy grin.

"Susanne, I'd like you to meet Quang Nguyen. He's our translator and guide." Dave playfully slapped Quang on the back, almost knocking him over. "He's a man who knows how to get things done!"

"I am pleased to meet you, Ms. Bennett," Quang said. "Welcome to my country. I help with all your needs. Nothing too big. Nothing too small. You ask; Quang helps." He bowed several times.

"Thank you, Mr. Nguyen." Susanne turned toward Dave. "Shall we find our team and get to work?"

Quang Nguyen bowed again then signaled to a man sitting in a white van. Susanne wondered where Dave had found him and what qualified him for the job. He certainly didn't look like a professional who could effectively translate her words during an intense negotiation. She decided to keep a close eye on him.

The van darted in and out of traffic on the way to the hotel, passing hundreds of people in cars, bicycles, and motor scooters. Vehicles vied for unlined road space, and exhaust emissions colored the air a noxious brown. The whole scene resembled an anthill where everything looked chaotic yet operated with a purpose.

The energy and vibrancy of Ho Chi Minh City surrounded her at every turn. Market stalls lined the street, and vendors waved all kinds of items—hats, jewelry, chickens, black eels—to catch a passerby's attention. A motorcycle whizzed by, transporting two children in front of the driver and a woman behind him who carried a baby strapped to her back. Susanne looked away, shocked at their disregard for safety.

Her driver stopped in front of a five-star hotel called the Rex, a stylish historical landmark in the heart of town. Susanne wiped perspiration from her forehead as Dave guided her to the registration desk.

Once inside her spacious suite, she showered and put on a silken gold robe provided by the hotel. She stood by a window and looked down at a small greenway in an otherwise concrete city, barely able to comprehend her presence in Saigon, the prewar name for Ho Chi Minh City. Did Stephen drive through this town? Did he eat at one of the noodle shops? Or buy souvenirs from a street vendor?

A large bowl filled with round pinkish-red balls with pointy green leaves caught her eye. She held one, careful not to prick her fingers. She touched it like a blind person reading Braille, then spotted a card that answered her unspoken question: *Dragon fruit for your enjoyment.* The sharp knife lying next to the bowl would definitely be needed to slice through its thick, intimidating skin. She returned the fruit to the bowl, doubting her tongue would ever taste it.

After dressing, Susanne walked to a hotel conference room to meet Dave and his team. Members included two manufacturing leaders from California, and the vice president of a private corporation in Houston who handled acquisition logistics for overseas manufacturing ventures. Their local support was four Vietnamese consultants who had expertise in project management, human resources, training and compliance, and accounting. Quang Nguyen sat quietly in a corner with his eyes lowered.

After introductions, Susanne faced the team and began speaking. "As you know, Vietnam is a dynamic country with a strong middle class. The government is stable and committed to growth. Labor costs are fifty percent less than China. The country's workforce is seeing an annual increase of one and a half-million people, and its workers are young and increasingly higher skilled."

She paused and gave each person eye contact before continuing.

"Six months ago, we decided to move a production plant from the United States to Vietnam for economic reasons. A month later, this group was tasked to make that happen. Two weeks ago, Chairman Thanh signed a letter of intent." Susanne stood and strolled to the window, staring at hundreds of people milling around the street below. She turned around and slowly asked, "Can someone please explain to me why we still don't have a signed contract?"

She calmly returned to her chair, sat down, and waited for an explanation.

Dave's face reddened as he thumbed through a stack of papers. Everyone else either looked at him or down at the table.

Susanne waited.

Finally, Dave spoke. "As I mentioned the other day, the Vietnamese rescinded our agreement for a ten-year land lease. That decision—"

"No need to repeat facts, Dave. Why did the breakdown occur and what is our recovery strategy?"

He rubbed the back of his neck and glanced around the table. "Those are good questions without clear answers."

Susanne looked at him with unflinching eyes.

"I believe they're testing our commitment. That plastics factory is an antique and should be condemned. They need us more than we need them, but won't take this last step. Maybe Chairman Thanh has a better offer. Who knows?" Dave tossed the question to his partners. "Other opinions?"

Anh Phan, the lead project manager, spoke. "Chairman Thanh is a shrewd man, Ms. Bennett. He knows the value of your company. I believe he wants your business."

"But?" Susanne molded the word into a question and waited for an answer.

Anh blushed and looked away briefly. "The chairman appreciated meeting you during videoconferences, but he looks forward to greeting you in person. In Vietnam, we believe the true nature of business is about people. You are demonstrating your commitment to this project by being here. I think that will please Chairman Thanh very much."

"What I'm hearing is that Dave should have summoned me here weeks ago."

Anh lowered her eyes and didn't respond.

Susanne knew her team had worked diligently to get this far. All land in Vietnam was government owned, but foreigners could lease property by forming a joint venture with a local partner. Dave's team had evaluated multiple properties and selected Chairman Thanh's because of its size and location. His decaying manufacturing plant outside city limits needed capital for modernization, which her company could provide. Vietnam offered financial incentives to grow foreign business, and an abundance of natural resources helped fuel a manufacturing boom that could increase profits substantially for both parties. Susanne had spent hours pouring over the schematics of the property and knew it was a good fit.

Over the next three hours, Susanne and her team examined all the relevant facts. They brainstormed ideas on how to move the negotiations forward, identified critical success factors, and created an agenda that would drive to outcomes for tomorrow's meeting with Chairman Thanh. Susanne concluded the meeting after reminding everyone to meet in the lobby the next morning at eight-thirty sharp.

Small talk filled the room as the team rehashed discussions before leaving to go their separate ways. Dave wanted to have dinner with Susanne, but she politely declined, wanting to fine-tune tomorrow's presentation. After working for an hour or so, she looked up and saw Quang Nguyen standing at the door.

"I'm staying at the hotel tonight so I won't need your services, Mr. Nguyen. You may go home."

Quang smiled. "May I come in?"

Susanne sighed and didn't try to hide it. She had work to do and didn't need this distraction. "What is it?"

"I would like to show you my city if you not too tired. Help you learn about my people. It's pretty at night. You can relax." He stared at her with a wide jack-o'-lantern smile, the kind that made one's eyes disappear.

Susanne glanced at the door wishing Dave would magically appear so he could deal with this intrusion. Quang waited patiently like he expected her to say yes, so she finally did.

"What time shall we leave?" She viewed the invitation as an opportunity to get to know him better. After spending an evening together, she would know whether or not he was up to the task at hand.

"I meet you in front of this hotel in one hour. Does that please you?"

After they left the Rex, Quang led Susanne down the street on a walking tour. "I take you to a nice place to eat your first Vietnamese dinner. Good food, cheap prices." He didn't say much else but focused his attention on navigating through the crowd and traffic.

He stopped at a busy intersection. "We cross here." They stepped off a curb and moved slowly in a horizontal line without the safety of a crosswalk or street light as hundreds of cars and motorbikes maneuvered all around them, coming within inches of touching their bodies. Susanne gripped Quang's arm in panic until they were safely on a sidewalk once again. She glanced back at all the chaos and felt a burst of anger, wondering why he would put her life in such danger.

She had no idea where they were going or how long they would be gone. That thought prompted fears about being alone with Quang, a man she barely knew. The whole thing felt like a kidnapping. How much ransom was a CEO worth? Would they find her body in a field on the outskirts of town tomorrow morning?

She distracted herself from the irrational thinking by asking, "Where were you educated, Mr. Nguyen?"

Quang smiled, ignored the question, and pointed to a building that had a blue neon sign with the number "2000" flashing brightly. "This restaurant got its name when your president Bill Clinton visited my country in the year 2000. He ate here and liked the noodles. You like noodles, too."

The restaurant was located on a busy street corner, and it had two open sides that allowed humid air, car exhaust fumes, and distracting noise to fill the space. A room full of locals sat on backless stools in front of plain wooden tables. They chattered so loudly that Susanne could barely hear Quang speak as he guided her to an empty table.

"I order the food. It is our custom to welcome you."

Quang hurried away and left Susanne alone, causing her to ponder the kidnapping scenario once again. She wanted to rush back to the hotel, hoping never to see Quang Nguyen again, but thoughts of crossing the street or trying to hail a cab gave her heartburn. What was she thinking? How could she be so foolish to let him talk her into coming here alone?

Quang returned with a tray, and set two bowls of steaming rice noodles, spring rolls, and bottled water on the table. The restaurant certainly didn't qualify as a Michelin five-star, and Susanne became nauseated when she spotted a fatty piece of chicken skin floating in her bowl. Quang handed her a spoon and motioned for her to take a bite while he reached for a plastic bottle that contained a foul-looking, dark liquid. He started to squirt some into her soup, but she held his wrist.

"What's that?"

"*Nuoc-mam*. Fish sauce makes food taste real good. All people in Vietnam eat it. You will like it."

"No thank you, Mr. Nguyen." Susanne had discovered the end of her patience.

Quang returned the bottle to the table after squeezing some sauce into his bowl. He slurped a few bites then pointed at a portrait of President Clinton. "We love that man. He lifted trade embargo that help Vietnamese economy. He good person. Like you good person. A real smart lady. We love Americans!"

Susanne eyed Quang, feeling like he was directing a play without sharing the script. She finally relaxed, deciding to make the best of a bad situation. She thanked him for dinner, then bit into the spring roll, finding it tasty but on the greasy side.

Quang smiled and nudged her soup bowl closer, so she took a bite of the noodles. "May I ask you a question, Mr. Nguyen?"

"Of course, of course! You ask Quang anything!"

"You've worked with Dave for several months now, correct?"

"Oh, yes! Mr. Dave is nice man. Very smart and hardworking. A good businessman."

"You've heard all conversations between him and Chairman Thanh?"

"Yes, yes. Everyone very dedicated. Do good work."

"Why won't Chairman Thanh sign our contract?"

Quang just laughed and laughed, like he was in an

audience watching Jerry Seinfeld perform on stage in New York City.

"Did I say something funny?"

"No. You smart lady, I can tell. Very, very smart."

Susanne couldn't remember the last time someone had acted so brazen in her presence. She wanted to wipe the perpetual grin off his face. "What makes you say that?"

"Because you ask good questions."

"You never answered my good question about your education."

Quang laughed at that one, too. "See? Smart lady never forgets anything!"

Susanne finally had endured enough of his insolence. She pushed back from the table and stood. She would demand this mindless little man take her back to the hotel right away. Dave would hear about—

Quang ceased smiling and patted Susanne's chair. "You don't want to know about Quang. You want to know Chairman Thanh is scared of smart lady."

What? Susanne was too stunned to respond.

"Chairman Thanh never work with important lady before. Doesn't know what to do."

Susanne returned to her chair, sipped some water, and leaned forward to listen carefully.

"Chairman Thanh is old way. Women take care of home, not business. Women don't shake hands; women bow. Women don't push. Women patient, no rush. You can do that. You very smart lady."

Quang finished his noodles, wiped his mouth on his shirtsleeve, and then announced, "We go now. You have big day tomorrow." He bowed and started walking as Susanne followed, puzzled by his abrupt change in behavior. *Who is this man?*

Quang retraced their steps back to the hotel, bowed and left Susanne standing at the front entrance with many questions swirling in her head. She stared at him until he disappeared into the night. What was he telling her? What was he *not* saying? Was Chairman Thanh unwilling to work with a woman? If so, why did he demand she fly to Vietnam? And what made Quang Nguyen such an expert?

She walked inside the hotel pondering the role of a powerful woman working in a male-dominated society. Bowing, handshaking, patience. As she waited for an elevator, Susanne replayed the whole night in her head and sensed that Quang Nguyen had orchestrated the event for a reason. Perhaps his comments weren't random but deliberate. Did he say what others were too afraid to declare?

Susanne closed her eyes and sighed after stepping into the elevator as a rare moment of insecurity pressed against her chest, causing discomfort. She thought about tomorrow's meeting with the chairman and knew that relief from her anxiety would only come after a night of further research.

Eighteen

Oregon

Muriel's bedroom faced the lake, and she never took the spectacular view for granted. Four lofty windows and French doors joined together to form a graceful curved wall opposite her queen-sized bed. Natural light filled the room with calmness, like being in a Zen monastery on a remote mountain top.

Matt kindled a fire in the room's wood-burning stove as Lilia helped settle Muriel into bed. After five nights in the hospital, it felt heavenly to lay her head on feather pillows once again. Rain began pelting the glass as she nestled under a plush down comforter. She felt grateful to be back home but also guilty.

Lilia wasn't supposed to visit Oregon during the winter holidays, yet here she was, functioning as a caregiver. And poor Matthew. Not only had he lost his beloved grandfather, but his family had sent him here alone to settle the estate. Such a heavy burden for a young man to bear. And now, she added to his woes with her problems.

Muriel knew Susanne would be livid when she discovered what had transpired. Maybe the time had come to accept outside help. At least she could stay in her own home instead of living in some tiny apartment where everyone knew her business. She didn't want to eat her meals with a bunch of strangers, play bingo twice a week, or take bus trips to smoke-filled casinos. That life wasn't for her.

Muriel decided to enjoy a few days with Lilia but had no intention of disrupting her blossoming career. She felt too tired to say or do anything today, but would talk with her soon. Perhaps Lilia could find a reliable caretaker for her, and then return to school. Muriel yawned, feeling hopeful about the idea.

Lilia tucked a quilt around her. "You've had a busy morning, Gran. It's time to rest."

"You sure take good care of me."

Matt slid his hands into his back pockets. "I hope you feel better real soon, Mrs. Bennett." He glanced at Lilia. "I'll leave you two alone. Call if you need anything."

"Thanks for your help, Matthew," Muriel said. "The fire feels wonderful."

He nodded and started moving toward the door.

"I'll walk you out, Matt." Lilia glanced at Muriel and held up a finger. "I'll be right back."

"No hurry." Muriel closed her eyes, feeling every one of her eighty-two years and then some. Just yesterday, Lilia and Matthew had been carefree kids kayaking on the lake, and now here they were, young adults with the weight of the world on their shoulders. Where did the time go? She yawned again, closed her eyes, and drifted into a late-morning nap.

Lilia handed Matt an umbrella from a container sitting by the front door. "You'll need this." She pointed up at the pouring rain.

He thanked her and accepted the loan.

Without thinking, she blurted out, "Catherine and Robin are fixing dinner tonight, and we're all eating together. Want to join us?"

He played with the umbrella's latch for a few moments. "I'd like to, but I'm not sure when I'll return."

"From where?"

"I'm visiting my grandmother after I leave here. Don't know what I'll find."

"Ben took me to visit Esther last summer."

"Yeah, he told me." Matt smiled. "Granddad said you spent lots of time together."

Lilia nodded. "I'd go with you but"—she tipped her head toward Muriel's bedroom—"I can't leave her."

"I understand."

"Umm, back to dinner…you need to eat and, well, Gran would like to…you know, thank you for helping her." Lilia felt tongue-tied and didn't know why.

Matt tilted his head. "Well, I wouldn't want to disappoint her. What time?"

"I don't know. Anytime really. Maybe around six?" *What a dumb answer.* Lilia hoped her cheeks weren't as red as they felt.

His lips edged into a kind smile. "Six sounds good." He opened the umbrella, looking at her. "I've missed you, Lilia."

"Me too…missing…seeing you, I mean." Lilia felt mortified and wanted to hide as her face burned with embarrassment. She hadn't uttered a single coherent sentence since they had started talking.

Matt said his goodbyes and headed home. Lilia watched him walk away, closed the door and flopped back against it, releasing a loud sigh. *What was all that about?* She waited for her pulse to slow, and then walked to the kitchen to tell Catherine and Robin about their additional dinner guest.

A truck delivered Muriel's medical equipment in the early afternoon, and her physical therapist arrived shortly thereafter. The therapist encouraged Muriel to sit on the edge of the bed as Lilia stood in the corner and observed.

"You have a lovely home, Mrs. Bennett."

"Thank you." Muriel swept her hand in front of the walker, commode, and cane. "Guess they're moving the hospital to me."

The therapist smiled. "Let's get you up." She helped Muriel stand then spoke to Lilia. "Your grandmother can walk by herself, but you should follow close behind as she rebuilds her strength." The therapist extended her arms on both sides of Muriel's body without touching her to demonstrate the point.

"You're doing great, Mrs. Bennett. There's no need to rush."

Muriel winked at Lilia. "Guess I better quit showing off so much."

Muriel turned a corner and saw Catherine sitting at the kitchen table and said, "Surprise!" She continued walking but pushed the walker too hard, causing herself to stumble. The therapist quickly caught her and guided her to a chair.

"You OK, Gran?" Lilia bent down in front of her, wringing her hands.

"Yes, yes. No need to fuss." She quickly changed the subject. "It smells good in here. What's cooking?"

Lilia backed away and looked at the therapist who shrugged. Catherine pointed to a Crock-Pot. "A roast with onions, carrots, and potatoes for dinner."

"Makes my mouth water," Muriel said. "Are we having corn bread, too?"

The therapist redirected the topic. "What just happened, Mrs. Bennett?"

All eyes fell upon Muriel, which made her uncomfortable. She wanted to minimize the incident, so everyone didn't worry but decided it wasn't fair to withhold information. Lilia and Catherine were caring for her, and they deserved the truth.

"Everything started spinning and my legs gave out. But I'm fine, now."

"Let's get you back to bed," the therapist said. "A nurse was scheduled to come here tomorrow, but I'll see if she can swing by today. Just to be safe."

Muriel offered no argument and followed all orders.

Some time later a nurse arrived, assessed Muriel, and shared her findings. "Other than low blood pressure you seem fine, Mrs. Bennett."

"Should we worry about the dizziness?" Lilia asked.

The nurse shook her head no. "Your grandmother's pressure normally runs low. I think we're dealing with postural hypotension."

"Postural what?"

The nurse explained that Muriel had low blood pressure, which can cause dizziness if a person rises too quickly, if they stand for extended periods of time, or if they don't stay hydrated.

"Your grandmother's body's been through a major trauma, Lilia. She needs time to heal. It's best to take things slowly for the first few days."

Muriel listened without asking any questions.

"Should I take her back to the hospital?" Lilia asked the nurse.

"If she doesn't overdo her activity, drinks more water, and adds additional salt to her diet, I think she'll be fine."

"More salt?" The advice confused Lilia. "Isn't that bad for you?"

"Only for people with high blood pressure," the nurse explained. "Salt raises the blood pressure, so it helps stabilize people with low pressure like your grandmother."

"Guess I'm special." Muriel winked at Lilia.

The nurse gathered her things. "You're healing nicely from the pneumothorax, Mrs. Bennett. If you become dizzy again, sit immediately and put your head between your knees until you feel normal. And remember to use that." The nurse lifted the tri-flow sitting on the nightstand. "It's important to keep exercising your lungs."

So much to remember, Muriel thought as she settled into bed, wanting to rest and be alone to ponder the nurse's advice.

"You'll come again tomorrow?" Lilia asked with a shaky voice.

"I will." The nurse handed her a business card. "If Muriel continues to feel light-headed, gets weaker or becomes confused, please call me right away."

After the nurse left, Catherine made corn bread while Robin left to retrieve Jasmine from school. Once Muriel fell asleep, Lilia gathered her music and an old cello that she kept at Muriel's house and carried both to the art studio. She needed to release some tension and music provided an outlet.

After tuning the instrument, she started with

Beethoven—the piece the quartet would play on Saturday night. She didn't want to give Peter any additional reasons to complain, so she practiced the music all the way through, then focused on several difficult passages.

Her mind began to wander, so she quit playing, unable to focus. As rain pelted the redwood deck, she started quivering inside. Watching her grandmother nearly fall caused her to doubt herself. Did she make a mistake in bringing her home? What if Muriel fell and broke a hip? Lilia would never forgive herself.

Then Peter's face merged into her thoughts, creating more angst. His perfectly coiffed hair, stylish dress, controlled smile, and demand for perfection haunted her. No way would she make tomorrow's practice. She'd be lucky to return by Saturday.

Lilia touched her locket. It had been one of the most difficult days of her life when her grandmother had placed the delicate chain around her neck after the birth of her baby. That day, she had been the one in need and Muriel had been the pillar of strength. Gran had murmured encouraging words, asking her to be strong and telling her that everything would turn out fine. Now their roles were reversed, and she had to be the sage.

She positioned her bow against the strings and began playing a different song, one called "Benedictus." The name came from the Gospel of Luke, and it was a song of praise spoken by Zechariah at the birth of his

son, John the Baptist. Artists such as Simon and Gar-
funkel had put music to its words, but two Croatian cellists, Luka Sulic and Stjepan Hauser, had truly captured
its essence. Lilia had listened to their interpretation
many times and had played various renditions of the
song. The melody soothed and comforted her, reminding her of pure love—the kind she felt for her grandmother. She played until a tear splashed on the cello.
After drying the wood with the edge of her shirt, she
stared into the dark night, consumed with worry about
Muriel's future.

While Lilia played the cello, Catherine answered Matt's
knock on the front door. After a brief conversation,
Catherine returned to the kitchen to help Robin with
dinner, and he drifted toward the music. Lilia had often
complained about her mom pushing the cello on her,
but Matt knew how much she loved the instrument. It
had become her life, and he never doubted that a bright
future awaited her on the concert stage.

The sounds led him to Muriel's art studio where he
quietly leaned against the doorframe, choosing not to
interrupt Lilia's performance. At first she played a classical piece but switched to a song he had never heard
before, a melancholy tune. Her posture shifted from
rigidity and intense focus to a more relaxed stance. She
closed her eyes and looked like the person in granddad's
photograph.

After she stopped playing, she wiped away a tear. He slowly backed out of the room to give her privacy, but a floorboard creaked, causing her to turn around.

"Matt?"

"Sorry. I heard the music and…" He shrugged and looked away.

Lilia set the cello aside. "How's Esther?"

He rubbed the back of his neck. "She didn't even know me." He entered the room and sat next to Lilia. "And I barely recognized her."

"That must have been so hard for you."

He shrugged again, not knowing what else to say. No one could begin to understand his pain after seeing his grandmother in that condition. It shattered him. The combination of Ben's death and Esther's deterioration had nearly caused him to pack up and return home. If he hadn't promised to have dinner with Lilia, he'd probably be at the airport right now.

"What'll happen to her now that Ben's gone?" Lilia asked, using a soft tone.

"That's the million-dollar question, isn't it?" He placed elbows on his thighs, chin resting on folded hands. "Her caregivers seem to be doing a good job. Who knows? Maybe we'll just leave her there."

Lilia gently rubbed his arm. "I'm here if you need to talk. About anything."

He liked that touch. He wanted to pepper her with questions about her apparent sadness, the melancholy song she played, school life, and how long she would be staying with Muriel. Instead, he simply said, "Guess we both have our hands full."

Lilia glanced at a wall clock, and then smiled for the first time that evening. "You're early."

Early? He had no idea what she meant.

"Dinner isn't until six. It's only five."

Her green eyes washed over him, looking like polished emeralds and causing a jolt inside his chest. He had glanced into those eyes hundreds of times, but today was like seeing them for the first time. He regained his composure and held up a black case. "I thought you might like to play backgammon before dinner."

Lilia started to respond, but her phone vibrated. She glanced at the screen, then frowned. "Sorry. I need to take this. We'll play after I'm done. OK?"

He nodded and left the room, thinking about those green eyes and wondering who had the power to steal her smile.

Lilia pressed the green button on her cell phone, dreading the call.

"Hi, Joel."

"Oh, good. I thought I'd get your voicemail."

Lilia waited.

"Peter told me what happened. How's your grandmother doing?"

She described Muriels's health problems.

"Guess you're not flying back tomorrow." He paused. "What about Saturday?"

She answered honestly. "I don't know. I'm needed here right now."

He sighed loudly into the phone.

"Joel? What is it?"

He finally blurted out, "I don't know how to tell you this without hurting your feelings, so I'm just saying it, and you need to listen *very* carefully."

His serious tone caused her pulse to race, like being in the middle of a final exam and forgetting the answers. She sat down with the phone glued to her ear. "OK. You have my attention."

"You know that guy who owns the house where we're playing on Saturday night?"

"Doctor Williamson?"

"Yes. He is—I mean, he has a daughter who is…"

"Joel! Just say it!"

"Peter's dating his daughter. They met last summer, and she's a cellist. They've been spending lots of time together. They seem to be getting close."

Lilia listened, wondering where the conversation was going.

"You need to return to Boston before it's too late."

"Too late for what?"

"She's a cellist, Lilia. A *cellist*. And they're *dating*. Think about it."

Lilia's throat grew dry.

"All I'm saying is you need to be here on Saturday. Otherwise, I'm not sure what Peter will do. *Please*. Listen to what I'm telling you."

She could barely breathe as Joel's message became painfully clear. Peter wouldn't replace her in the quartet, would he? Not after three years and playing hundreds of hours together. Not after all their concerts. And certainly not for someone he had met just a few months ago. What about their career path? The Boston Symphony?

"Thanks for the heads-up," she managed to say. "And for being a good friend."

"I care about you, Lilia. Please come home."

She hung up and called Peter right away, but got his voicemail. She left a message explaining her grandmother's tenuous situation and begged him to call her, saying nothing about the conversation with Joel. She slid the phone into her back pocket and stared mindlessly through a window into the darkness.

Catherine strolled into the studio and announced dinner was on the table.

Lilia studied Catherine's reflection in the window as she calmed herself.

"Are you all right, Lilia?"

Was she all right? Of course not. Nothing was right. What should she do about Peter? Saturday night's performance? The quartet? School? Gran? Her mom? Ben had died, and she would never see him again. Life was so overwhelming and complicated. She pulled her shoulders back, took a deep breath, and turned around.

"I'm fine. Let's go eat that pot roast."

NINETEEN

Oregon

When Lilia entered the dining room, all thoughts of Peter vanished as she glanced around the table. Gran sat at her usual place, a queen's throne in her castle. Her hair had been styled. She wore a brown suede vest over an ivory turtleneck sweater and had applied a touch of pink lipstick that brightened her face.

Matt was showing Jasmine something on his phone, and they both looked up at Lilia, but the spry ten-year-old promptly tugged on his arm, pointing at the phone. He smiled, shrugged and continued conversing with the girl.

Lilia strolled into the kitchen and saw Robin arranging meat and vegetables on a large oval platter. "Mmm, that looks good. Need any help?"

Robin motioned toward to a plate of corn bread and a pitcher of water sitting on the kitchen island. "Those can go on the table."

After everyone had taken a seat, Muriel cleared her throat. "I don't always pray before meals, but today feels special." She held out both arms. "Will you join me?"

A chain reaction began as Catherine held Muriel's hand and reached for Lilia's. Once Matt held Lilia's other hand, he caressed her palm with his thumb, giving her a warm rush. Jasmine leaned over and scooped up Matt's free hand, then turned and held her mom's as Robin closed the circle with Muriel.

With heads bowed, Muriel began speaking. "Dear Lord, thank you for bringing everyone together and for watching over us with your love. Thanks to Robin for preparing dinner and for my dear friend Catherine who looks out for me. Thank you for bringing Lilia home in my hour of need. Lord, we miss Ben so much and pray for his soul. We thank you for sending Matthew to be with us tonight."

"And bless Mr. McKnight, so he gets better real soon!" Jasmine blurted. "Amen."

Everyone looked up, startled by the outburst.

"Who is Mr. McKnight?" Catherine asked.

"My music teacher."

"What happened to him?"

"His heart is hurt, but Momma can tell you better."

Robin began filling Jasmine's plate as she explained, "He had chest pains last evening at home. He's in the hospital now."

"That doesn't sound good," Muriel said. "As I recall, he's not that old."

"Only fifty-eight," Robin said. "We're all worried about him. He's worked so hard to create the children's choir, and now…"

"What about Saturday's concert? Who'll lead the kids?" Muriel asked as she placed some corn bread on her plate.

"The director is trying to find a back-up—just in case." Robin rubbed Jasmine's back. "We can't disappoint our little ones."

Jasmine looked at Lilia, and her face suddenly brightened. "Maybe *you* could!" She turned toward her mom, bouncing in her seat. "Maybe Lily can take Mr. McKnight's place!"

Robin rubbed her back. "Sweetie, Lilia needs to take care of Muriel right now."

Jasmine crossed her arms and grunted, throwing a mini-tantrum that everyone ignored.

Lilia empathized with Jasmine's disappointment and wished she could help her, but she needed to return to Boston to play in her own concert.

Everyone complimented Robin on the scrumptious food, and the dinner conversations ranged from the perils of hospitals to the weather on both coasts. Robin had just placed a German chocolate cake on the table when Lilia's phone vibrated.

She glanced at the screen and jumped up. "I'm sorry, but I need to take this." She rushed to her bedroom and closed the door.

"Thanks for calling, Peter."

"You're missing practice tomorrow?"

"I just brought my grandmother—"

"I listened to your message."

"Then you know how impor—"

"What I know is you're letting the quartet down."

"But I've been practi—"

"Will you be here on Saturday?"

Lilia almost screamed. How could she explain herself when he kept interrupting?

"It's a simple question, Lil."

"I'll do my best to be there."

"That sounds like a no."

"It's a maybe, not a no."

"If it's not a yes, it's a no."

Lilia wanted to explain that she would return to Boston as soon as possible, hopefully by Saturday. She wanted to reiterate how much her grandmother needed her right now while expressing her commitment to the quartet. She wanted to tell him all these things, and to compliment his leadership to boost his ego, but she didn't get a chance.

"You've made your choice, and now I'm making mine. You're out."

Out? What's he talking about?

"It's my responsibility to make sure we honor our commitments. It was a hard call, but you left me no choice. I need a person we can depend on."

Lilia felt a trace of relief. She didn't feel too bad about missing Saturday's performance, although she would never admit it to Peter. She would use this time to help her grandmother, and then return to school with a renewed commitment to the quartet.

"I understand, Peter. I promise to focus when I get back. No more excuses."

"No, Lil. This isn't just about Saturday."

"What do you mean?"

"You're out of the *quartet*."

Lilia nearly dropped the phone.

"You forced my hand, Lilia. "

"It's only a couple of *days*!"

"This isn't about time; it's about priorities."

"I know my priorities."

"My point exactly. We're headed for the big stage, and you're in Oregon instead of Boston. It's all about choices."

At that moment, she hated Peter Tremblay. She detested his arrogance, lack of compassion, and insensitivity. She tried her best not to let her emotion get the best of her, but tears soon filled her eyes.

"I'm sorry, but you gave me no other option." *Click*.

The line went dead, and Lilia stared at the phone. She couldn't believe Peter had actually hung up on her. No discussion. No empathy. She's out of the quartet? Forever? A sinking sensation filled her chest, and she began to panic like being caught in quicksand, descending deeper into the spongy soil with no way out. She replayed the conversation repeatedly in her head, trying to make sense of his words.

She finally admitted to herself that she didn't hate

him. His brilliance had led them to the Boston Symphony, and she loved playing in the quartet. Peter, Joel and Viktor were her musical family, and Peter did have a point. She had let them down by missing Saturday's performance.

Lilia sat up, knowing she had a house full of guests and needed to pull herself together. She blew her nose and dried her eyes, promising herself she would find a way out of this mess. She would help Muriel get settled, and then head back to Boston and talk with Peter in person, certain he would eventually forgive her. Music was her life, the quartet her destiny.

Matt glanced at his watch for the third time and grew concerned knowing Lilia had been gone for a while. She had seemed distracted all evening, first in the art studio, and then over dinner. He finally relaxed when she joined them in the living room.

"Everything OK?" Muriel asked.

Lilia nodded as she placed a big pillow in front of the fire and sat down. "Just some school stuff."

"Do you need to return to Boston?"

She offered a half-smile. "Actually, I have good news. My schedule changed, and I don't have to get back right away."

Muriel spoke to Jasmine. "Honey, why don't you bring Lilia her cake?"

The energetic ten-year-old jumped up and rushed

to the kitchen.

Matt could tell something wasn't right. Lilia's eyes had a hint of pink, and her monotone belied her confidence. He wanted to bridge the distance between them, so he scanned for ideas. A possibility surfaced, and he gave it a shot. "I run most every day and wouldn't mind some company. Care to join me tomorrow?"

Lilia slowly moved her head from side to side while wrinkling her nose. "I'm not much of a runner." Her eyes flickered toward the window. "Besides, we're in the middle of a major storm."

Matt leaned forward. "Tell you what. If it's not raining in the morning, we'll run. Otherwise, we'll stay here and play backgammon. Deal?"

Catherine, Muriel, and Robin remained quiet, eyes glued to Matt and Lilia as they continued to banter back and forth.

Lilia gazed at him with a relaxed smile. "I'll set up the backgammon board tonight."

Matt motioned toward the front door. "And I'll be here at nine wearing running shoes."

Catherine chimed in with perfect timing. "And I'll be here at eight-thirty to visit Muriel no matter what you two decide."

Everyone had a good laugh.

Matt couldn't believe his good luck, knowing he would get to spend more time with Lilia. He didn't want to overstay his welcome, so he said his goodbyes and stood to leave.

Lilia followed him outside and closed the door behind her. They huddled together under an awning, trying to avoid the downpour. "Get ready for a gammon. Ben taught me some great moves."

Matt liked that she felt comfortable enough to tease him. "Granddad may have shared a strategy or two with me, also." He reveled in her warmth, catching her fragrance, a citrusy rose blend that suited her. He wondered about the two phone calls that had upset her tonight, but didn't ask any questions. "You know, things often seem better after a good night's sleep."

She tilted her head and gave him a curious stare.

"Pleasant dreams, Lilia." He pulled a hood over his head and walked home, wishing dawn had already arrived.

TWENTY

Oregon

Lilia woke early the next morning and glanced at her slumbering bedmate who needed help only twice during the night. Muriel had wanted to sleep alone, promising to ask if she needed assistance, but Lilia didn't trust her. No way was her grandmother falling on her watch.

The rain had stopped, and the sun began poking through gray clouds. She couldn't believe how Matt had looked at her last night. He had said things would seem better in the morning as if he could read her mind. Even though he knew nothing about her problems, he was surprisingly accurate. The same issues troubled her, but the pressure to solve them had lessened.

Muriel continued to sleep, blowing puffs of air through her lips. Lilia needed to return to Boston sooner rather than later, but didn't want to rush her grandmother's recovery. Gran had been a source of strength and inspiration for her over the years and—

"I can feel you staring at me." Muriel opened her eyes. "You didn't need to sleep here." She winced as she slowly opened and closed her hands.

Lilia gently touched Muriel's swollen finger joints. "Do they hurt?"

"They're a little stiff in the morning."

Lilia kissed Muriel's cheek as a distraction from her pain. "Remember how I used to crawl into bed with you when I was little? Being here always felt safe and secure. It still does."

"But you're not a little girl anymore. You have school. Big year, remember?"

"I'm not leaving until you're better."

Muriel sighed, staring through a window. "Can we have an honest conversation?"

Lilia rolled up on her elbow. "Is there any other kind?"

Muriel playfully pinched her nose. "My best days are behind me, Lilia. I need to face that reality." She paused. "I love having you here, but we both know where you belong."

Lilia listened without interrupting.

"Your mother wants me to move into that assisted living place. Maybe it's time."

"Is that what you want, Gran?"

"I need to stop being such a cranky old lady."

"I'm asking again. What do you want to do?" Lilia sat up and faced Muriel. "And remember, this is an *honest* conversation."

"The truth?" Muriel gazed outside for a few moments. "I'd like to stay in my own home. In this bed for as long as possible."

"Then let's build a plan around that goal."

Muriel chuckled. "You sound just like your mother right now."

"Don't go there." Lilia narrowed her eyes, then relaxed. "Let's find a home care worker to come here. A person you like and trust."

"Not like those other two. I want someone who won't fuss over me all the time."

Lilia pointed outside. "It's not raining, so Matt and I are going for a run. When I return, let's do some research. We'll find the right person."

Muriel placed her hand over Lilia's. "I'd like that."

Lilia narrowed her eyes again. "And you won't fire her like the others, right?"

Muriel's expression grew soft. "No, sweetheart. This time I won't. Cross my heart."

Lilia hoped Matt didn't laugh at her old gray sweats and tennis shoes that had been in the closet for at least three years. The shoes were for hiking, but she guessed they'd be fine for running, too. She had just finished tying the laces when a doorbell rang. She rushed to answer the front door.

Matt greeted her by raising a white bag. "Got some treats for you and Muriel from the local bakery."

"Good morning to you, too." Lilia held the door open. "Come in."

He kicked off his shoes and entered the house. "How'd things go last night?"

"I didn't sleep much, but Gran's better. She and

Catherine are in the kitchen."

He lifted the bag again. "Let's give this to them and get moving"—he raised his chin toward the window—"before the rain starts."

Lilia tried unsuccessfully to control the flutters erupting inside of her. She couldn't stop staring at his eyes, and his hair had a controlled messiness that made him look so hot.

Matt guided Lilia along the highway for a couple of miles before turning into Honeyman State Park. He stole glances at her bouncy ponytail and couldn't believe they were actually running together. He had planned an easy route, nothing like his normal run, and knew exactly where he wanted to end up.

They followed a well-maintained path inside the park, and soon arrived at an old moss-covered gazebo surrounded by water and pine trees. During the summer, crowds often swarmed the area, but not during winter—especially after a major thunderstorm.

Lilia bent over and placed both hands on her thighs as she caught her breath. She raised her head and looked around. "This place is gorgeous, Matt. So peaceful and calm."

"Yeah, the view's pretty amazing." He leaned on the railing, gazing into the distance. "The park has so many textures; lake, trees, wildflowers, and dunes. I like coming here to think."

Lilia continued to look around as Matt stole more glances. Her face glistened with sweat, and her cheeks had a pinkish glow. She started shivering and folded her arms for warmth, so he removed his sweatshirt and offered it to her.

"You sure?"

"I'd take it off even if I were alone."

She dropped it over her head and thanked him.

Matt sat on a bench facing the lake. "So, how's school? Life in Boston?"

Lilia drew a deep breath and released it loudly as she tapped a finger on the gazebo wall.

"That bad?"

She glanced at him with eyes that had darkened in the cold air, then looked out toward the lake, planting both hands on the railing and leaning forward. She eventually turned around and said, "Do you really want to know?"

"I'm a good listener."

She studied him while biting her lower lip. She pulled a locket from under her shirt and mindlessly zipped it back and forth on its chain.

He waited.

She finally began talking and told him everything on her mind. She described Peter's threat, Muriel's uncertain future, Louis's musical advice, her dad's remarriage, her mom's trip to Asia knowing Muriel was sick. She went on and on, finally coming to an abrupt stop.

"Wow. I'm sorry, Matt. You shouldn't have to listen to all my troubles."

He didn't want her to apologize. Walls were tumbling, and he wanted to keep them falling. "You sure have a lot going on."

Her face grew flush. "How about you?" She looked up. "What's your life like these days? Family? Work?"

"Oh, I have a few stories, but let's save them for another day." He could have easily bent her ear for the next three hours, but sensed she had more to say, so he nudged her to continue talking. "Tell me about Peter and the quartet. What brought you together?"

Lilia recapped the quartet's history as Matt listened.

"So…Peter handpicked you?"

She nodded. "I wanted to be a soloist, but Mom pushed me toward the quartet." Lilia sat up straight like she had to defend herself. "Don't get me wrong. I enjoy playing with Peter, Joel, and Viktor. Peter has opened important doors for us. And we're getting great press."

"What happens when you return to Boston?"

"I'm sure Peter didn't mean what he said. He's just disappointed in me."

"Because you're helping Muriel?"

"No. Because I chose her over music."

Matt had a few choice things to say on that topic but remained silent.

"What should I do?" Lilia asked.

"About Muriel?"

"No. About Peter."

Matt gave the question some thought as he stared at the dunes. "When I returned home after graduating from college, my friends thought I was crazy." He glanced at Lilia. "I had a good job, and a couple of buddies wanted to rent a house together, but leaving my parents when they were struggling didn't feel right. They needed help, so I stayed." He paused. "It was the right choice for me."

Matt didn't want to discuss any more of his life at that moment, so he stood and brought Lilia up with him. He gave her hand a reassuring squeeze. "You've turned into an amazingly beautiful and talented woman, Lilia. I like what your music coach said about not trying to please everyone. I say do what makes you happy and the rest will follow. That's my best advice."

A flash of lightning brightened the sky, followed by a crack of thunder. "We better get back." Matt released her and pointed at the sky. "Maybe we can still fit in a game of backgammon."

She hugged him like a treasured friend. "Thanks for listening, Matt. And for bringing me here." She stepped back, pink creeping across her cheeks.

He wanted to fold her in his arms and kiss her, but she didn't need any more complications in her life. What she needed was a friend, and he could be that for her. "You're welcome."

By the time they returned home, the heavens had opened and drenched Matt and Lilia from head to toe. He raised his chin toward Ben's house. "I'll get cleaned up then come over, OK?"

"Sounds good." Lilia started to remove his sweatshirt, but Matt stopped her.

"Don't you want it back?"

"I'll get it later." He motioned toward Muriel's house. "Please get inside before you drown."

She stood on her toes and kissed his cheek. "Thanks again for listening." She hurried away but turned and shouted over her shoulder, "See you later," before returning to Muriel's house.

He waited until she closed the front door as adrenaline pumped through his body. "What a woman," he mumbled to himself as he raced toward Ben's house to get out of the storm.

Muriel and Catherine caught all the action from the living room window. "What do you make of that?" Catherine smiled, tipping her head toward Lilia and Matt.

"They sure make a cute couple," Muriel said.

"Wouldn't Ben have enjoyed seeing this unfold?"

"We probably shouldn't jump to conclusions." Muriel pushed herself out of the chair and started walking to the front door, excited to tell Lilia her health news: she no longer had a chest dressing, and her blood pressure was normal.

The front door burst open.

"Hey, Gran!" Lilia stood dripping wet as she kicked off her shoes. "You're looking good!"

"And you're shivering. Go take a hot shower. We'll talk afterward."

Lilia nodded and waved at Catherine before sprinting to her bedroom.

Muriel returned to her chair and chuckled. "Who was that girl and what did she do with my granddaughter?"

"Oh, there's love in the air." Catherine chuckled, too. "Isn't it wonderful?"

Thirty minutes later, Lilia came into the living room with her hair wrapped in a towel, carrying a tablet and looking at her grandmother. "How was your morning?"

Muriel glanced at Catherine and grinned. "We were about to ask you that same question."

"You first," Lilia volleyed back.

Muriel relayed her health update. "The nurse said I should still use the walker if I feel unsteady"—she lifted the cane—"otherwise I can use this to get around."

"Any dizziness?"

"None."

Lilia powered up the tablet. "Did you talk with her about home care workers?"

"Didn't have to." Muriel handed a folder to Lilia. "She gave me this."

Lilia scanned the material and found information about several companies that provided in-home services, as well as, a list of local people who performed that type of work. "This is perfect! She just made our job a whole lot easier."

The three women were sorting through the list and reading bios when someone knocked on the door. Lilia pulled the towel off her head and ran her hands through her hair before rushing over to answer it as Catherine and Muriel smiled at each other.

"Oh. Hello, Robin."

"Am I disturbing you?"

Lilia started to respond, but Muriel spoke first. "No, of course not. Come in." She waved her hand. "Come sit with us by the fire."

"I saw a woman come and go. Was she your nurse?"

Muriel updated Robin about her health, then showed her the papers scattered on the coffee table. "I need help, so Lilia and I are sorting through options."

"That's great news, Muriel." Robin looked heavenward and released a happy sigh. "I'm glad you're better." She paused, losing some of her enthusiasm. "I have sad news about Mr. McKnight."

"Jasmine's music teacher?" Catherine asked.

Robin nodded. "He's having heart surgery today. A bypass. It'll keep him out of work for several weeks."

"Poor Jasmine," Catherine said. "What'll happen with the children's choir?"

"Don't know yet. The community director is still working on finding a replacement." Robin lowered her eyes as Catherine and Muriel shook their heads.

Lilia sat back, taking in the conversation. Gran looked less pale and had reclaimed her smile. She had no signs of infection and was gaining strength. Robin had worked hard to prepare the homecoming dinner last evening, and Catherine was everyone's rock, willing to do anything for anyone. Matt's words about doing what made her happy echoed in her mind and she made a spur-of-the-moment decision. She turned to Robin and said, "Do you suppose they'd let an outsider help out?"

Robin, Muriel and Catherine all stared at Lilia as though they didn't understand the question.

"Since I'll be here over the weekend, I'd be willing to lead the choir. But only if Catherine can stay with Gran while I'm gone."

"You'd do that?" Robin covered her cheeks with her hands. "You have no idea what it would mean to Jasmine and the rest of the children."

Lilia knew exactly what volunteering would mean to her little protégé. "Why don't you call the director? If she hasn't found anyone, offer my services."

Robin rushed over and hugged Lilia. "Thank you, thank you, thank you!"

Catherine volunteered to stay with Muriel, and the women talked about the concert for a few more minutes before Robin returned home.

"She's such a terrific mother," Muriel said, watching Robin walk away. She turned to Lilia. "And that was one generous offer."

"It's the least I can do considering how hard Jazzy has worked."

Catherine switched topics. "I'm getting hungry. How do tuna sandwiches sound for lunch?" She stood. "We can use that nice organic bread Matthew gave us."

"Sounds yummy." Muriel used her cane to stand up. "I'll help you."

Lilia marveled at the difference a few days at home had made in Muriel's life. Her optimism had returned, and each day brought increased strength to her body. By agreeing to accept help from an outsider, she could remain here, the place she loved. Lilia felt a sense of pride knowing she had played a role in making it happen.

Then a sinking sensation filled her chest as she thought about her mother, the great and powerful CEO.

Lilia picked up her tennis shoes, opened the front door and banged the soles together, knocking crud off. Her mother had asked her to run countless times, but Lilia had always refused, not wanting to relinquish any more control of her life than necessary.

She set her shoes on the floor then checked her phone for messages: nothing from the busy executive. She wondered if her mom ever planned on telling her about Gran's accident. Did she actually think the news wouldn't slip out?

Lilia didn't understand her mother at all but decided to take the high road. She started composing a message to her but kept pressing the delete key, sensing that anything she said would backfire. She finally returned the phone to her back pocket without sending anything.

Susanne would learn about Muriel living at home soon enough. For now, Lilia had more important things to think about. She had a gourmet sandwich to enjoy, home care workers to screen, and a backgammon game to win. Plus, she needed to prepare for a kids' concert. The activities weren't part of her normal routine, but they sure were a pleasant distraction.

TWENTY-ONE

ಬಂಡಚ

Vietnam

Susanne woke early Thursday morning feeling fatigued after a restless night's sleep as family and work issues wove themselves into her dreams. The Rex, her luxury hotel, was located in the former Saigon, the place where the war had ended, but not before ripping Stephen from her family's arms. There was something surreal about building a manufacturing plant in a country that had been tainted by such sorrow, and Susanne struggled to wrap her head around it.

A part of her wanted to tell her family about the business venture, but Muriel would only suffer, having to relive Stephen's death once again. Susanne couldn't endanger her mother's health by resurrecting old memories. And Lilia wasn't interested in the business world, plus Susanne couldn't risk her inadvertently telling Muriel about the factory.

The pressure to keep secrets weighed heavily on her, but it was the right move to maintain everyone's wellbeing. Lilia's youth and Muriel's years sometimes prevented them from making the best decisions, and it was her job to look after them.

Susanne needed to clear her mind of family matters, so

she dressed in her workout clothes and visited the hotel's gym. She set the treadmill at a brisk pace and began running while thinking about today's meeting with Chairman Thanh. She had stayed up late reviewing the data compiled by her research team and had scanned the Internet to learn more about the cultural differences between the United States and Vietnam.

Quang Nguyen had drawn a realistic picture of a woman's role in his country. Even today, Vietnamese women were still considered to be inferior to men, although the government touted equality between the sexes.

Traditionally, Vietnamese women were brought up in a strict, disciplined manner. Since they often received less formal education than men, women rarely entered the job market. They married, assimilated into the husband's family, and assumed responsibility for household chores and childcare. A woman was expected to obey her husband in all matters, sacrificing herself for the benefit of the family.

Another set of rules applied for educated Vietnamese women. They often performed lower level jobs and rarely worked in public service or administrative roles. If a woman attained a position of authority, tradition dictated that she blend in and not overly distinguish herself. Success and reward belonged to the collective group, never to the individual contributor.

Conservative clothes and deferential behavior ruled

the day. A woman could shake a man's hand only after she had earned the right, and the act must be done with great respect and humility. Susanne increased her pace to release growing anxiety and counted her blessings to have been born in the United States.

After working up a decent sweat, she returned to her room to shower and get ready for the day. She realized that Vietnamese business meetings required a specific style, so she dressed in a conservative black suit, white blouse, and low-healed pumps. She wore no jewelry, not even modest earrings. Satisfied with her appearance, she gathered the gifts she had brought from America and walked to the hotel lobby to meet her VP of manufacturing, Dave Simms, and their team.

After zigzagging through town, their van pulled in front of Chairman Thanh's business complex. Susanne's entourage entered a tall building and rode an elevator up eleven stories to a large conference room. Six men wearing dark suits, white shirts, black ties, and dour expressions looked up when the door opened. The environment felt more like a funeral service than a business meeting as Susanne entered the room. She immediately recognized the chairman from pictures and videoconferences, but allowed Dave to make formal introductions.

The chairman smiled broadly. "Madam CEO. Welcome to my country. I trust you had a comfortable trip and are enjoying your hotel."

Susanne bowed. "*Xin chào*. It is my great privilege to meet you, Chairman Thanh. My accommodations in your city are quite pleasing. Thank you for your graciousness."

"Please allow me to introduce my colleagues." The chairman shifted his eyes to the man on his left who introduced himself, bowed and handed Susanne a business card. She mirrored the behavior by greeting him by name and title, then giving him her card. Once finished, the man nodded to the man on his left and the ritual continued until Susanne had met each executive on Chairman Thanh's leadership team.

She faced the chairman and bowed again. "Thank you, Chairman Thanh, for your kind welcome." She motioned toward a bag. "If I may, I would like to honor you with a small gift from my country." She spoke in a respectful tone and waited, eyes lowered.

"That is not necessary, Madam CEO, but I am happy to receive your graciousness."

Susanne reached into the bag and pulled out six packages wrapped in saffron-colored paper and tied with gold ribbon, colors that symbolized wealth and prosperity. She handed the largest gift to Chairman Thanh before distributing the others.

Everyone waited for the chairman to open his gift, and then followed suit. Each man received a framed watercolor of the San Francisco skyline. They chatted among themselves in Vietnamese while examining their gifts. Susanne turned to Quang, seeking a translation.

He whispered, "Men like art. You do good."

Susanne didn't believe that was all they said and wished she understood the language. She disliked relying on others and wanted to know exactly what was being discussed to determine if it impacted the negotiation.

Chairman Thanh silenced the room and looked at his second-in-command, Director Vo, who motioned for everyone to take a seat. Susanne sat across from the chairman, and everyone else sat in descending order according to title.

Director Vo spoke to Susanne. "Thank you for your kindness, Madam CEO." He turned and looked at Dave. "Thank you, Mr. Simms, for sending us your agenda. Shall we begin?"

The next three hours felt like weeks as broad discussions and politeness usurped focus and results. Susanne had never seen anything like it. None of their topics were discussed. Instead, Director Vo talked about tooling and factory production, quality inspections, shipping options and customs protocol as if the contract had already been signed. Nothing made sense.

Susanne wanted to focus on the nuances of the contract to determine sticking points. She asked questions that resulted in indirect answers but didn't probe, fearing she would break an invisible protocol. If someone on the Vietnamese team lapsed into his native language, Quang whispered a translation in her ear. She had hoped to gain insight into their thinking during those unguarded conversations, but the vagueness continued.

As the clock ran out, Susanne occasionally glanced at Chairman Thanh, who sat quietly at the head of the table. She prided herself on being able to read body language but found the chairman's facial expressions impossible to decipher. Lowered heads could indicate a reason to hide something or uncertainty, but he observed all the action, sitting upright in his chair with perfect posture and a stone face.

For Susanne, the morning had been a complete waste of time, and she breathed a sigh of relief when Director Vo ended the session at noon. The chairman stood. "Thank you for a productive morning." He bowed toward Susanne. "Now you will be my honored guests for lunch."

Susanne fantasized about leading the afternoon session where she would do three things: develop a shared vision for the manufacturing plant, surface conflicts, and openly address each one. She would lead by intention, directly asking Chairman Thanh to sign the contract by day's end.

Instead, she bowed and said, "Thank you for your kindness, Chairman Thanh. We will be most pleased to join you." She hoped her facial expression didn't reveal her true feelings.

After lunch, Susanne slipped away to a grassy square next to the chairman's building, needing time alone to clear her head. The morning had ended in complete disappointment. Polite talk supplanted analytical discussions that could have advanced the negotiation. She had started to rethink her decision to partner with the chairman when someone tapped her shoulder, causing her to turn around.

"You do real good this morning, Ms. Bennett. Make excellent progress," Quang said.

What? He couldn't be serious. "Thank you, Mr. Nguyen, but it doesn't feel that way."

"No! You must stay positive. Keep moving forward."

Susanne sighed loudly, wondering what qualified Quang Nguyen to dole out advice when he knew nothing about the business world.

"Vietnamese people prefer a broad overview, then discuss issues. Point by point. You are smart lady who knows to go slow. Walk before run."

"But we're not accomplishing anything. Everyone talks in circles."

Quang became agitated. "No! No circles! Chairman Thanh sizes you up. Likes what he sees. Be patient. He works different than you but has same goal. Make money." He winked at Susanne. "You make lots of money and maybe give Quang a little tip."

Susanne listened without responding.

Quang dropped his smile. "The chairman allows Director Vo to lead, but not make decisions. Only chairman decide. He is patient. You must be patient, too."

"Do you think he's serious about doing business with me?"

"I am only a humble servant and know nothing, but you might like him to show you factory. Give you chance to appreciate his success."

Susanne intuitively knew that Chairman Thanh wanted her company as a partner; otherwise she wouldn't be here. But what was he not saying? Why did he allow the meeting to drag on? What prevented him from signing the contract? Maybe touring the factory, their common ground, would shed light on his thinking. Susanne carefully studied Quang, wondering if he hid wisdom behind a humble facade.

Director Vo conducted the afternoon session with the same ineffectiveness as the morning, yet he professed satisfaction about their accomplishments. He suggested they resume talks tomorrow at the same time to continue the negotiation.

Susanne glanced at Quang, who remained straight-faced, as Dave and his team enthusiastically shook hands with their counterparts, acting as if they had cleared a path through a dense jungle and discovered hidden riches. Dave's behavior disappointed her, and his complacency explained why he hadn't closed the deal after working with Chairman Thanh for weeks. Susanne pondered her earlier conversation with Quang and decided she had nothing to lose.

"Chairman Thanh and Director Vo, this has been an informative day. Thank you for your leadership." She bowed. "With your permission, I would like to ask a favor before we adjourn."

The two men exchanged glances before the chairman said, "What is it, Madam CEO?"

"I am sorry to be ill informed, but I have never seen your factory. Would you do me the great honor of taking me there? You have achieved much success, and I can learn from you." She bowed and waited for a response.

Chairman Thanh and Director Vo whispered back and forth in Vietnamese; then the chairman looked at Susanne. "I appreciate your interest in my business, Madam CEO. Are you available tomorrow morning at nine? I will send a car for you."

His rapid response surprised her, but she hid her reaction under a veil of poise. "Thank you, Mr. Chairman. I accept your kindness."

Susanne glanced at her interpreter and suddenly saw him in a whole new light.

The next morning, a driver arrived at the Rex and whisked Susanne and Quang away. They drove from the city into the countryside for a short while, finally arriving at the factory. Chairman Thanh met her out front and greeted her. An assistant provided earplugs and hard hats for them to wear before starting the tour. The dank building felt like a mammoth tomb, dark and smelly, with row after row of machines churning out parts that fed an assembly line. The workers never looked up, and the whole scene reminded Susanne of early twentieth-century American factories, crowded and noisy, with few exit doors. The place needed to be demolished, but the acreage offered room to construct a massive new building.

At the conclusion of the tour, Susanne spoke. "Your business is quite impressive, Chairman Thanh. Congratulations on your success."

Quang stood next to her with his eyes lowered.

Chairman Thanh bowed. "You honor me, Madam CEO. One day I must tour your American factories."

"It would be my privilege to host a visit for you, Mr. Chairman."

He briefly smiled then cleared his throat. "I understand your daughter plays music and attends school on your east coast."

Susanne did a double-take, wondering if she had heard him correctly. *How did he know about Lilia? And why mention her?*

"Yes. My daughter plays the cello in a quartet, Mr. Chairman. With your permission, I will send you a sample of their music."

The chairman smiled broadly. "Certainly. And I can do the same. My son studies the violin. Maybe they play music together one day. At Carnegie Hall." His eyes lit up with pride.

Carnegie Hall? This man is full of surprises. "That would be a most enjoyable concert. Your son is success-ful, just like his father."

The chairman's smile faded, and he grew serious. "Your man, Tom Reynolds. Does he need to be involved in our business?"

Susanne struggled to maintain her composure as she pondered his second non sequitur. Tom worked for a Houston-based company that had pioneered the art of importing high-quality products made overseas. He had mastered foreign manufacturing, including language and culture, and had been an invaluable resource to advance this project. Susanne wondered what Tom had done to rile the chairman, causing this breach of trust. Chairman Thanh's steady voice and well-articulated question implied sincerity. More importantly, his direct-ness suggested he had begun treating her as a peer. She replied accordingly.

"Mr. Reynolds has expertise with overseas manu-facturing that my company does not possess. That is why we hired him, Mr. Chairman. Would you honor me by sharing your thoughts?"

The chairman didn't respond right away, but placed

his hand on his chin and looked down, taking a few moments for himself. Finally, he raised his eyes and spoke. "Mr. Reynolds is a good man who has served us well but is no longer needed. Perhaps you and I can move forward alone. This would be more efficient and save money."

Susanne could hardly believe her ears. The chairman had never spoken to her so directly or with such clarity. She performed a quick mental analysis and decided Tom wasn't critical to the negotiation's success. She would retain him as a consultant and tap his expertise behind the scenes as needed. A part of her wanted to probe for reasons why the chairman disliked Tom, but she decided against it, sensing her questions might be perceived as a challenge to his leadership.

"That's an interesting idea, Mr. Chairman. Very creative thinking."

"Thank you, Ms. Bennett." The chairman relaxed his brows and tilted his head. "My suggestion does not offend you?"

At that moment, Susanne knew the man standing in front of her would become her business partner. He had demonstrated respect for her by treating her as an equal. They arrived at outcomes differently but shared the same business goals. Susanne glanced at Quang, feeling a great affinity for him. His guidance had led her to this moment, of that she was sure.

"I value your ideas, Chairman Thanh. You do me a

great honor by telling me your truest thoughts."

He smiled broadly. "You are a trusted friend of Vietnamese, Ms. Bennett. I think you and I could build a new factory together." He fanned his arm toward the deafening machines. "Do you agree?"

"Yes. I would enjoy working together very much, Chairman Thanh."

"Maybe I sign that contract." He winked at her. "Shall we tell our people?

She bowed toward the chairman. "If you think the time is right."

"Could you and your team return to my office this afternoon at three?"

"It would be my privilege. Thank you for your wisdom, Mr. Chairman."

As they returned to the car, Susanne glanced at her interpreter who wore a modest smile. Quang Nguyen, the jovial man of mystery, had just become her most trusted Vietnamese advisor.

TWENTY-TWO

Vietnam

Susanne Bennett and Chairman Thanh reconvened at his office later that afternoon with their teams except for Tom Reynolds, who was flying over the South China Sea toward home. Neither Susanne nor Dave understood why the chairman disliked him, but the reason didn't matter. As a deal breaker, he had to go.

Tom's absence shifted the mood in the room, and while formality still prevailed, everyone seemed more relaxed. The chairman served afternoon refreshments: green tea and Vietnamese crepes called *bành xéo*, a rice-flour layer stuffed with pork, shrimp, and bean sprouts. Quang winked at Susanne after she poured a tiny bit of fish sauce on her crepe. He moved a bowl filled with chunks of white fruit containing black seeds closer to her.

"This is called dragon fruit, Ms. Bennett. I think you will like it."

Susanne placed several chunks on her plate and took a bite. It tasted sweet, like a cross between kiwi and pear. She thanked Quang for his recommendation.

Following afternoon tea, a photographer took pictures of Chairman Thanh and CEO Bennett signing a contract for their joint venture. The picture and story would make headline news in tomorrow's edition of the *Saigon Times*. Dave took a few personal photos, then he and Director Vo huddled together in a corner, outlining their next steps as Chairman Thanh and Susanne said their farewells.

"I hope this will not be your only trip to my country, Ms. Bennett. Next time you bring your daughter, and I will introduce her to my son. We will have a concert." The chairman held out his hand. "We are friends now. You may call me, and I will call you."

Susanne shook his hand and nodded graciously, feeling on top of the world. This negotiation had been one of the strangest and most satisfying of her life.

Dave and his team stayed behind to sort through the contract details as Susanne, Quang, and their driver returned to the hotel. Once on the open road Susanne laid her head back, closed her eyes and yawned. Conducting business in Vietnam had been exhausting. She recalled the steps that had led to the signed contract and chuckled to herself, thinking the facts would make an interesting case study for MBA students.

While she knew challenges lay ahead, she felt confident about moving forward after weighing the risks and rewards of the joint venture. At the end of the day, she saw an exciting and profitable partnership between her and Chairman Thanh.

Susanne massaged the back of her neck. She had

never bowed to anyone in her life, and now her neck hurt from doing it so often. This year's bonus had better include generous stock options and a substantial check.

As they entered the city, an enormous structure in the distance caught her attention. "Quang, what's that building over there?"

His eyes followed her finger. "That is Reunification Palace. On April 30, 1975, North Vietnamese tanks crashed through the gates to show war had ended. VC soldiers hang flag off balcony. Our world changed that day. Very symbolic place."

Work had consumed her during the past few days, but now Stephen's ghost had returned. Her brother had fought and died in a war that nobody had won. What would he be like today if he'd lived? Would they be close?

"When do you fly home, Ms. Bennett?"

"Tomorrow morning."

Quang pointed out a window. "It is a shame to come so far and not see more of my country. Maybe you take one or two extra days? I show you good sights. Busy lady need break."

Susanne gazed out the window again. Busy lady definitely needed a break, more than Quang could possibly realize. She hadn't thought much about Muriel during the past two days, but family obligations soon filled her mind. She needed to fly to Oregon and move her mother into an assisted living apartment. It was the right step to take, but she dreaded the responsibility, knowing she faced an uphill, thankless battle. She wasn't one to delay the inevitable, but perhaps taking an extra day to relax before she faced the arduous task wasn't such a bad idea.

Susanne rubbed her forehead and laid her head back. She took a few cleansing breaths, reminding herself that she had made the right decision on Muriel's behalf. She glanced out the window and began thinking about Vietnam's tragic history and how it linked to her family. Slowly, her entire body grew heavy, and she began to shiver. She crossed her arms for warmth and closed her eyes, trying to understand what was happening to her.

Quang spoke. "Are you sick, Ms. Bennett? We can pull over."

Susanne shook her head no. The odd feelings continued, pulling her to a dark place of shadows and remembrances. Suddenly, she wasn't a passenger in a van, but a patient lying on a psychiatrist's couch, spewing her secrets.

She told Quang about Stephen dying in the war and how her mom had cried for years afterward, and still grieved today. She explained how her dad had buried himself in work, pretending that nothing had changed when the opposite was true. Joy and happiness had vanished from the Bennett home, and suppressed feelings became the norm. She described a shrine to Stephen that Muriel kept on her fireplace mantel.

Susanne admitted how much she resented it, telling Quang she never understood how a dead son could trump a living daughter. She went on and on until she stopped herself, feeling embarrassed by the emotional breakdown. She prided herself on not losing control, yet here she was acting so foolishly, sharing her inner-most thoughts with a man she barely knew. She sat up and dried her eyes.

"I'm sorry, Quang. I don't know what came over me. Please accept my apology."

He looked at her with a vacant stare, then turned and gazed out the window.

Susanne felt ashamed for allowing her emotions to get the best of her.

Quang continued staring out the window as he spoke. "I serve in war, too, Ms. Bennett. With Ameri-cans. It was a sad time." His voice seeped with melan-choly. "Difficult for both soldiers and families."

Susanne observed Quang closely. His eyes had red-dened, and his shoulders slumped forward. Her rant had obviously stirred painful memories for him, and she felt even more guilty about her silly outburst. She could only imagine the tragic ways the war had affected him and his family.

The next few miles were filled with silence as she scrolled through her calendar. Her commitments blur-red together, and she had an overwhelming urge to toss the phone out the window to free her from obligations.

"Are you available tomorrow, Quang?"

He nodded while removing a handkerchief from his back pocket and blowing his nose. "Do you remember where your brother died, Ms. Bennett?"

Quang's question instantly transported Susanne back in time to when she was a nine-year-old girl living with her parents in Oregon. A black sedan had parked in the family's driveway late one afternoon. Her mother glanced through a curtain, and after two men wearing military uniforms started walking toward the house, she screamed, "No! No! Please God, no!" She collapsed on the floor in agony. Her father rushed in from the kitchen and knelt beside Muriel, trying to understand what was wrong. A knock on the front door forced him to look up.

Edward Bennett didn't invite the soldiers into the house that day. Instead, he stood at the door and calmly received the news of his son's death while Muriel wept. His voice cracked as he thanked the men for coming, then closed the door, and rested his head against it. He soon fell next to his wife and pulled her into his arms, wailing and asking "Why?" repeatedly.

The two of them had lost all sense of time and had forgotten about Susanne completely. She ran to her bedroom, slammed the door and threw herself on the bed, sobbing uncontrollably. She would never forget the name of the battle where Stephen had died. It had been seared into her brain.

"Have you heard about the New Year's Day Battle in the Tay Ninh province?"

Quang's chin began to tremble. He started to speak but stumbled on the words, so he turned away and stared out the window. Several miles later, he wiped his eyes with the back of his hand and faced Susanne. "Yes, Ms. Bennett. I know about that battle. I know it very well."

TWENTY-THREE

๛)๖

Oregon

Lilia arrived at the community center to meet the director and to lead the children's choir through a dry run. As she glanced around the place, memories of carefree summers came flooding back. She had taken swim and tennis lessons there, and Gran had taught watercolor classes as she sat in the back of the room, doodling on paper.

Anticipation grew as she entered the auditorium where the choir would practice. After the director handed her a participant roster and left, Lilia strolled onstage, sat down with her legs dangling off the edge and closed her eyes.

Her music coach, Louis, had taught her to visualize success, and his words echoed in her head: "All things are created twice, dear Lilia, first in your mind, and then in real time. You must leave your own thoughts behind and travel into the composer's world. What did he feel as he wrote the notes? What was he trying to express? Once you have those answers, play the piece in your head before you pick up a bow. After that, your interpretation will be meaningful."

For today's rehearsal, Lilia pictured well-behaved children standing on stage and singing like little angels.

They skillfully hit their notes and proudly remembered every word of their three songs: "Jingle Bells," "The Twelve Days of Christmas," and "Let It Snow." Jasmine hit each key on the piano with perfect timing.

Lilia was ready for them.

Jasmine and her mom arrived first, and within twenty minutes, Lilia had fifteen children milling around the stage, laughing and chasing one another playfully.

"May I have your attention?" Lilia said.

The kids completely ignored her and continued their silliness.

Lilia clapped her hands and raised her voice. "Will everyone please listen?"

Only Jasmine looked up.

Her chest tightened when the kids didn't respond. Compliance was her norm, and she wondered how to get the kids to pay attention. Jasmine standing next to the piano gave her an idea, and she silently prayed it would work.

She sat on the bench and faced the keyboard. She took an extra breath to center herself, flexed her fingers a few times, and then began playing a lively version of "Santa Claus Is Coming to Town." The kids quickly gathered around her, humming and singing, and Lilia didn't stop until she had finished the entire song, performing just for fun.

Afterward, she swung around and faced the kids.

"I'm sorry Mr. McKnight isn't here. We all hope he gets better soon. Meanwhile, if we work together, I think your part in the program will still be lots of fun." She glanced around, not stopping until she had given each child eye contact. "What questions do you have for me?"

"Who are you?" a red-haired girl asked.

"My name is Lilia Bennett-Parker. I've spent time every summer here with my grandparents, but I grew up in California. Right now, I live in Boston where I attend music school."

"How come you have two last names?" a freckled-faced boy asked.

"Bennett is my mom's last name; Parker is my dad's. Both wanted me to have their name, so I ended up with two."

"You play really good!" another boy exclaimed. "That was a cool song!"

"Thank you." Lilia smiled at her angels. "I've told you about me; now I want to hear about you."

She asked each child to say his or her name, tell everyone his or her favorite song and describe why. She listened carefully to the responses, sizing up each child. After the last one had spoken, she organized them onstage and asked them to sing "Jingle Bells" as Jasmine played the piano. Each child carried a bell to ring at appropriate intervals throughout the song.

Lilia almost covered her ears after they began singing. Their voices were out of key, their sense of timing was way off, and they rang bells whenever they wanted, not with the beat. She silently pondered what to do, given the circumstances. A metronome sitting on the piano generated an idea. She lifted the device high into the air so everyone could see it. "Have you ever used one of these?"

Several of the kids nodded while others wore blank expressions.

"Want to try something really fun?"

"Yeah!" they yelled in unison.

Lilia started the metronome and motioned for everyone to settle down. "Can you hear it click when it moves back and forth?"

The kids nodded and started moving with the beat.

"Now I want you to clap every time you hear that click." Lilia demonstrated the behavior she sought from the children.

"But Mr. McKnight only uses the metronome for the piano," Jasmine whined.

"It can be used in different ways. Would you like to be my assistant?"

Her eyes lit up, and she quickly stood next to Lilia.

"Let's try this. Every time you hear a click, I want you to clap your hands like Jasmine and me." Lilia started with a slow tempo, making sure Jazzy had mastered the beat, and before long, the kids were hitting the mark most of the time. Lilia had them sing "Jingle Bells" again. Even though the performance wasn't perfect, their timing had improved. She started the metronome again, but this time she had the kids ring a bell to the beat instead of clapping. Finally, she asked Jazzy to play a few scores on the piano so the kids could practice with the music.

"That was fun!" two kids squealed at the same time.

"Can we do it again?" a shy girl asked.

Lilia had the choir sing "Jingle Bells" once more, then rehearsed the other two songs. The children seemed to take feedback well, and Lilia breathed a sigh of relief after the practice ended, feeling cautiously optimistic.

"Good work, everyone. See you tomorrow at six." Lilia chuckled to herself, thinking she sounded a little like Louis. She made a mental note to call him about missing Sunday's coaching session.

Parents gathered in the auditorium, waiting to take their children home. Several of the kids hugged Lilia before leaving, and Jazzy practiced the piano until Robin arrived. Lilia finished cleaning up and was walking out when she spotted a familiar face sitting near the back row. Matt stood and approached her with a kind smile.

"You're a nice surprise," Lilia said, trying to understand his visit.

"So are you."

She pointed toward the stage. "Umm, I think you knew I'd be here."

"You were great with those kids, Lilia. You're a gifted teacher."

She felt her cheeks warm. "Thanks."

"Care to give a guy a lift home?" He pointed to his running shoes. "I told Muriel and Catherine we'd bring dinner with us."

Lilia couldn't think of a better way to end her day.

Matt and Lilia stopped at a Chinese restaurant and bought honey-sesame chicken, broccoli beef, chow mein, fried rice, and egg rolls. Once they arrived back home, Matt slipped away to shower at his house before joining Lilia, Catherine, Robin and Jasmine around Muriel's table. Catherine didn't bother transferring the food to serving plates. Instead, she opened the white cartons, stuck big spoons in each one, and placed them on the dining room table as Robin and Lilia set out dishes, glasses, and silverware.

After enjoying their feast and cleaning up, everyone gathered around the living room fire and swapped stories. Before long, Jasmine yawned and curled up on the couch, laying her head on her mother's lap. "I better get this little one to bed. She's had a busy day."

Catherine stood. "I'm rather tired myself." She turned toward Muriel and asked, "Do you need anything before I leave?"

"No, and I appreciate you for staying with me this afternoon."

Muriel pushed up from her chair to walk her guests out and bid them farewell.

Matt cautiously watched the exodus, not wanting to return to his grandfather's cold house where nothing but memories awaited him. The crackling fire, heavy rain, and full stomach made him want to stay with Lilia, so he didn't move. He hoped neither she nor Muriel would chase him away.

After Muriel closed the front door, she looked at Lilia and Matt. "Do you care if I go to bed? It's been a long day and I'm pretty tired."

"No, of course not." Lilia started to rise. "I'll help you get ready."

Muriel shook her head. "You stay here and keep Matthew company. I'll let you know if I need anything."

"You sure?"

"Yes. I'll be fine. Just remember to put out the fire," Muriel said before walking to her bedroom and closing the door.

Matt wanted to high-five the universe. He stretched out his legs and patted the seat next to him. He couldn't believe they were all alone. He thought about setting up the backgammon board but decided in favor of something more personal. "How about a foot rub?"

Lilia's eyes flickered as she looked at him with a mischevious grin. "For you or me?"

He enjoyed her wit and liked how she blushed and

smiled at the same time. "Either way works."

Lilia hopped on the couch, settled into a stack of pillows and placed her feet in his lap. "Act quickly, think slowly," she teased. "Famous Greek proverb."

Matt smiled and began massaging her feet, moving slowly and methodically. Before long, Lilia's eyes closed, her body relaxed, and she yawned without apologizing as the fire made her complexion glow.

"Mmm, that feels amazing."

"It's your reward for working with those kids."

"They were a handful." She peeked at him with one eye. "When did you arrive at the center?"

"During 'The Twelve Days of Christmas.'"

"What'd you think?"

"That they have an awesome teacher." He pressed his thumbs into her arches, rubbing back and forth. "Pressure OK?"

"Mmm, heavenly. You get an A-plus."

Matt continued massaging her feet, enjoying their quiet time together.

Lilia broke the silence. "May I ask you a question?"

"Of course. Anything."

She sat up, tucking her feet underneath her body. "I'm curious. Why didn't your parents come with you? Are they OK?"

Matt leaned forward and looked into the flames, and didn't respond right away. Finally, he spoke. "They're fine. Just busy with the store"—he looked at Lilia—"and other family stuff."

"Sounds like they have a lot going on."

"You could say that."

"Want to talk about it?"

He considered the offer but decided not to ruin the mood. "Maybe one day, but not now." He didn't want to think about anything tonight except Lilia.

"Let me know if you change your mind." She tossed him a tender smile. "I'm a good listener, too."

"You know what I'd like to talk about?" he asked, making a bold move.

Lilia tilted her head and waited for him to explain. "Head rubs." Matt tugged at his hair. "I wouldn't say no to one."

She hesitated a moment, then gingerly patted her lap. Matt quickly crawled over and laid his head down, stretching his legs out the length of the couch.

He and Lilia had never been this intimate with each other, and as he caught her eye, she turned away, blushing. He closed his eyes, hoping darkness would soften the uneasiness between them. But as she began massaging his scalp, her touch felt awkward, like standing too close to a stranger on a crowded bus during rush hour.

Since arriving in Oregon, a question had plagued him. He decided the time was right to get it out of the way. "You dating anyone back in Boston?"

Lilia stopped massaging for a second and chuckled.

"If my cello's a guy, I'd have to say yes. Otherwise, the answer's no."

He opened his eyes to catch her expression. She wore a playful smile, and when their gaze met, she held it briefly.

"What about you?" she asked in a demure voice. "You seeing anyone?"

He closed his eyes again and nuzzled closer. "Not in Boston, but I have a few hundred ladies waiting for me back home in Williamsport."

She giggled and tugged his hair. He kept his eyes closed, not wanting to break the spell. Her touch became bolder as she increased the massage's pressure using her nails to scratch his scalp, stirring all kinds of pleasant sensations.

He marveled at how Lilia had changed from a girl who tattled on him for pulling her pigtails to an accomplished young woman waiting to be discovered. Although work consumed most of his time, he'd had several relationships, but none of the women had held his interest for long.

Lilia Bennett-Parker had never been far from his thoughts, and now, here they were together, touching and being touched. Their proximity seemed dreamlike, and he breathed in her scent to make sure he was actually nestled in her lap, on this couch, at this moment.

Her fingers left his scalp and gently explored his face, causing him to sigh contentedly. He hadn't felt this happy in a long time. Her touch awakened something deep inside of him, and he opened his eyes and caught her stare. He smiled; she smiled and neither turned away.

He reached up and caressed her cheek. "Are we becoming more than friends?"

Her body tensed, and she slowly withdrew her hand. "I…I don't think I'd be very good for you."

He sat up, confused by the sudden mood shift. "Why would you say that?"

"Oh, Matt, you know better than anyone how crazy my life is right now. I don't have time to breathe." She brought her legs close to her body and wrapped her arms around them, lowering her head.

Matt struggled to reconcile the swift change in her behavior. They were back to square one, all trust disappearing in an instant. He racked his brain for possible explanations. A busy schedule? School? Peter? Her grandmother? Her mom? Something else?

"Can you just forget I said that?" he begged.

Her chin began trembling, and he drew her into a soft embrace. "Hey, what's wrong?" He gently rubbed her back. "You can tell me anything."

She laid her cheek on his chest, making no effort to talk or move.

He held her, continuing to rub her back and giving her all the time she needed.

After a few minutes, she pulled back. "Maybe I'll

talk about it one day, but not now."

Matt's mouth dropped open to feign disbelief. "Did you just steal my line?"

She gave him a half-smile then looked down, pressing her lips together.

He wanted to leave on a semi-positive note, so he stood up. "Thank you for tonight." He shrugged on a jacket. "I had a good time."

She followed him to the front door, looking like a child waking from a bad dream, frightened and in need of comforting. He hugged her again and kissed her cheek, but when she made no move to return his affection, he backed away and decided to call it a night.

"Sleep well, Lilia."

She leaned against the doorframe and murmured, "You too."

He tucked his hands in his pockets and strolled home alone, wanting to be with her, but unsure how to make it happen. An invisible door held her back, and he had no idea how to unlock it. He wondered if their relationship wasn't meant to be. Perhaps he should finish business, return home, and put this part of his life behind him. Maybe chasing past dreams wasn't such a great idea after all.

Twenty-Four

‾‾‾

Vietnam

Susanne dressed in running gear and braved the morning streets of Ho Chi Minh City. Even on Saturday, traffic jammed the city center as she ran along a boulevard lined with evergreen trees and high-rise buildings. Tiny packed stalls inside a large market sold produce, flowers, lacquerware, jewelry, apparel and so forth.

Vendors of all ages sold drinks and noodles at roadside stalls throughout the city. The Communist town even offered its rendition of Beverly Hills' Rodeo Drive with high-end shops such as Louis Vuitton and Chanel. If consumerism offered a glimpse of how people live, some Vietnamese were doing quite well.

She passed a toddler sitting happily in a child's seat behind a man riding an old bicycle. She wore a white hat with large, pink bunny ears. Susanne waved at her, and the little girl smiled, revealing a dimple in her chin.

A woman wearing peasant clothing and a conical hat shouldered a basket while walking past another woman in a business suit carrying a briefcase. *A time warp*, Susanne thought, marveling at the contrast between them as she turned down the street leading back to her hotel.

She ran up the stairs to the rooftop bar where she

rested and drank a full bottle of water while looking over the city. Where would Quang take her today? She stretched her leg to relieve a muscle cramp then glanced at her watch. He and the driver would arrive soon, so she headed down to her room to shower and change.

A van parked in front of the hotel and Quang jumped out to greet Susanne. His business suit had been replaced by blue jeans, a white shirt with rolled sleeves, tennis shoes and a Red Sox baseball cap.

He bowed. "Good morning, Ms. Bennett. We have one day and many things to see."

Susanne bowed even though she didn't have to. "Where are we going?"

"Places that will interest you." He opened the back door. "Are you ready?"

Susanne nodded. By now, she had learned to trust him, so she stepped into the van and buckled her seat belt.

The first stop was the Reunification Palace, headquarters of the South Vietnamese presidency until 1975. "This place is like a castle. You see pretty rooms, then I show you two interesting things before we leave."

The building had a 1960s architecture look that was more municipal than regal. Formal meeting rooms contained shiny black lacquered furniture, and the palace lacked warmth; more museum than home.

Quang guided Susanne down a flight of stairs.

"The basement not changed since war. This place called war room. Make you feel like a CEO general." Quang's jack-o'-lantern grin had returned.

Old maps cluttered the long tables. Ancient phones and radio transmitters collected dust as bulky ceiling fans chopped the stale air. While the rest of the palace had been renovated, the communications center had been left untouched as a tribute to history. Susanne imagined military men hovering around the tables and strategizing about their next move, similar to her executive meetings back in California.

"We go now." Quang led Susanne up from the basement to the roof where a restored Huey helicopter awaited. No doubt he had seen the big bird hundreds of times, but he observed it like a first-time visitor.

"Have you ridden in one of these, Quang?"

"I attend naval academy in Nha Trang. We ride in boats, not helicopters." He smiled and said, "But I ride in a few of those, too," as he pointed at the Huey.

Susanne observed Quang, a complex man with a secret past. "Where'd you learn to speak English so well?"

"I study in Vietnamese school"—he looked at her with a sly grin—"then in San Diego."

"San Diego? As in California?"

He touched his lips with a finger. "I study with US Navy to decipher codes, but don't tell anyone." He winked at her and said, "We go to next place now."

They left the city and drove about twenty miles to the countryside, parking next to an enormous crater created by a five-hundred-pound American bomb. Quang talked about the huge pit as if it were a museum exhibit instead of a death sentence for hundreds of people.

"Quang, you don't seem...how can I say this? You and other Vietnamese are quite forgiving of Americans considering our forced presence in your country." Susanne motioned toward the crater.

"No sense in living in the past, Ms. Bennett. We look to future. My children and grandchild have better life than me. That's all that matters."

Quang amazed Susanne with his positive outlook given the obstacles life had tossed his way. He never seemed to have a bad day. The tour continued as she followed him along a path toward a series of buildings that looked like army barracks.

"In 1948, Viet Cong dig first tunnel in Cu Chi. They hide guns, then hide themselves underground. Americans bombed this area. Try to destroy tunnels, but can't. They are part of large network that run through my country. You see one now." Quang spoke in Vietnamese to a young man dressed in a khaki uniform, handed him some local currency, then motioned for Susanne to follow the guide.

"You go in tunnel now, Ms. Bennett." Quang refused to enter but nudged Susanne forward. "Very interesting, you learn. Home to Viet Cong during war. You see how enemy lived."

She followed the guide, dipping her head to enter the manmade cave. She walked hunched over for twenty or thirty yards, feeling claustrophobic the entire time. Damp earth, dim lighting, bugs and narrow dirt walls caused her heart to palpitate. She hurried toward the exit, desperate for sunlight and fresh air.

Susanne sat on a bench staring at the tunnel's exit wondering how the Viet Cong could live in a place like that for weeks at a time. She sipped bottled water, waiting for her breathing to return to normal.

When Quang started to talk, she held up a hand. "No more tunnels." Her body shivered as she recalled the movie *Platoon* where US soldiers had tossed explosives into holes, then climbed into them to search for VC. Was Stephen forced to do that terrifying job? She hoped not.

Quang sat beside her bent over with elbows on his thighs, chin resting on folded hands. "I spend eight years in prison camp after war. For rehabilitation. Do hard work in mountains, only have dirty rice to eat. Always cold and sick, barely stay alive. Tunnel not so bad."

Susanne stared at him. "What did you just say?"

"Camp was terrible place. Many people die. I pretend to be re-educated, so I can go home to my family." He abruptly stood. "We leave now."

Quang's words left Susanne dazed. Crawling

through the tunnel and hearing about his ordeal, combined with her brother's death, became too painful. She remained seated and crossed her arms.

"I'm not going anywhere until you tell me the plan."

He patted her shoulder. "I take you to Tay Ninh province. You pay respect to Stephen."

She unfolded her arms and slumped back. "I...I don't think I can go there, Quang." She glanced away, unable to look him in the eyes. "Please take me back to the hotel."

He patted her shoulder again, causing her to look up. "You do this for Stephen. You will be fine. We all fine." He motioned for them to leave. Knowing where they would end up, Susanne stood and reluctantly followed him to the van.

During the drive to Tay Ninh, they passed a portion of the Mekong Delta where acres and acres of fields supported rice paddies. Fisherman trolled in muddy waters with large nets, as rickety houseboats floated nearby.

Quang continued to point out various sites along the way but kept mostly to himself. As they entered the town of Tay Ninh, Susanne tensed. She questioned her sanity for allowing Quang to bring her here. What possible good could come from it?

Quang interrupted her thoughts by motioning toward the most intricate structure Susanne had ever seen. "That temple is for Cao Dai religion. It combines

Buddhism, Taoism and Confucianism. Makes all people happy."

The structure appeared to be equal parts pagoda, cathedral and mosque. Fluorescent shades of pinks and yellows illuminated the area, and its mosaic-mirrored tiles glinted in the sun. Multi-colored dragons of all shapes and sizes accessorized the building. *How fitting,* thought Susanne, *to find a temple of immense beauty in a place of war-torn sadness.*

As they moved through town, Quang lifted his chin toward a mountain range and wooded area in the distance. "The Ho Chi Minh Trail is over there. More tunnels, too. VC uses both during war. Very dangerous place for American and South Vietnamese armies."

They drove toward an open field, and Quang directed the driver to pull over to the side of the road. He glanced at Susanne and said somberly, "We walk now, Ms. Bennett."

He rubbed his lower back while strolling through the tall weeds, looking here and there, picking up an occasional rock and tossing it at nothing in particular. Susanne gently touched his arm.

"What happened here, Quang?" she whispered.

He took out a handkerchief and blew his nose, then stuffed it back in his pocket. "At the end of 1967, Pope John Paul ask all soldiers to observe a thirty-six-hour cease-fire. To begin New Year in peace. Both sides agree to the request."

Quang paused and looked toward the mountain and trees in the distance.

"Six hours before truce ended, Viet Cong attack. It was heavy mortar strike late at night." He paused again. "Your Stephen fight here. Many people die." He glanced at Susanne with a mournful expression. "I am sorry about your pain, Ms. Bennett." His eyes drifted over the field. "Your brother die trying to help people like Quang. You honor him now." He bowed and eased away, slowly crossing the field and leaving Susanne alone with her thoughts.

Most of her life, she had lived in Stephen's shadow, never quite understanding what really happened to him, never accepting her parents' pain as real. She had seen the war movies, studied the history of Vietnam, but nothing prepared her for this moment.

The field seemed to welcome her like an expected guest, opening its door and ushering her in. She smelled the pungent earth and closed her eyes as a warm breeze blew across her face, taking her to a place far away. She felt mortar shells erupting, smoke and fire, screams in the darkness, cries of pain, shouts of fear from hundreds of soldiers, blood flowing like a river all around her.

She held out her arms to embrace the sorrow as she meandered across a grassy knoll. She imagined Stephen dressed in his military uniform—the picture on Muriel's fireplace mantel. He had fought to provide freedom for others, like Quang. He died honorably while serving his country. She suddenly realized how much she loved and missed him.

She took a deep breath and allowed herself to feel everything; the loss, the bitterness, the tragedy, the emptiness. Wind brushed her face, cooling perspiration that had accumulated on her skin. The war never ended for people like Quang and Muriel, nor for families of other dead soldiers. It never ended for a sister who grew up in an older brother's shadow. But right now, here in Tay Ninh, Susanne finally understood what Stephen's sacrifice was about.

She looked up at the clouds and thought about her mother. Susanne couldn't imagine losing Lilia like Muriel had lost Stephen. She couldn't bear the crushing sensation filling her chest as she pictured him gasping for air under a starless night, taking his final breath alone as death and destruction surrounded him. Why hadn't she been able to understand her mother's pain before today—*especially* after giving birth to Lilia? Had Muriel been living in this kind of perpetual grief since Stephen's death?

Susanne watched Quang pick a wildflower and toss one petal at a time into the wind, freeing them from bondage. She moved next to him and clasped his hand in friendship.

"Thank you for bringing me here, Quang. It means more than you'll ever know."

He nodded. "You honored your brother, Ms. Bennett. Now you both free."

Susanne looked at him with reverence. She did feel a sense of freedom and wanted to share the experience with her mother more than anything. She would tell Muriel about Quang and others like him whom Stephen tried to save from tyranny. She would describe her brother's courage in the middle of a dark night, caught in an ambush that wasn't supposed to happen. Perhaps she and her mother could make their peace before it was too late. Maybe that's why fate had brought her halfway around the world to Vietnam.

"I'm ready to go home, Quang."

TWENTY-FIVE

ଔୗଔ

Oregon

On Saturday morning Lilia woke from a distressing nightmare about Peter Tremblay. In the dream, she had returned to school, but Peter wouldn't acknowledge her presence. She saw him everywhere—in class, practice rooms, the coffee shop, the library—but he completely ignored her. She begged him for a second chance, but he turned his head and refused to listen.

Lilia realized it was only a dream, but if Peter knew she was leading a kids' choir tonight, he'd write her off permanently. Although she enjoyed helping her grandmother and Jazzy, she needed to quit sabotaging her career and return to Boston pronto.

For that to happen, three things needed to occur, and hiring a qualified home care worker topped the list. She and Muriel had reviewed many résumés and had narrowed the list to three candidates. They would conduct interviews on Monday and select Muriel's favorite. Once the caretaker had been recruited, Lilia needed Catherine to stay with Gran until the worker started. They already spent most of their time together, but Lilia wanted to formalize an agreement for her own peace of mind.

The final part of the return-to-Boston plan depended on a factor totally out of Lilia's control: Susanne Bennett's compassion. After her mom returned from Asia, Lilia would call and explain the past week's events to her. She expected her mother to be irate about Muriel living at home instead of East River. But she trusted that Gran's improved health, combined with a commitment to hire and retain qualified help, would trump all anger. If all that happened, and if Muriel's health continued to improve, she could return home with a clear conscious. She still had an uphill battle with Peter but believed it was a fight she could win.

Just as the plan fell into place, she pictured Matthew Campbell's light brown eyes gazing at her.

Their time together last evening had stirred some unexpected feelings. She had always been drawn to him but figured it was because they had grown up together during summer vacations. Last night, friendship had morphed into something more, and they both knew it. She felt a strong physical attraction for him—a longing —that frightened her. A relationship between them could never work because he only knew the innocent girl from his past. He didn't know the real her, the secret part she kept locked away. If he learned about her baby, he would return home and never look back. She'd rather keep him as a friend. Besides, she had a music career to consider, which left no time for romance.

She glanced out the window toward Ben's house, thinking about Matt. *Was he awake? Was he thinking about her at this very moment? How would he spend the day?*

Lilia heard a noise outside her door, so she got up to explore and found Muriel banging around in the kitchen. She had dressed herself, combed her hair, and was using her cane for support even though it seemed like she didn't need it.

"Looking good, Gran."

"Hello, sleepyhead." Muriel motioned toward the coffeemaker. "Your caffeine's almost ready."

"How 'bout I make scrambled eggs and toast?"

"Sounds like a winner."

Lilia set the table and served the food. As they were eating breakfast, she gazed out the window toward Ben's house.

"Thinking about Matthew?" Muriel asked with a teasing smile.

"Nope." Lilia tried to be serious as she pointed to a feeder that hung outside the window. "I was searching for rare birds."

"I'm not blind, you know."

"I like him, Gran, but…"

"You're too busy to fall in love?"

Lilia didn't want to go there, so she redirected the conversation. "Do you have any chores for me today?" She pointed at a wall clock. "I don't have to be at the community center until five."

"Would you mind driving me to a couple of places?"

"Of course not." Lilia tilted her head. "Where to?"

"Not far."

"What kind of answer is that?"

Muriel winked at her without explaining.

Lilia turned onto the main highway and drove south toward an unknown destination. Several miles later, Gran gestured toward a market and asked her to stop so she could buy three flower bouquets, but wouldn't say why. Lilia rolled her eyes but helped Muriel with her mission. Soon they arrived at the Collier Memory Center, and Lilia glanced at her grandmother as she rolled into the parking lot and turned off the ignition.

"Why are we visiting Esther?"

"I thought you might like to see her before returning to school. You know, just in case…"

Lilia could have filled in the blank with "in case she *dies*," but didn't, knowing the words would make them both sad. She helped Muriel out of the car without asking further questions so they could visit Matt's grandmother. Muriel held a bouquet in one hand while clutching Lilia's arm with her other as they entered the nursing home.

Forty-five minutes later, they left the facility with Lilia shaking her head. Esther's deterioration had devastated her, and she wondered what would happen now that Ben was gone. Matt sure had some important decisions to make about his grandmother's future before returning home.

"Where to now?" Lilia asked, trying to distract herself from thinking about Matt and Esther.

"Drive toward my house, but we'll turn off before the usual exit."

"You're enjoying this little game, aren't you?"

Muriel smiled, then turned to watch the scenery. Miles later, she directed Lilia to turn into the Pacific Memorial Cemetery.

"We're visiting Gramps?"

"And Stephen."

Once she parked the car, Lilia assisted Muriel over a small hill toward the Bennett family plots, carrying two bouquets. Days of rain had soaked the earth, and walking through the muddy grass proved challenging as their shoes sank into the moist ground. Lilia held Muriel's arm securely, making sure she didn't fall.

Edward Bennett had died fifteen years earlier at the age of seventy-two, and Stephen Bennett had died at age nineteen in the Vietnam War. Lilia had never met her uncle and barely remembered her grandfather, and she wondered why Gran had brought her here today.

After arriving at the two gravesites, Muriel closed her eyes, bowed her head and began praying. Lilia bowed, too, as she held her grandmother's arm. Later, Muriel bent over and began removing overgrown grass and weeds that choked Stephen's headstone while Lilia worked on her grandfather's marker. Muriel unearthed two vases and handed both to Lilia.

"Would you mind filling these with water?" She gestured toward a faucet about thirty yards away.

Muriel artfully arranged the flowers in the vases and returned them to the earth. She brushed both hands on her pants, then kissed the inside of her fingers and pressed love on the two names etched in stone. "Your Uncle Stephen was more like me, but your mom was closer to her dad."

Lilia listened to a few stories about each man without asking questions. Soon, Muriel motioned toward a cement bench. "May we sit for a couple of minutes?"

Lilia helped her grandmother walk over to the bench, mentally chalking up the entire morning to nostalgia. Once seated, Muriel casually looked around the cemetery, taking in the birds and flowers. She chuckled as two squirrels chased one another in a nearby tree.

Lilia waited patiently.

Muriel pulled her jacket tighter as a sudden gust of wind blew past. Her eyes grew moist. "Do you know what Matthew is doing right now?"

Lilia shrugged. "No idea."

"He's with his grandfather." Muriel reached into her purse and pulled out a tissue. "He's having Ben's body cremated."

Lilia felt as though an arrow had pierced her heart.

She stood abruptly, unable to fathom why Matt hadn't told her. "He shouldn't be alone, Gran. We need to find him."

Muriel held her arm. "I asked if he wanted company. He said no. We need to honor his wishes."

Lilia returned to the bench but had an overwhelming urge to flee. She wanted to escape from this day of sickness, death and sadness, and return to school where demanding routines made sense.

"Why'd you bring me here, Gran? I mean, why today of all days?"

"I love you, Lilia." Muriel reached over and touched her locket. "And I'm worried about you because of your baby."

What? Lilia drew back, feeling like she'd taken a wrong turn down a dark alley and shadows were closing in. No one ever mentioned the baby, an unspoken pact between family members who pretended the pregnancy had never happened. She sat back, pulling away from her grandmother.

"I'm sorry, Lilia."

"For what?" She twisted the locket and looked at Muriel. "You're the only one who didn't want my *problem* to go away."

"It's time you and I talk about her."

"Why now?" Lilia crossed her arms. "Nothing good can come from it."

"I want to apologize. I stood by without saying a

word to keep the peace. It was wrong."

Lilia squeezed her eyes shut, trying to understand why her grandmother was forcing her to relive painful memories. She didn't want to talk about the baby. She had moved on, and saw no purpose in rehashing the past. Especially when she couldn't do anything to change it.

Muriel clasped Lilia's hand. "Will you tell me how you felt back then? What you wanted?"

Lilia slumped forward. Pain, guilt, and doubt bubbled up from her heart. "What do you expect me to say?" Her eyes filled with tears. "She was my little girl. I loved her."

"I know you did, sweetheart." Muriel paused. "And I need your forgiveness."

Lilia looked into her grandmother's eyes. "Mom and Dad forced everything, not you. You were the only one who understood. There's nothing to forgive."

Muriel swallowed a few times before speaking slowly. "I want to apologize for burying her in that piece of jewelry." She touched the necklace. "That was a mistake."

Bury her? Lilia covered her mouth to stifle a gasp.

"You know my greatest fear?"

Lilia stood and began pacing back and forth, not understanding her grandmother's renewed interest in her past. She didn't want to know Muriel's greatest fear. She wrapped her arms across her body, wondering how to escape from the inquisition.

Muriel stood and lovingly placed her hands on Lilia's shoulders. "I bought that necklace to comfort you during a time of great sorrow. Now I worry it'll weigh you down for the rest of your life." She lifted Lilia's chin, forcing eye contact. "You gave your baby to a loving family. That took tremendous courage. Now it's time to forgive yourself and move on with your life."

Lilia backed away and looked defiantly at Muriel. "I *have* moved on. I'm in college. I get good grades. I play the cello. I do *everything* I'm supposed to. Isn't that good enough for you?"

"Oh, Lilia, I see your struggle. I'm not blind. You pick up that locket and hold it at least ten times a day. You sleep with it." Muriel caught her breath. "And moving on and forgiving yourself…well, those are two very different things, aren't they?"

Lilia's eyes blurred with more tears, and she crumpled on the bench.

"I don't expect you to forget your baby, but her birth and adoption shouldn't dictate your future. I want you to do more than persevere. I want you to soar to the stars."

"It's not that easy, Gran. *I* signed those papers. *I* gave her away."

Muriel sat next to her and lifted her chin. "You did your very best under challenging circumstances. It's all we can ask of ourselves." She patted both their eyes. "Now…I've said my piece and won't harp on the subject anymore. I only ask that you think about what I've said. You get one shot at life, Lilia. Please carve out one that brings you joy."

Time grounded to a halt as Lilia slid into her grandmother's arms, finding understanding and unconditional love. She had her dreams and tried not living in the past, but whenever she opened up, something or someone usually shut her down. Even the news about her dad's baby had set her off. She knew she had overreacted, but didn't know what else to do. After a while, she asked Muriel a question that haunted her. "How do I move on, Gran? I mean, really move on and put the past behind me?"

"Here's how you do it, sweetheart." Muriel held her tenderly, stroking her hair and not rushing time. "You allow your baby girl, Gramps, Stephen, Ben and Esther to remind you how precious life is. You move forward by choosing a path that makes sense for you. No one—not your mom or dad, not Peter Tremblay, not your professors and certainly not me—has any right to tell you how to live your life."

Lilia's body began shaking as she spoke in a strained whisper. "Everyone's always dictating my life, Gran. It's all I know."

"Not anymore, my sweet girl. You're all grown up now. You've certainly proved that this week by coming here to take care of me."

Lilia lost track of time as she and her grandmother spoke of their lives. They shared secrets that would never be revealed to anyone else. They prayed for Lilia's little girl just like they prayed for other lost loved ones, no longer pretending she didn't exist.

When it was time to leave, Lilia opened her locket and kissed her baby's tiny lips, then closed the clasp. The necklace still dangled from her neck, but it felt so much lighter as she and Muriel returned to the car for the drive home.

TWENTY-SIX

~

Oregon

Lilia arrived at the community center for the holiday program after spending an emotionally charged day with her grandmother. Not only was she coping with the rawness of her and Muriel's conversation, she also agonized over Matt having to coordinate his grandfather's cremation by himself. No one should have to go through something like that alone. For now, she needed to focus on the children's choir, but would check on Matt afterward in case he wanted to talk.

The event doubled as a fund-raiser, and the place buzzed with activity as crafters organized tables to showcase creations such as Christmas tree ornaments, tablecloths, placemats, cards and other festive items. Lilia spoke with the director to learn where her choir would sit, and then visited backstage to make sure the props were in place. Now all she had to do was wait for her angels to arrive.

Robin and Jasmine strolled in early, providing a welcome distraction for Lilia. Jazzy wore a black velvet dress with red ribbons, and her hair had been curled and tied back with a red bow. She looked adorable. Soon Lilia spotted other familiar faces, and she greeted the children while chitchatting with their parents.

The director walked onstage holding a microphone. "Good evening ladies and gentlemen, and welcome to our annual holiday gala! Will everyone please take a seat so we can begin the show?"

Lilia quickly gathered her young charges and sat with them near the stage. Attendees continued milling around gift tables until the lights dimmed, causing them to scurry for a chair in the auditorium.

The director continued, "Thanks to your generous donations, we've already raised close to a thousand dollars for our community programs. Isn't that wonderful?" She basked in the applause. "Now it's time to sit back and enjoy the performances, beginning with a holiday classic: a reading of 'A Visit from St. Nicholas.'"

The curtain opened, and a spotlight illuminated three teenagers sitting in wooden rocking chairs on center stage. A painted fireplace with bright red and yellow flames offered a colorful backdrop for the teens who were dressed in red-footed pajamas and stocking caps. Each one held a book as a boy began reciting, "'Twas the night before Christmas when all through the house, not a creature was stirring, not even a mouse." A girl read next. "The stockings were hung by the chimney with care, in hopes that Saint Nicholas soon would be there." The story continued until the conclusion of the beloved tale.

An elderly barbershop quartet wearing peppermint-striped vests and black bow ties replaced the three teens for the next performance. After warming up, they belted out a lively and creative rendition of "Rudolph, The Red Nose Reindeer." The audience rewarded them with shouts of "Encore! Encore!"

Butterflies invaded Lilia's stomach, fluttering away as she guided her children backstage. Louis used to say, "My dear Lilia, when butterflies flap their wings, you thank them. They bring energy to the performer. Your job is to make them fly in formation." She took a few deep breaths to try and tame them.

The director returned to the stage. "What a wonderful performance! I know all of us will be looking for our red-nosed friend on Christmas Eve! Let's give our barbershop quartet another round of applause."

As the audience clapped, Lilia ushered the children onstage, nudging them into position. Once everyone stood in place, she turned around and waited for a formal introduction.

The director began, "I'm happy to report that Mr. McKnight is recovering from surgery, and his family thanks you for your prayers." She smiled at Lilia. "We're fortunate to have Lilia Bennett-Parker with us tonight to take his place. Please join me in welcoming her and the children's choir."

Some kids fidgeted while others chewed their fingernails, but all maintained their stage position. Lilia lifted the metronome to remind them to keep the beat. Once they returned her smile, she knew they were ready to start. She nodded at Jasmine, who began playing the first song with gusto.

Lilia had been on the stage hundreds of times in front of thousands of people, but until tonight, she had never seen pure performance joy. The kids didn't care if their singing wasn't perfect or Jasmine missed a note. They were having fun, warbling from their hearts while ringing bells. Their voices squeaked at times, and the audience laughed with them. They ended the performance with a lively rendition of "Let It Snow," swaying with the music as tiny pieces of white paper floated from the ceiling. The audience stood and cheered, whispering to one another as Lilia and the children bowed. Once backstage, she hugged each child before leading the group back to their seats.

The next act was an adult choir who sang soulful renditions of "Hallelujah" and "Amazing Grace," and the evening ended with a high school string quartet that played a festive Christmas medley. After everyone returned to the stage for final bows, the director gushed, "Hasn't this been a wonderful evening? Let's give all of our performers another round of applause!"

The audience responded with a standing ovation as one man yelled, "That's my boy!" while pointing to a violinist. The director motioned for the performers to exit the stage and return to their seats.

"Before we leave tonight, one of the children has asked for a special favor." She waited until everyone quieted. "Some of you may not know that Lilia Bennett-Parker is a senior at the New England Conservatory of Music in Boston."

Lilia's face warmed as she closed her eyes. She had no idea this was coming.

"A little elf told me she plays the cello quite well." The director winked at Jasmine, then smiled at Lilia. "I'm wondering if you would grace us with a short performance to show our children what can happen with hard work and determination." Two high school students carried a cello and a chair on stage, then left.

The audience broke into applause, and Lilia surrendered. She returned to the stage and settled into the chair, sensing the audience's energy and eyes upon her. She positioned the endpin securely on the floor, curved her body around the cello and began playing a song that every decent cellist knew by heart: Bach's "Suite Number 1 in G Major," a harmonically rich crowd-pleaser.

She hit each note, taking advantage of the natural resonance of the cello: an open G, an open D, and a B one full step above the open A string. The resonating G and D defined the essence of the piece, soothing and... poor Matt...

Lilia continued playing as she thought about Matt and Ben. Her hand started shaking as she tried to finish the Bach, but the music fell flat and she couldn't go on. For the first time in her life, she stopped playing in front of a live audience. She fought back tears as she stood, unable to see specific faces because of the spotlight shining on her, so she spoke to the shadows.

"Please forgive me, but my mind is elsewhere. Many of you know Benjamin Campbell recently died in a car accident. He was my surrogate grandfather, and with your permission, I'd like to start over and play a different song in his honor." Lilia lowered her head and waited for the audience to respond.

Clapping came from somewhere in the room and was soon followed by an uproar that sounded like a train racing through a sleepy town. Once the noise subsided, Lilia continued, "The Gospel of Luke inspired a song called 'Benedictus.' It's a simple melody that speaks of love and thanksgiving, and I dedicate it to one of the most kindhearted men I have ever known."

Lilia channeled Ben's spirit by picturing him sitting on his backyard deck in the glow of a magnificent sunset. After taking a few slow breaths, she pulled the bow across the strings while closing her eyes and clearing her thoughts. She slowly left earth, drifting toward the heavens, passing through selflessness, kindness, goodness and love as angels lifted her higher and higher into the colors of joy and happiness. Time and space lost meaning as she played from her heart. She eased back down, gently and quietly on a compassionate breeze, until she returned to earth in peace, feeling grateful for all her gifts—especially Ben's love. She thanked the audience for their indulgence, bowed and left the stage.

Everyone erupted into applause. Afterward, many people offered condolences and praised Lilia's music, but she only wanted to see and talk to only one person: Matthew Campbell. She excused herself to leave and had almost reached the exit when she bumped into five familiar faces: Muriel, Catherine, Robin, Jasmine and Matt.

Lilia looked at Matt, feeling breathless. "I can't believe you're here." She eased next to him and whispered, "Gran told me about Ben. Are you all right?"

"I am now," he said softly, pointing at the stage.

"Oh, Lilia, your music sounded incredible!" Catherine gushed.

"I'm sorry," Robin said. "I had no idea Jasmine would do that."

"I'm not sorry." Muriel held Lilia's hand. "I'm so proud of you, sweetheart. Ben would've loved that tribute."

Catherine motioned toward the exit. "Shall we head home? Robin has a cherry pie and vanilla ice cream waiting for us at Muriel's."

As the tight-knit clan walked outside, Lilia glanced at Matt, and when their eyes met, she slipped her hand into his as they made their way through the parking lot. Even though a different reality awaited her in Boston, she refused to give the future any attention tonight. She granted herself a temporary reprieve from all wor-

ries surrounding the quartet, school, and family. This
one special evening belonged to remembrance and
friendship, and she would spend it with Matthew Benjamin Campbell.

TWENTY-SEVEN

Oregon

Lilia and Matt followed everyone out of the community center. They moved in step as if they had done it for years, which, in a way, they had. She used to follow him out into the woods where they played hide-and-seek and searched for flowers and rocks. One year they built a fort and stocked it with snacks, gadgets and books. Only Ben knew the location of their secret hiding place because he provided the supplies.

Lilia wanted time alone with Matt so they could talk about Ben. She gently squeezed his hand to get his attention. "You up for buying a Christmas tree?"

He smiled and directed his chin to Catherine and Muriel. "I am, but you'd better ask them."

Lilia tapped Gran's shoulder, causing her to stop walking. "Tonight's show put me in the mood to decorate a tree. Do you mind if Matt and I get one? We can trim it at your house after dessert."

"What a lovely idea." Muriel exchanged looks with Catherine and Robin. "OK with the two of you?"

Catherine raised her thumb and Robin nodded.

"Oh! Oh! Can I go with Lily and Matt?" Jasmine begged, jumping up and down. "*Pleeeease!*"

Lilia's eyes pleaded with Robin, and she quickly

intervened, speaking to her daughter. "Honey, I could use your help getting dessert ready."

Jasmine folded her arms and pouted, but Robin stayed the course, nudging Jazzy to their car with promises of buying their tree the next day.

Matt bent over and whispered in Lilia's ear, "That was a close one."

She giggled and began searching for Muriel's car, feeling like a teenager sneaking out a bedroom window after curfew.

Matt and Lilia stopped at a Christmas tree lot and found a nicely shaped Douglas fir that wasn't too tall or short, nor too dry. The owner helped tie the unruly beast to the car's roof, and then offered them a cup of hot cocoa, which they graciously accepted. They cuddled together next to an outdoor heater to stay warm while sipping their drinks and making small talk.

When the time seemed right, Lilia asked, "Why didn't you tell me about Ben?" She touched his hand and searched his eyes. "I would've gone with you."

Matt shrugged. "Guess I didn't want to bother you."

"I loved him, you know." Lilia became teary-eyed, still trying to come to terms with Ben's sudden death. "I thought of him as my grandfather, too."

Matt looked at her for a few moments, then removed the Styrofoam cup from her hand and put them both on the ground. He folded her into his arms and kissed her with a passion that took her breath away. She melted in his embrace as the cold air, his warm chocolate breath, and strong arms created a euphoric moment she never wanted to end. Then several kids, laughing and shouting, raced past them and disrupted everything.

Matt pulled back and watched the urchins run away. "Just my luck."

Lilia turned his chin toward her. "I liked that kiss."

He wrapped his arms around her shoulders and nuzzled her nose with his. "I like that you liked it."

Lilia drew back, playing with his fingers. "Are you available tomorrow morning?"

"My schedule's pretty open. Why?"

He brushed her lips again, stirring all kinds of sensations inside her body.

"There's a place I want to show you."

"A mystery date?"

"Nothing big. Don't get too excited. It's a quiet location where we can talk without being interrupted."

"Talk?" He nibbled on the side of her neck, his beard grazing her skin. "About what?"

Lilia moaned softly. "You are very distracting."

He sat back and smiled. "What time?"

"If Catherine can stay with Gran, would ten work?"

"Ten's good." He stood, bringing her with him. "We have people waiting for us. Shall we go and decorate our tree?"

"Yes…and bring a warm jacket tomorrow."

He nodded, then laid his arm over her shoulder and pulled her close. "A date, huh?"

She glanced up and gave him a contented smile while coiling an arm around his waist as they strolled back to the car.

The next morning, Lilia and Matt drove north on the central Oregon coast. Gray clouds and wind ruled the day, and Lilia thanked her good luck when the rain stopped once they neared their destination.

"We're visiting Heceta Head?"

Lilia nodded. "Gran brought me to this lighthouse during summers. I loved playing on the beach while she painted."

"I've visited it a few times." Matt looked out the window. "Kind of a busy place."

"Not during winter." Lilia drove into a nearly empty parking lot. "We'll have lots of privacy."

Matt reached over and massaged her shoulder. "Sounds good to me."

After paying a parking fee, Lilia slipped her hand in Matt's as they strolled up the half-mile paved path toward the lighthouse. Soon they arrived at the hilltop and took in the immense Pacific Ocean as waves with white foam crashed against the jagged rocks below.

"The place sure looks different in December," Matt said. "More mystical because of the fog."

Lilia closed her eyes, embracing the contrast between the biting wind and Matt's warmth. She hugged him tighter, feeling secure and vulnerable at the same time. She had no idea where to begin her story.

He lifted her chin so he could see her eyes. "You can tell me anything."

Matt carried a tender expression as hair blew across his face. Lilia wrapped her arms around his neck and whispered in his ear, "I need you to just listen, OK? No questions until I'm finished."

He nodded as the two of them settled on a bench that overlooked the sea.

She removed the silver locket from her neck and placed it in his hand. "Please open that."

He undid the clasp and stared at an inch-sized picture of a baby's face.

"That's my daughter," she said softly. "I had her when I was seventeen but gave her up, so I never got to know her." Lilia looked away. "I met her father at a music camp and things happened so fast. I didn't even realize I was pregnant until three months later. My mom hid me in Oregon with Gran for a year." She paused a few moments gazing into the distance, then continued, "Mom said she didn't want my reputation to be tarnished"—Lilia shook her head— "but I think I actually embarrassed her."

Matt leaned forward and gently stroked her hand with his thumb.

"Anyway, Mom coordinated the adoption and forced me to sign papers right after I gave birth." Lilia cried, "I only got to hold my little girl once."

Matt listened, giving her all the time she needed.

"My baby's father attended Juilliard and wanted no part of her. Mom talked his parents into the adoption" —Lilia turned toward Matt—"but no one asked what I wanted."

Matt kissed her forehead and gently tucked loose hair behind her ear. "I can't imagine how difficult that must have been. For you to give her up."

She laid her head on his shoulder while shivering and looking out to sea. "It was the worst day of my entire life."

They huddled together in silence for a long time listening to the crashing waves.

"Thanks for telling me." He paused, wiping away a tear from her cheek with his thumb. "Do you wonder what happened to her?"

"All the time."

"Is there a way to find out?"

"What I want and what can happen are two different things."

Matt waited for an explanation.

"It was a closed adoption. All records were sealed."

"Can't a lawyer unseal them?"

She searched his eyes for a clue to explain his calm demeanor. She imagined him reacting to her secret with disappointment, becoming restless and wanting to leave after hearing the story. Instead, he became a pillar of strength, showing empathy and concern. He seemed to accept her past without any judgment whatsoever.

"A lawyer could probably find her, but it's not what I want anymore."

"Why's that?"

Matt's simple question surfaced more painful memories. At seventeen, she had wanted to keep the baby, but now she knew that would've been a mistake, given her age and immaturity. Casting blame on her parents had been easier than facing the harsh truth that the baby's father didn't want either of them. He had returned to school like nothing had happened while she spent a miserable year muddled in doctor appointments, giving birth, and feeling like a failure to everyone around her.

"She deserves a mom and dad who both love her. Now that she's five, I have no intention of disrupting her life."

"You seem at peace with that decision."

Lilia tilted her head. "And you don't seem all that surprised with my news."

"The truth?" He brushed some stray hairs away from her face. "Granddad told me all about her."

"You knew?" She perched on the edge of the bench and stared at him. "And didn't say anything?"

"It wasn't my story to tell."

"But…"

"I knew you'd confide in me eventually."

Lilia dropped her head, swallowed a few times, then asked, "And you're not running?"

Matt returned the locket to her neck and straightened the chain. "I care about you, Lilia. We've both had some crazy twists and turns in our lives, but here we are."

Lilia looked at him in wonder. Last evening, he had asked if they were more becoming more than friends. She knew the answer was yes, but was afraid to admit it.

Matt continued, "I like when your eyes change color with the weather. I love hearing your music and watching you perform. You are beautiful, intelligent, kind and one of the hardest working people I know. Your smile lights up a room. You're strong and focused." He kissed her forehead. "Thanks for trusting me enough to tell me about your baby. It meant a lot."

Matt's words made her feel light-headed like she had stood up too fast, causing everything around her to spin. *I can't believe this is how he sees me. How could he think I'm strong? Focused maybe, but not strong. And I do trust him. I wonder if—*

Matt touched her temple. "I can feel the wheels churning." He paused and took a moment to consider his next words. "Here's the thing. I don't know what will happen between us, but I'm not running from it. Maybe things won't work out. I mean, who can predict the future? But I wanted you to know how I felt."

Lilia glanced at the waves crashing over the rocks

as she searched her heart. Finally, she turned to him and kissed him gently on the lips. "I feel it too, Matt." She hugged him tenderly, then pulled back, shaking her head. "But I don't know how to fit everything in. You know, school and music. You living in Williamsport, me in Boston. And there's my concert schedule. How could this ever work?"

"I'm fine with not knowing all the answers." He kissed her forehead and grazed her lips. "We'll figure out a way to be together."

"But...what about the quartet?"

He brushed his nose along her neck, nibbling along the way. "What about it?"

She pushed back to look into his eyes. "It's real, you know. The quartet consumes my life."

He wrapped his arms around her, then brushed her lips again. "This is real, too."

After spending time at the lighthouse, Matt and Lilia returned to the car. "Thanks for planning our mystery date." He pulled her close. "For the record, I'm also available tonight, tomorrow, the day after..."

She gave him a half-smile. "The only mystery is how we'll work this out."

He tapped her temple again. "Don't overthink it."

She playfully side-bumped him. "You act like it's not a big deal."

"Your music?"

"No!"

"Me living in Pennsylvania?"

"No! Well, yes, but…"

Matt enjoyed teasing her and making her laugh. They would have challenges like every couple, but now she knew how he felt. "You're a very big deal, Lilia Bennett-Parker." He paused, turning the moment serious. "And I'm sorry I didn't tell you about Granddad yesterday. I would've liked having you with me."

Lilia reached over and hugged him for a few minutes before asking, "What happens with his ashes?"

"They're flying back home with me. My folks will coordinate a service, but I don't know when."

"Will you keep me posted? I'd like to be there."

He wanted to make many promises: to support her aspirations, to find a way to blend their lives, to tell her about his dreams. "You can count on it."

Just as they started kissing again, her phone vibrated. She pulled it from her back pocket and stared at the screen.

"Oh, no!" Lilia cried, covering her mouth.

"What's wrong?"

"My mom's back from Asia! And she just landed. In *Portland*." She pressed a hand to her chest to soothe the discomfort. "She thinks I'm in Boston and Gran's in that rehab place." She looked up. "We need to get home, Matt. Fast! Gran can't be alone with her."

He opened the passenger door and motioned for

her to get in, holding out his hand. "I'll drive. You call Muriel."

Lilia tossed the keys to him and pressed Gran's speed dial, praying she would answer right away. They needed to align their stories before it was too late.

TWENTY-EIGHT

Vietnam and Oregon

Susanne boarded the corporate jet early Sunday morning along with Dave and his two managers. After weeks away from their families, the three men were glad to be going home for a much-needed rest before work on the factory began in the new year.

Quang joined Susanne on the jet for a quick tour. "One day you take me with you." He sat in a leather chair, swiveling back and forth. "Maybe I go to America for holiday." He laughed and laughed.

Susanne felt like they had known each other for months instead of days. He had opened her eyes in ways that were difficult to articulate, but she tried expressing gratitude via a generous tip. "Here's a token of my appreciation, Quang." She pointed to his Dodgers baseball cap. "When I return to California, I'll send you a Giants hat to add to your collection."

"You are a kind lady, Ms. Bennett." He slid the envelope into his back pocket without opening it. "You do good work in Vietnam. Everything will be OK."

She recalled the disdain she held for him at their first meeting, but now marveled at his ingenuity. "I think you may be right."

He smiled and bowed; she reached out and gave

him a genuine American hug.

After leaving the jet, Quang walked to the hangar then turned around and watched the crew prepare the aircraft for departure. Susanne buckled her seat belt and glanced out the window, waving one last time. She couldn't wait to tell Muriel about the entire experience, hoping the story would bring her some peace.

The jet landed in Portland to drop off Susanne before continuing to San Francisco. She had chased the dawn during the flight, recovering a day as she crossed over the International Date Line, and was elated to walk on American soil once again.

Susanne rented a car and drove to Muriel's home as she mentally planned her visit. She would sleep at the house and lead Monday's executive meeting via video link. Afterward, she'd call East River about Muriel's apartment. Once it was secured, she would find out what Muriel wanted to bring to the new place, then hire a moving company. Susanne saw no need to sell the lake house right away. She would take things slowly and give Muriel a chance to settle in before listing the place with a real estate broker. If Muriel's health had improved, perhaps they could lunch together at a nice restaurant, and then find a quiet place to talk about Vietnam and Stephen.

Susanne's thoughts shifted to her daughter. Lilia hadn't responded to the text she had sent after land-ing in Portland. In fact, there'd been no messages from her all week, Susanne realized. That fact didn't surprise her given how their last conversation had ended. She wondered if Lilia was still moping. Her moodiness these days made having simple conversations nearly impossible.

Susanne continued to think about Lilia as she turned onto Lakeshore Drive until she saw smoke coming out of Muriel's chimney. Her breathing halted momentarily as she looked closer. Was someone in the house?

Susanne quietly closed the car's door and inched toward the front steps while scanning the neighborhood. Everything looked normal; no suspicious activity with the exception of an unfamiliar car parked in Ben's driveway. *Maybe he had purchased a new one?* She pressed an ear to Muriel's front door and heard no sound. She jiggled the door handle and found it unlocked, so she turned it slowly and stepped inside. Flames in the fireplace warmed the room, and she had her phone out ready to call the police when a familiar voice startled her.

"East River ran out of rooms, so I came home," Muriel said. "And Lilia missed my cooking."

Susanne gasped, fanning her fingers out against her breastbone as she stared at her mother and daughter sitting side-by-side on the living room sofa. She calmly shut the door, then placed her purse and keys on a table while assessing the situation. She didn't know whether to scream or cry as she wrestled with her erupting emotions. Muriel's toothy grin made her blood boil. The woman had returned to her old tricks, but this time she had crossed the line by dragging Lilia along with her. "Would someone care to fill me in?"

"It's pretty simple actually," Muriel said. "I fell, spent a few days in the hospital, Lilia flew here to take care of me and now I'm better." She waved her cane. "Want to hear about our plan?"

Susanne opened and closed her hands a few times to release tension. She wanted to scrape the smirk off Muriel's face. She focused on Lilia as she sat down across from her. "Why aren't you in school?"

"I came home because Gran needed help." Lilia reached for a glass and eyed her mom as she gulped down some water.

"This isn't 'home,' and you have an ambitious concert schedule. You don't have time for this childishness."

Lilia ignored her mother's comment and retrieved a folder from the coffee table. "Gran agreed to have in-home help. Tomorrow we're interviewing—"

Susanne raised her voice. "It's *not* your job to take care of her. You need to focus on your music."

Lilia's cheeks grew flush. "As I was *saying*, tomorrow we're interviewing three home care workers. Gran's picking her favorite." She tipped her head toward Muriel. "She knows she needs help around here. We're working on making it happen."

Susanne idly slid her finger around the rim of a glass vase, wanting to throw it against the wall and shatter it into a million pieces. "I've been down this path with her many times before, but that isn't the point." She glared at Muriel then focused back on Lilia. "Your grandmother is not your responsibility. You have more important things to think about."

"But I—"

"You're leaving for Boston right away. End of the discussion." Susanne held up her phone. "Either you make the reservation or I will."

Lilia's face reddened, and she pulled her legs close to her body, looking down and not speaking.

Muriel pushed up from the sofa and stood. "I think Lilia can make—"

"I'm not interested in what you think, Mom. What you've done here is reprehensible. You need—"

"Don't talk to her that way!" Lilia shouted. "You have no idea—"

"And you don't talk to *me* that way!" Susanne yelled back. "Do you know—"

"Don't interrupt me, Mom! I have something to say to you!"

Susanne gasped at her daughter's outburst. Lilia had never spoken to her with such disrespect. She studied Muriel's face, wondering what nonsense she had stuffed inside her daughter's impressionable head.

Muriel sat down and focused on Lilia.

"I'm so angry you didn't call me about her accident. I had a right to know." Lilia glared at her mother. "Gran needed help from family. Not from strangers. And look how well she's—"

Susanne interrupted Lilia, unable to take any more verbal abuse. "You know what I—"

"Please! Let me finish!" Lilia screamed, her entire body shaking.

A coldness ripped through Susanne as her daughter's insolent voice slapped her across the face. *What's her problem? Who does she think she's talking to?*

Lilia picked up the file again and offered it to Susanne with a shaky hand. "Will you at least look at this? Gran knows she's getting older and needs help, but doesn't want to live at East River. It's *her* choice, Mom, not yours. She really wants…"

Susanne took the file and mindlessly glanced at a list of names as Lilia kept talking, but her words blurred into nothingness. Every one of Susanne's good intentions had completely evaporated. She wanted to leave this place, to fly home to California, away from the ambush and her ungrateful family. *Let them figure out how to make things work. They'll soon learn—*

"Mom!" Lilia shrieked. "Are you listening to me?"

Susanne didn't respond nor look at her daughter. She calmly set the file on the coffee table as her life began caving in all around her. Lilia and Muriel didn't care about her feelings or listen to her, so why should she bother with them? She strolled over to the fireplace mantel and studied all the photos, ignoring her family's incessant chatter. *Stephen in his military uniform, Stephen in a football jersey, Stephen fishing on the lake, his high school graduation photo. Stephen. Stephen. Stephen.*

She fingered his silver star, closed her eyes and mentally returned to the field in Tay Ninh, trying to recall her feelings from that sacred day, but she only felt hollow and alone. Stephen haunted her; Lilia and Muriel disrespected her. Jim had left her. Everyone wanted a piece of her. She became an abandoned nine-year-old girl once again, and couldn't take the pain anymore.

She swiftly raised her arm and...*wham*! With one clean sweep, everything on the mantel crashed on the floor, shattering glass everywhere. Susanne rushed to her childhood bedroom and slammed the door.

Lilia and Muriel stared in disbelief, unable to comprehend Susanne's bizarre behavior. Lilia expected Gran to cry and carry on, but she looked surprisingly calm.

"Should we go talk to her?" Lilia finally asked.

Muriel shook her head slowly. "This has been coming for some time." She rubbed her forehead. "Would you mind visiting Matthew or Catherine for an hour or so? I'd like to talk to your mother alone."

"Are you kidding?" Lilia motioned toward the broken glass. "After that?"

Muriel knew this was a "now or never" moment.

The incident had caught Lilia in the crossfire of her and Susanne's private war, and she wanted to spare her any more drama.

"Gran? Are you sure?"

"I'm not sure of anything except for trying to make this right."

"But you didn't do anything wrong!"

"Oh, but I have, Lilia. And it's time for amends."

"But…I don't understand."

"I'll explain later, but I'd like to be alone with your mother. I'll call when we're done. Please, sweetheart, I need you to do this for me."

Lilia slowly stood. "I'll go, but…"

"We'll be fine." Muriel hugged her. "Please try not to worry."

Lilia waved her phone and threatened, "It'd better ring soon." She opened the front door, looked over her shoulder and gave her grandmother one last chance to change her mind.

"I'll call." Muriel drew a cross over her heart.

Lilia sighed, then reluctantly moved outside and closed the door behind her.

Muriel knocked on Susanne's bedroom door. "It's me. May I come in?"

No response.

"Susanne, please. We need to talk."

Still no response.

"Lilia isn't here. We're alone, and I'm not leaving. Please unlock this door."

A few minutes later, a latch sounded, and Susanne pushed the door open while keeping her head lowered. "I'll clean up the mess." She started walking out of the room, but Muriel held her arm.

"Don't fret about the pictures."

Susanne sighed loudly and sat on the bed.

"Please, Susie. I just want to talk."

Susanne glanced up with red, swollen eyes, an image that broke Muriel's heart. She had never seen her daughter look so defeated. Muriel tried to recall the last time they had been genuinely happy in one another's presence, but couldn't remember. She crumpled next to Susanne, falling on her shoulder.

"Oh, Susie." Muriel wept. "I'm so sorry."

Susanne bore the weight of her mother's limp body but didn't move or speak.

Muriel sat up, sniffling and brushing away tears. Getting through to her daughter would not be easy, but she knew what needed to be said. "I want to tell you something"—she touched Susanne's hand—"and it has nothing to do with what just happened in the living room."

Susanne didn't respond or look at her.

"I wasn't a good mother. You deserved so much more." She paused, rubbing her chest to soothe the heartache. "When Stephen died, a part of me died, too.

You were a child and I neglected you, pure and simple."
Muriel wrung her hands and looked at her daughter.
"I buried myself in art and let Dad raise you. It wasn't
right for you or me, and I lost your love. I'm so sorry I
let you down."

Susanne didn't speak, remaining distant and cold.

Muriel stood, unwilling to give up. "Will you come
with me?" She extended her hand. "Please, Susie?"

Susanne ignored her mother's gesture, but slowly
stood on her own.

Muriel swallowed a few times, hurt by her daughter's reluctance, but remained committed to making
amends. She lowered her arm and left the room, breathing a sigh of relief when Susanne followed.

Once they arrived at the living room, Muriel stood
by the mantel and began speaking. "I allowed the grief
over losing my son to affect our relationship. I erred on
every level, and I'm deeply sorry. I can't change the
past, but I can do things differently now."

Muriel bent over to pick up the photo of Stephen
in his military uniform, carefully removing shards of
glass. "I love and still miss him every day. Even after all
these years." She placed the frame back on the mantel
then faced Susanne. "And I love you too. But I don't
show it very well."

She clasped Susanne's hands. "I'm proud of you,
Susie. Of who you are and what you've become. You've
raised a wonderful daughter. You work hard leading

your company. And you've taken care of me, even when I didn't deserve it."

Susanne studied Muriel's face but said nothing.

"I want to start over. Do things differently. I'll go to East River tomorrow. It's the best place to live so you and Lilia won't worry about me." Muriel softly squeezed Susanne's hand. "No more games. I mean it."

Muriel released her daughter's hand and backed up to give her space. She meant every word of her promise. She didn't expect Susanne's forgiveness right away but hoped to make things better over time. If living in an apartment could help heal transgressions, so be it. And Lilia could return to school, which is where she belonged. Most of all, she wanted to heal her fractured family before time ran out.

Susanne took a deep breath. She glanced at her mother, then turned toward the mantel, staring at Stephen's military picture.

"Susie?" Muriel spoke softly and with respect. "Did you hear what I said?"

Susanne turned around and embraced her mother with a token hug that slowly grew stronger. She spoke to her in a loving whisper, "I heard every word. Your candor means a lot to me. Your sincerity, too."

Muriel glanced up with tears in her eyes and pulled her daughter close to her heart. The moment of forgiveness had arrived at last, and she never wanted to let Susanne go.

After a few minutes, Susanne guided Muriel to the sofa where they sat contentedly next to one another. Susanne scooped up her mother's hand and cradled it securely in her lap while glancing at the shattered glass on the living room floor. She took a few deep breaths, dropped her head back, and gazed at the ceiling.

"For the past week I've been in Vietnam, Mom." Susanne pulled a few tissues from a box with her free hand and patted her eyes. She mindlessly wove the white gauzy material through her fingers while gathering her thoughts. Finally, she said in a trembling voice, "May I tell you a story?"

TWENTY-NINE

Oregon

Lilia sat on the front porch for a few minutes wondering if she should leave the two women alone. She couldn't believe how her mom had destroyed the mantel pictures. Lilia had never seen anything like it. She felt guilty about the way she had spoken to her mom, but how else could she get her to listen?

Lilia glanced at Matt's house, then Catherine's. Where should she go? The road leading toward the main highway caught her eye, and she took off. She ran faster and faster, ignoring her aching lungs. She finally arrived at the gazebo in the state park where Matt had taken her several days earlier, a sanctuary where she could be alone with her thoughts.

She waited for her breathing to return to normal while looking at her phone. No new messages. What were Muriel and Susanne discussing? Her mother calculated every move of her life with precision and never lost control. What had set her off? Could Gran stand up to her?

Lilia decided she shouldn't have left them alone together and started down the steps just as her phone rang. She nearly fainted when Peter's name flashed across the screen. Yesterday the quartet had performed without her. Was he calling to gloat?

"Peter?"

"Hey, Lilia. How are you?"

"Uh, I'm fine. How'd things go last night?"

"That's why I'm calling. Can you talk for a couple of minutes?"

His friendly tone confused her as she sat on the steps. "Sure."

"I…we…the quartet wasn't the same without you. I'm sorry about our earlier conversation. Forget what I said about leaving. I reacted out of anger and made a mistake."

A mistake?

"By the way, how's your grandmother doing?"

Seriously? "Peter, why are you calling?"

"To find out when you're coming back. We need you here in Boston."

"I'm still part of the quartet?"

"Let's just say we're better with you."

"What happened? I mean, why the change?"

"Please don't make me beg, Lil. I said my apologies, now let's move on."

Beg? About what? "I still have things to settle here."

Peter sighed loudly. "Do you want back in or am I wasting my breath?"

Lilia's chest tightened as the performance clock resumed ticking. Of course, she wanted to be part of the quartet, but she couldn't leave Oregon right now with things so unsettled. "I need a few more days."

He sighed even louder and said, "Don't make me wait too long."

Lilia stared at the phone for a long time after their call had ended. Peter had never apologized to her for anything. What made him change his mind about the quartet? What happened at that party? Should she call Joel to find out? Did it even matter?

She reviewed her phone messages: still nothing from Gran and nearly two hours had lapsed. She pictured Susanne driving away in the rental car, leaving Muriel heartbroken and in tears. Suddenly, Peter didn't seem as important. Lilia tucked her phone away and quickly retraced her path back home.

Once Lilia arrived at Muriel's house, she took a minute to catch a breath as she kicked off her shoes and pressed an ear to the door. No yelling. She listened closer. Was that laughter?

She entered the house slowly, not knowing what to expect. Her mother and grandmother both glanced up, smiling. They sat next to each other on the sofa, surrounded by a bunch of books.

Gran patted the seat next to her. "Come in and see these old pictures, sweetheart. You won't believe how much you look like your mother when she was your age."

What? They were looking at old photo albums? Together? Why hadn't they called her? Lilia tried to comprehend the strange turn of events. First Peter and now this? Nothing made sense. "I guess you two worked things out?"

Susanne pointed to a page in the album. "Come see this picture of me water-skiing. I look pretty good!"

Lilia sat and listened for a few minutes, but couldn't stomach the charade. She released a loud, frustrated sigh, then stood abruptly. "I'm glad everyone's so cheery, but we have important things to discuss."

Susanne and Muriel looked at her with curious expressions.

"Unlike you, I can't pretend everything is fine when our world's upside down, inside out. Good one day, bad the next. Half-truths. How am I supposed to…" Lilia flopped down and covered her face with her hands.

Susanne leaned forward. "What's wrong, Lil?"

She raised her head and stared. "Seriously, Mom? Two hours ago you destroyed Gran's photos and made her cry!" Lilia jerked a finger toward the mantel. "Now you're looking at old pictures and laughing together. I don't get it."

"Your mom and I had a good talk." Muriel ambled over and gave Lilia a warm, generous hug. "And we came to an understanding."

Lilia stepped back. "Oh yeah? But for how long? We all know how this works. Today we're fine, but tomorrow we're back at one another's throats. Tell me I'm wrong." She stared angrily at both of them.

Over the next several hours, the Bennett women talked about many things: Stephen's death, Muriel's grief, Vietnam, Susanne's childhood, aging, Ben's accident, the quartet, college life, Peter Tremblay, Lilia's dad, directing children's choirs, Fortune 500 companies, and family memories. They answered questions without being defensive while putting regrets behind them.

Something happened between them that afternoon, a genuine shift toward understanding and acceptance. Lilia wanted to build on the momentum.

"Can we try something?"

"What would you like us to do, sweetheart?"

"Things are good between us right now, but I'm worried it'll be short-lived." Lilia held up a small rectangular pillow. "I want this to become a talking pillow."

Both Susanne and Muriel looked at her like she was crazy, so she explained.

"In class one time, we were all talking at once and the professor blew up. He said we didn't know how to listen. He tossed a cushion to a guy who got to speak all by himself. We couldn't interrupt no matter what. We had to try and understand his view." She paused to catch her breath. "I want us to do that. To have an honest conversation."

Muriel smiled. "Is there any other kind?"

Lilia gave her a "don't go there" look and continued, "I want each of us to hold the pillow and describe what she wants for her life. No interruptions, no judging. Just listen and respect what the other person has to say. Can we do that?"

Muriel nodded, then settled into her chair.

Susanne shrugged. "I'm willing to try."

"Gran, will you go first?" Lilia handed the pillow to her. "Tell us what's most important to you. Describe what you need from us. And *please*. Be sincere."

Muriel held the pillow and traced its floral embroidery with a finger. "Ben's wife made this for me many years ago. A birthday gift, I think." She studied the pattern for a long time without speaking, then glanced out the front window.

"I know my health is declining"—Muriel looked at Susanne—"but I don't want to end up in a place like Esther. Or at East River. It's not for me. I want to stay here, in my home. But I need help." She paused. "Lilia and I are interviewing caretakers tomorrow, and I'll hire one. I don't know if she'll be full time, at night or during the day. We'll have to see." She lowered her eyes, tracing the floral embroidery again. "What I won't do is fire her as soon as you leave. Those days are over." Muriel handed the pillow to Susanne. "That's my truth."

Susanne pressed the pillow to her chest. "Honesty, huh?" She glanced at her mother and daughter, considering her words carefully. "Most of my life I've lived in Stephen's shadow. I never felt good enough or completely loved for who I am, so I threw myself into work."

She focused on Muriel. "In Vietnam, I stood in

the field where Stephen had fought and died. I get your grief, Mom. I couldn't bear something like that happening to Lilia. You did your best to raise me. And I know you love me."

She turned toward Lilia. "You're the light of my life. You make me so proud, and I want you to have the best of everything. You're strong and compassionate, coming here to take care of your grandmother. I regret not telling you about her accident. I should have trusted your judgment."

Susanne took a minute to compose herself. "I won't apologize for enjoying my work. I love what I do, but my company isn't the most important thing in my life." Susanne sat forward. "Even though I don't always act like it, you two are my top priorities." She handed the pillow to Lilia. "That's my truth."

Lilia clutched the pillow, sensing an opportunity. She took a few deep breaths and decided not to hold back. "I don't want to be your top priority, Mom." She covered her eyes to hide from Susanne's reaction as she said, "It's too suffocating."

Lilia's heart thumped as she peeked through her fingers and caught Susanne grimacing. Her mother remained silent, however, so Lilia continued speaking.

"Being your top priority means you're in my business. Sometimes it's good but other times, not as much." Lilia opened her locket and looked at her daughter. "I blamed you for forcing me to give up my baby. For not giving me a choice. But there was no way I could have taken care of her. I know that now." She closed the locket and pressed her lips together, thinking about her next words. "Sometimes it's easier to blame others when things don't go right. But I want to stop doing that. I need to take responsibility for my life."

She held the pillow tighter, wishing the cushion could speak for her given what she was about to say. Peter's call had triggered thoughts about her career, and she had made an important decision that her mom wouldn't like. She picked up her glass of water, took a couple of swallows to buy time, then faced Susanne and began speaking.

"I don't want to play in the quartet anymore. I've made a decision to—"

Susanne immediately sat up straight. "But that's—"

"No, Susie," Muriel said softly. "Please don't interrupt. Ler her finish."

Susanne covered her mouth and sat back.

Lilia continued, "I don't want to be part of Peter's world anymore. It isn't fun or rewarding to play music with him. He fired me once, and he'll do it again. He's rude and condescending. He doesn't respect me. And he never listens to any of us. It's not for me."

Lilia stood and paced, gathering the courage to make her final announcements. "I'm calling Peter to tell him my decision. He won't like it, but that's his problem. I'm also staying with Gran during the holidays."

Lilia looked at Muriel. "You've always been there for me. Now it's my turn to help you." She turned toward her mother. "I'm returning to school in January to finish my degree." She closed her eyes and pushed the words out. "And I want to compete in the Naumburg as a soloist. I love the cello, but want to play on my terms."

Lilia paused as tension eased from her shoulders. It felt euphoric to be this honest with her family, so she continued with some bonus news. She felt her lips crack into a wide grin. "And I want Matthew Campbell in my life. Don't ask any questions because he and I are figuring things out. But I like him and wanted you to know."

Lilia ignored Susanne's raised eyebrow and sat next to her. "Mom, you've been more than generous with me, paying for college and all my expenses. Please know how much I appreciate you. My decisions have nothing to do with not being grateful. I know how lucky I am to have you as my mom. But I need to direct my future. It's time." Lilia's hands trembled as she set the pillow on the Queen Anne chair, returning it to its proper place.

"That's my truth." Lilia glanced at her mom and grandmother as she sat back and waited for their reactions to her announcements.

Silence.

Painful silence.

"The pillow game's over. You can talk now." Lilia said cautiously.

More silence.

"Mom, *please*. Say something."

"How long will Matt be here?"

Lilia relaxed her shoulders. "He flew to Oregon to take care of Ben and the estate. He's headed home soon, but I don't know when."

"What's he doing now?"

"What'd you mean?"

"Where does he live? Is he in school? Working?"

"He lives with his parents and works for a company that makes educational software. He and two buddies are designing a video game. I can't explain it very well, but he gets all excited when he talks about it."

"Your face sure brightens when you talk about him."

Lilia wanted to press an escape button and disappear, so she didn't have to answer more questions about her love life.

"Can we shift this conversation to music?" Susanne asked as she folded her arms.

Familiar territory, Lilia nodded as she braced herself.

"Please help me understand why you'd leave the quartet after investing so much time and energy. You're on the brink of launching your career, Lil. I know Peter's demanding, but that's what an effective leader does. And what's your career path as a soloist?"

Fair questions without easy answers. Since today was about honesty, Lilia chose not to hold back. "Playing with Peter feels stifling. I want something different for my professional life. I may go the orchestral path or teach. Maybe I'll go to grad school. I don't know, Mom. I'll graduate, compete at the Naumburg and see what happens from there."

Stillness.

Lilia waited.

Finally, Susanne spoke. "You should know it's taking all of my self-control not to tell you what I really think versus what you want to hear."

Lilia tensed, waiting for a lecture, but it never materialized. Susanne Bennett had never held back a day in her life, and Lilia tried to make sense of her mother's puzzling behavior. She started to second-guess herself, but halted the thought pattern, realizing things could be different. Today was about new beginnings and owning her future. She explored her mother's eyes and detected an equal mix of apprehension, concern, and most importantly, love. Lilia relaxed her shoulders, picked up the talking pillow and tossed it over to her.

"Go ahead. Tell me what you think. I can take it."

Susanne tilted her head, studying Lilia then Muriel, and finally settling back on Lilia. All of a sudden, she started laughing. A genuine belly laugh that made her eyes water. Her gaiety incited laughter in Muriel, too.

"Care to let me in on what's so funny?" Lilia felt like the only adult in the room.

"Lilia Bennett, you're a woman who will get things done." Susanne smiled. "After what you've accomplished this week with your grandmother, who am I to interfere in your life?" She stretched her back and released an audible sigh. "This has been one insightful afternoon."

What? Lilia could barely comprehend her mother's words. She had readied herself for a big fight, not this surrender. She had no idea what to do next.

Once Muriel stopped laughing, she asked Susanne, "Will you help us interview the home care folks tomorrow. I'd value your opinion."

"Oh, why not." Susanne tickled her mom's knee with her big toe. "It'll be tough to find someone who'll put up with you, though."

Gran laughed again. "Too right."

Lilia felt like she had entered an alternate universe, arriving at a happy, but unfamiliar place. "Is this real, Mom?"

"Is what real?"

"Umm, this sudden shift in you." She pressed her lips together and slowly turned her head from side to side. "I'm not sure I buy it."

Susanne blew out a lung's worth of air, taking a minute for herself. She finally looked at Lilia. "Oh, it's real." She pointed toward the front door. "When I arrived here today, I'll admit to having a very different agenda." She tossed the talking pillow back on its chair and stood. "I'll always have my opinions, Lil. But I see things differently now."

She moved over to the window and gazed out, stretching her back again. "We are three adults with the right to live our lives as we see fit." She turned and faced her family, giving Lilia and Muriel equal time. "Each of us gets to make our own decisions"—she held up a finger—"and live with the consequences." Susanne strode over to Lilia and embraced her. "That responsibility doesn't seem to frighten you anymore."

Susanne stepped back and held her daughter's hands. "And that's why this change is real." She drew a cross over her heart.

Lilia's gut told her that this moment was genuine, a breakthrough of epic proportions. She threw her arms around her mom's neck. "I love you, Mom."

Susanne held her tenderly. "And I love you. More than you'll ever know."

After a few minutes, Lilia spoke to Muriel. "You know how you don't have a picture of the three of us on your photo wall?"

Muriel wore a blank expression, so Lilia explained.

"When Mom and I were here last August, you said you didn't have a picture of the three of us. You asked if we could take one the next time we were together. Remember?"

Muriel tapped her head and smiled. "Ahhh, the light just came on."

"How about sitting for a formal portrait tomorrow?

Before Mom leaves for home."

"I'd like that." Muriel turned to Susanne. "Is it OK with you?"

Susanne smiled. "I'm all for immortalizing the Bennett women."

"All right, then. I'll find a studio and make an appointment." Lilia offered.

"Sounds good." Muriel stood. "Anyone want to help me fix dinner?"

Susanne's arm shot up in the air like an overachieving sixth-grader in math class.

"But you never cook."

"If one can read a recipe, one can prepare food."

Lilia hopped up. "While the two of you figure things out, do you mind if I visit Matt?"

"How about inviting him to dinner?" Susanne suggested. "I'd enjoy seeing him again."

Lilia threw her arms around her mother's neck again, then rushed out the door.

Susanne and Muriel watched from the front window as Lilia skipped over to Matt's house with a smile plastered across her face. "Have you ever seen her so happy?" Muriel asked.

"No, but she has no idea the difficulties that await her as a soloist. She's talented, but so are hundreds of other cellists. At least with Peter—"

"You've raised her to be self-sufficient, Susie. Let's

support her decision."

"But I could help guide her. I see things she doesn't. Isn't that my job as her mom?"

Muriel gave Susanne a look.

Susanne released a hearty laugh. "If you'd micromanaged me the way I do her, I'd have run away."

Muriel smiled and held her tongue.

Susanne watched as Matt open his door, and Lilia stepped inside. "It won't be easy for her. School's a piece of cake compared to what comes next. I've sheltered her more than I'd like to admit."

"You've done a wonderful job raising her. She's ready to face the world. A few hard knocks won't keep our Lilia down. Never has. Never will." Muriel clasped her daughter's hand. "Besides, if she turns out half as good as you, she'll be fine."

Susanne rested her head on her mother's shoulder. "Thanks, Mom."

The two women stood by the window for a few minutes before Susanne spoke. "How about you getting dinner started while I clean up?" She gestured toward the broken glass in front of the fireplace. "I'll join you in a few minutes."

Muriel nodded and headed toward the kitchen.

Susanne swept the floor, placed the broken glass in the trash, removed the photos from the damaged frames, then stepped back to assess the mantel. She would replace the frames and life would go on. Muriel would live in her home for as long as possible while Lilia blazed a new trail. But what about *her* future?

She strolled over to the window and stared at Ben's house again, struggling to accept his death. He didn't deserve to die so violently when he had been such a gentleman his entire life. Had she ever thanked him for his kindness toward Muriel and Lilia? She didn't think so.

Now Lilia was in Ben's living room with his grandson. The next generation. What were they talking about? How far had their relationship progressed? As kids, they'd been inseparable during summer vacations. But they weren't kids anymore.

Susanne dropped into a chair, feeling physically and emotionally drained from business, traveling, and family drama. Perhaps she should take a page out of her daughter's playbook and reevaluate her priorities. Maybe she needed to slow down before life passed her by.

She closed her eyes and surrendered to all things possible. Contentment, a sensation she hadn't felt for a while, if ever, slowly filled her body as sleep arrived.

THIRTY

ᏸᎧᏣᏱ

Oregon

After Matt opened the front door; Lilia rushed into his arms. "Am I disturbing you?" she asked.

He smiled and used his foot to close the door. "Hello to you, too." He lifted his chin toward Muriel's house. "How'd it go over there?"

Lilia's eyes lit up. "Surprisingly well." She removed black-rimmed glasses from his forehead and waved them. "When did you start wearing these?"

"During college. They're only for reading." He motioned toward a stack of papers on the kitchen table next to his laptop. "I've been reviewing Granddad's files. Estate stuff." He retrieved his eyewear and set them on a table. "Tell me about your mom."

"She invited you to dinner."

"You told her about us?"

"It may have slipped out."

"And she hasn't called the cops?"

Lilia dropped her head back and laughed. "Not yet."

Matt sat down on the couch and pulled her into his lap. "You're full of surprises." He kissed the tip of her nose. "What'd the three of you talk about?"

Lilia relayed the highlights as Matt listened.

"So…you'll come to dinner?"

"Sure." Matt motioned toward a camera on the coffee table. "And I could take your family's portrait if you want."

"You ever hold one of those before?" Lilia teased.

Matt moved her off his lap and picked up the Nikon. He adjusted its settings, then started taking pictures of her. She ducked and hid, then darted around the house as he followed, clicking away. He finally trapped her in the den where he set the camera down and folded her in his arms. "Do you know how happy you make me?"

She moved back, holding both of his hands. "Umm, I hope you'll still feel that way after I tell you one last bit of news."

He steadied himself for the big reveal, thinking life would never be boring with her by his side. She had a playful spirit and an easy smile, two things he admired in a woman.

"Peter called and wants me back. He asked me to fly to Boston today."

"And?"

"Mom says I should go."

"And?"

"She doesn't think I can succeed on my own."

He would play this game all evening if doing so made her happy, but he wanted answers. From what he could tell, Peter excelled at messing with her head. "Bottom line?"

"I'm turning my life upside down."

Matt tried to follow her thinking, but was having difficulty and said so.

Lilia told him about leaving the quartet, staying with Muriel through the holidays, finishing school, and competing as a soloist. "I'll need to practice until I drop, but I think I can do it!"

"That's a lot of changes." Matt led her to a couch where they both sat down. "Tell me about the Naumburg. How does it work?"

Lilia's eyes lit up. "It's a big deal. A man named Walter Naumburg created a foundation that funds competitions. It's a great way for a novice musician to get noticed."

"Isn't your quartet competing in it?"

"That was the plan."

"And now you'll compete as a soloist?"

Lilia nodded. "Cellists from around the world gather. The winner wins cash and two subsidized New York recitals. It's a great career launcher."

Matt took a minute to decode the meaning behind her words. He hadn't considered the concert route, which probably involved travel and long absences. He wanted to support her dreams, but—

"Hey." She moved his chin until their eyes met. "What's with the funny look?"

He liked how lines formed on her forehead when she got serious or worried, and how her eyes sparkled when she was happy or excited.

"Funny? I'll show you funny."

He began tickling her until she begged him to stop. After she quit laughing, he kissed her with a passion that grew intense and she eagerly responded, releasing a quiet moan. She fit perfectly in his arms, and he could have kept going, but pulled back, wanting to slow things down. He knew they shared something special and saw no need to rush their relationship.

Matt gazed into her eyes and found desire, friendship and trust all waiting for him. He caressed her cheek. "This week has turned my life upside down, too. You and me, Granddad's death, seeing my grandmother. I'm just trying to absorb everything."

She responded by laying her cheek on his chest, her arm wrapped around him. He kissed the top of her head and held her securely.

Later in the day, Lilia and Matt returned to Muriel's home and found her and Susanne in the art studio standing next to the easel. Both looked up when they walked into the room.

Muriel's eyes brightened. "Well, hello, you two. We were just looking at my masterpiece."

"Hi, Matt," Susanne said. "It's been a few years." She reached over and gave him a hug. "I'm sorry about your grandfather. We all loved him."

"Thanks, Ms. Bennett." He stepped back and

slipped his hands into his back pockets. "It's good to see you again."

"Have you seen Lilia's portrait, Matthew?" Muriel asked, tilting her head toward the watercolor.

"Yeah. I saw it the other day. It's pretty special."

"It's her graduation gift," Muriel beamed. "But I need to finish it."

Susanne's eyes scanned the portrait. "You're capturing a striking image of her, Mom." She picked up several photographs of Lilia that were clipped to the easel. "Were these your inspiration?"

Muriel nodded, her eyes etched in sadness. "Ben took them last summer. Aren't they something else?"

All heads nodded in agreement.

"I bet Granddad enjoyed seeing his photography turn into that painting."

Muriel started to respond, but her voice choked with tears. Lilia handed her a tissue and changed the subject.

"I have good news. Matt found Ben's Nikon and offered to take our family photo." She playfully elbowed him. "I can attest to his superb camera skills."

"That's nice of you, Matthew," Muriel said. "Shall we wait until tomorrow when the light's better?"

Everyone agreed as Muriel sniffed the air. "That meatloaf should be ready soon. Who wants to help me set the table?"

Susanne spoke to Matt. "May we talk privately for

a few minutes?"

Lilia immediately tensed, fearing her mother would grill Matt like a prospective employee.

He nodded, then glanced at Lilia and silently mouthed "it's fine" while gently squeezing her hand.

Lilia spoke to Matt, "I'll be in the kitchen if you need me," then threw her mom a look before slowly following Muriel out the door.

Matt had watched Lilia argue with her mother many times over the years, but he knew how much they loved and depended on each other. He respected Susanne's intelligence and dedication to hard work. Although they hadn't seen each other in recent years, when he was a teen they had shared many stimulating conversations about technology and coding. She could explain complex concepts in simple ways that had made a lasting impression on him.

Susanne broke the silence. "Lilia tells me you write software."

"It pays the student loans."

"Where do you work?"

"I'm a partner in a small company called Knowledge Portal. We've created a platform to deliver self-paced tutorials covering most subjects taught through high school. We have almost three million users each month."

"Impressive. What's your contribution?"

"Mostly in design. Right now, I'm beta testing a trig course I wrote."

"You enjoy the work?"

"Yeah, I like playing with multithreaded algorithms and mucking around in user data."

"Computer science major?"

"Double major from Penn State, computer science and math."

Susanne sat in Muriel's artist chair, swiveling it back and forth and watching him. Matt lowered his eyes and waited for the next question as he hid his hands in his back pockets.

"Does my daughter know you're a computer geek like me?"

He looked up, caught off guard by the out-of-character question. He glanced at her, but couldn't decipher her facial expression. He decided to take a risk to renew the bond between them.

"No, and we shouldn't say anything." He held his breath. "I don't want her to run."

After a few moments, Susanne laughed, the real deal, and Matt started breathing again.

"Ms. Bennett, I've known you and Lilia practically my whole life. I know she's told you about us." He shifted his weight from one foot to the other. "Your approval would mean a lot. Please know I'll support her career."

Susanne tipped her head toward Lilia's portrait. "If

you keep her looking like this, you have my blessing."

Matt studied the painting. "She had that same look when she played a tribute to my granddad at the community center." He glanced down, thinking about his grandfather. Waves of grief hit at the strangest time, and he struggled to control his emotions. He took a few moments before saying, "Wish you had been there to hear it."

Susanne nodded then shifted the topic. "Some people call musicians road warriors because they travel all the time." She waited until Matt looked up at her, then continued, "It won't be easy to build a relationship around her schedule."

"Yeah, I suspect——"

Lilia entered the room and interrupted the conversation. "Dinner's ready." Her eyes flitted back and forth between Matt and Susanne.

"Matt was telling me about his work. Smart guy you have here." Susanne stood and left the room.

Lilia waited until she was out of earshot before saying, "Well? What'd you talk about?"

"Global warming and the World Series."

"Seriously! Did she make you feel uncomfortable?"

Matt used his thumbs to soften the worry lines on her forehead, and then tipped his head toward the portrait. "She said I could hang around if I keep you that happy."

She wrapped her arms around his neck. "Well, I

guess you'll be here for a very long time."

He could hold her all day, but knew dinner awaited. "Shall we join your family?"

She didn't move, and the worry lines deepened.

"Lilia? What's wrong?"

She waited a few moments, then blurted out, "When
are you going home? And what about Esther? Ben's
place? How will you, I mean we—"

"Hey, hey." He held her close. "Why all the worry?"

"There are so many loose ends, Matt. How do
things come together?"

He kissed her forehead. "I can work remotely, so
I'll stay here until you return to school. Since my grandmother is well-cared for, we're thinking about leaving
her put for now." He shrugged. "I don't know about
Granddad's house. My folks are talking about selling,
but who knows what they'll do."

"What about us? You know, after January?"

"Guess I'll get to know Boston a little better. Williamsport is only"—he tilted his head—"four hundred
or so miles away."

Lilia quickly added. "And I'll find a way to visit you.
Plus we can Skype and text."

"We'll figure it out." He patted his stomach. "That
meatloaf sure smells good. Shall we join your family
and find out how it tastes?"

Lilia linked her fingers around his neck. "If you're
lucky, I may give you another head rub after dinner."

"I'd like that." Matt kissed her forehead then draped his arm around her shoulder as they strolled out of the room together. "I'd like that a lot."

THIRTY-ONE

Oregon

The next morning, Susanne awoke with Lilia and Muriel on her mind. Yesterday's emotional conversation with them had filled her with equal parts hope and dread. Their heartfelt disclosures didn't change Muriel's age or lessen her declining health, but her mother was mentally stable and could make her own choices.

Susanne zipped up her fleece jacket as she looked out a window toward Ben's house, thinking about Lilia. Her daughter's overnight transformation into an independent woman had caught her off guard. She saw Lilia as an immature girl who carried a tenuous grip on life, a person who needed guidance. But this past week, she had shown herself to be a responsible and courageous young woman who could take care of business.

Lilia's impulsive choices about her career reflected her naiveté, but her daughter was an adult and deserved a chance to forge her own path. Susanne needed to find a way to let go while continuing to support her—not an easy balance to achieve.

She scanned her calendar: two hours to take a run, shower, and ready herself for a nine o'clock videoconference. She tied her shoes, left the bedroom, and promptly bumped into Lilia in the hallway.

"Good morning. Sleep well?"

Lilia yawned. "Uh-huh. Mind if I join you?"

"For a run?"

"Yeah. Turns out running is cathartic."

Another change. Susanne had asked Lilia to run countless times before, but never got a yes. She decided to simply enjoy her company and not probe for rationale. "I'll get water and meet you out front."

Lilia's stamina impressed Susanne as they returned to Lakeshore Drive after completing a short seven-mile run. She had watched her daughter closely for signs of exhaustion and had adjusted the pace accordingly.

"Good run, Mom. Thanks for letting me tag along."

Susanne returned the sentiment and discovered a potential answer to Lilia's sudden change in exercise habits: Matthew Campbell standing on his porch in running gear. He finished stretching his legs, then waved at them before taking off down the road.

They both returned the greeting, and Lilia couldn't take her eyes off him. Susanne wondered how their relationship could ever work given all the challenges they faced, but she kept her thoughts to herself. It wasn't her place to cast uncertainty over her daughter's life.

After returning home, Lilia rested on the edge of her bed, feeling proud about keeping up with her mom. As she sipped water, her thoughts shifted to Peter Tremblay. She had delayed calling him, wondering if a new day would alter her decision about turning solo, but nothing had changed. In fact, she felt more determined than ever to find success on her own.

She had Peter's number on speed dial but didn't want to rush the call, so she slowly scrolled through her phone's directory. Her throat tightened as she rehearsed her speech one last time, then pressed his number, halfway hoping to get voice mail. He answered right away.

"Lilia."

"Hello, Peter. Is this a good time to talk?"

"It depends."

Her mouth grew dry as she readied herself.

"What time does your plane land?"

His haughty tone rattled her, but she summoned her strength, knowing she had to push through the well-rehearsed words that would change her life.

"Lilia? I'm waiting."

"I won't be returning to Boston until January. My grandmother needs me here."

No response, no sound.

Lilia swallowed a few times. "And I'm not returning to the quartet. I've carefully considered my options, and I've decided to go solo."

No response.

"Peter?"

"You know what this means, right?" he finally spewed. "No one will want you after dropping out. I'll make sure of that. And you'll *never* succeed on your own. Trust me."

His words burned fear into her soul and made her feel like a nothing.

"Does Susanne support this ridiculous decision?" His voice shifted, becoming more condescending.

She gasped. How dare he play that card!

He laughed. "I bet you haven't even told her."

She struggled to control her temper.

"Too scared, aren't you?" he taunted. "You know she'll side with me."

Lilia had finally heard enough. She didn't care if she sounded angry. She blasted him. "It's *my* decision, not my mother's. And I'm not changing my mind. I'm sorry if you can't understand—"

"Grow up and face the real world, Lilia. You have no idea what it's like to—"

"No! *You* need to listen. I've given this a lot of—"

"Thought?" He finished her sentence, then chortled. "I do the thinking, not you. Your job is to—"

Lilia hung up. She ended his threats and contempt with the push of a red button. Peter called right back, but she ignored him. Days of one-way conversations with someone who had no respect for her had ended. She deleted his name from her phone book, then called Joel and told him everything. She wanted to say a proper goodbye before Peter bent his ear with half-truths and lies. She'd miss Joel, knowing he could never contact her again if he valued being in Peter's quartet.

She called her music tutor, Louis, and told him about the past week, highlighting her decision to fly as a solo artist. He offered to coach her extra days to prepare for competition, and she gratefully accepted.

Lilia tossed her phone on the bed, changed into a robe, and walked to the bathroom. She stepped into the shower and relished the hot water cascading over her body. Sweat, doubt, and dread disappeared down the drain as she emptied her mind of the past.

Afterward, she used her palm to wipe away steam from the mirror and studied her reflection. The person gazing back welcomed new challenges. She would make mistakes, but would learn and grow.

After dressing, she wandered into the kitchen and sat down at the table, sipping coffee and waiting for Matt to return from his run. Warmth filled her heart when he looked at Muriel's home before stepping inside his house. She forced herself to give him enough time to shower, and then scurried over to tell him about her morning.

After spending time together, Matt and Lilia returned to Muriel's home with a camera and a plan. Matt would photograph the three women, and then he and Lilia would select their favorite images to print and frame as early Christmas gifts for Susanne and Muriel.

Sunshine graced the day as Matt guided everyone

to Muriel's redwood deck. He staged the women with the lake in the background, then captured various formal poses. He encouraged them to relax and took many casual shots, trusting one standout image would emerge.

Matt returned home to sort through the images while Muriel, Susanne, and Lilia interviewed home care candidates. The first one spoke in a high-pitched voice that drove Muriel crazy, and she dismissed her halfway through the meeting. The second candidate looked at her phone repeatedly, told them she didn't do housework and used the word *like* so many times Susanne terminated the interview early. The final candidate looked promising until she informed them she couldn't work nights and needed every fourth Monday off for an undisclosed reason.

"What a waste of time." Muriel sighed.

"Don't worry, Gran. We'll find someone." Lilia encouraged. "We still have a whole bunch of qualified people on that list."

Susanne tapped a pencil on a sheet of paper. "Let's identify your top three must-haves for a worker, Mom. It'll help us narrow the search."

Muriel rested her chin on her palm, thinking. Finally, she spoke. "I'm feeling stronger each day and don't need someone with a medical background. What I need is help with bathing, washing my hair, laundry, grocery shopping and housekeeping. A good cook is a bonus. I'd like someone to drive me places such as doctor appointments." She crossed her arms. "And I don't want anyone hovering over me." She tapped her ear. "They need to listen and not treat me like an invalid."

Susanne rubbed her temple. "Do you think—"

A knock on the door interrupted the conversation, and Lilia answered it.

Robin stood holding a casserole dish. "I know you're busy with interviews, so I made lasagna for dinner."

"That was kind of you." Lilia opened the door wider and welcomed her in.

"Just stick it in the oven at three fifty for an hour." Robin set it on the kitchen counter. "I hope you enjoy the recipe."

Susanne, Muriel, and Lilia looked at one another and suddenly broke into big smiles.

"Robin, don't you clean Mom's house?" Susanne asked.

"Uh, yes, if she needs help."

"You shop for her and drive her around, right?"

"I'm happy to help out."

"Would giving her a bath scare you?"

Robin's eyes widened in surprise, but she slowly shook her head from side to side.

Susanne spoke to Muriel. "I think we just found your perfect candidate, Mom."

Muriel grinned, then pulled out a chair. "Robin, may we sit and talk for a few minutes?"

With a caretaker hired, Susanne pulled out a laptop to work before packing for her flight home. Lilia visited Matt at his house to review the photos while Muriel called Catherine.

A few minutes later, Catherine entered the house without knocking and found Muriel sitting in her living room admiring the Christmas tree.

"Such good news about Robin!" Catherine said. "Talk about a win-win!"

"Guess I took her for granted." Muriel shrugged. "I had no idea her only income comes from house cleaning jobs and occasional child support payments. She could sure use the cash." She pushed up from her chair. "Anyway, will you follow me? There's something I want to show you."

Catherine nodded and gave her a helping hand.

Muriel entered her bedroom and pointed toward a jeweled chest on the top shelf of her closet. "Will you please haul that thing down for me?"

Catherine set the chest on the bed as Muriel unlocked it and lifted its lid. She thumbed through a stash of pills they had collected over the past few years as part of their "death with dignity" plan.

"Since Ben's gone, I wanted to revisit our death pact." Muriel said.

"Our chest contains a lot of medications for just the two of us."

"Not for me, Cat. I've changed my mind."

Catherine looked at her with a quizzical expression and waited for an explanation.

Muriel picked up a container and shook it, turning the pill bottle into a maraca. "After what Lilia has done for me this past week, I could never hurt her by taking my life. I don't know how things will end, but I won't do anything to make my girl cry. I love her too much."

Catherine listened.

"I guess what I'm trying to say is I don't need the pills anymore."

"Are you sure, Muri? The chest seemed awfully important to you."

"I'm sure."

"Well then, would you like me to toss them?"

"Or keep 'em for yourself. Either way, they don't belong here anymore."

Catherine sorted through the bottles and examined the labels carefully. "We put a lot of thought into our little project "—she looked at Muriel with a knowing smile—"but I never believed we'd use them." She shut the lid and secured the latch. "I'll take the pills to my pharmacy. They'll dispose of them properly."

"You don't mind?"

"Of course not." Catherine clasped Muriel's hand. "This treasure chest represented choice, Muri. We're just making a different one now."

"What would I do without you?"

"You'll never find out."

The two friends shared a tender hug.

"Want to stay for dinner?" Muriel asked. "My new employee made lasagna. I hear she's a pretty good cook."

Catherine licked her lips. "I'll take the chest home and hurry back."

Muriel waved as Catherine walked away, then caught her reflection in a wall mirror. She barely recognized the old woman who returned her gaze. She closed her eyes and drifted back many years until a vibrant young woman with long flowing hair and a flawless complexion emerged.

The woman sat in a canoe holding a picnic basket containing roast beef sandwiches, two apples, and frosted brownies. Her handsome young beau paddled slowly across a lake toward an island on a lovely spring morning. He helped her ashore, then dragged the boat out of the water so it wouldn't drift away. They strolled hand in hand to a grove of Oregon myrtles where a spicy scent of bay filled the air. The tree's small yellow flowers created a romantic setting as they laid out a blanket to read poetry and enjoy a leisurely lunch.

After they had finished their meal, the man reached into his pocket and removed a small black box, got down on one knee and proposed. The woman agreed to be his wife without any hesitation, and he slid a diamond ring on the proper finger of her left hand. They embraced and made sweet, tender love under those myrtle trees, then talked for hours about their future together.

Muriel opened her eyes and smiled at her reflection, privately celebrating the wrinkles on her face. Each one captured a snapshot of a rich, full life, and she wouldn't erase a single one. She stepped outside onto the deck and closed her eyes as a cool breeze gusted past. She had made her peace and no longer feared that final curtain. She trusted Susanne and Lilia to care for her in ways that mattered as she lived out the rest of her days.

THIRTY-TWO

Oregon

Matt and Lilia huddled together at his house, viewing images from the photo shoot. Many good ones caught their eye, but two clear winners emerged. One was a formal pose, and the other showed three women of different generations, relaxed in one another's company. All wore playful expressions as Muriel stood in the middle with her arms tucked around Susanne's and Lilia's waists. Susanne's head dipped back in laughter while Lilia, wearing a carefree smile, rested her head against Muriel's shoulder.

"My mom rarely laughs. I can't believe you've captured it on camera." She reached over and kissed his cheek. "You're amazing."

"All three of you look great."

"Let's print and frame these two along with the others so Mom can take them home with her tonight."

Matt nodded and grabbed his keys.

Lilia continued to stare at the images for another minute, barely able to comprehend all the recent changes in her family. She knew her mother and grandmother loved her, but now felt more of an equal, one of three instead of a child who needed protecting. The insight filled her with all kinds of confidence.

After running errands, Lilia and Matt returned to Muriel's house and slipped three wrapped packages under the Christmas tree. They quietly hung a new picture on her photo wall and put new frames on the mantel before joining everyone in the dining room. Holiday music created a festive mood as the group gathered around the table, comfortably chit-chatting about this and that as they ate lasagna, salad and garlic bread. Lilia couldn't remember the last time she had felt so relaxed and happy.

Later, the group moseyed into the living room, and Lilia reached under the tree to extract the three gifts, handing one to her grandmother and two packages to her mom.

"Christmas is a couple of weeks away, but I'd like you to open these now."

Muriel needed no coaxing, happily ripping off the green paper. She held a framed photograph of three women standing together looking happy and relaxed. The image captured the essence of love without words. She pressed her hand over her heart, eyes watering.

"Gran? What's wrong?"

"What could possibly be wrong?" Muriel said sniffling. "I finally have a picture of me and both my girls." She couldn't stop staring at the photo. "Aren't we something else?"

Susanne gently rubbed Muriel's back to comfort

her while Catherine complimented Matthew on his keen eye for photography.

Lilia nudged Muriel toward the fireplace. "Mom and I have a surprise for you, Gran."

Earlier in the day, Lilia and Susanne had selected photographs from the family albums and had them re-printed and framed, changing the mantel's landscape. Stephen's military picture and silver medal remained on the shelf, but new images appeared.

As Muriel's scanned the display, her knees buckled and Lilia caught her arm.

"Whoa! You OK, Gran?"

"Oh, I'm more than OK." She moved closer to the mantel to get a better look.

"I loved that car." Susanne picked up a photograph of her and her father standing next to a red Mustang. "I remember when Daddy taught me to drive. He had such patience."

"Where'd you find that one?" Matt asked, pointing to a photo of him and Lilia sitting in a canoe.

"In a dusty album," Susanne said, smiling.

"How old were we?" Matt asked Lilia.

"I look about ten. That makes you what? Fourteen?"

"Boy, was I a skinny geek." Matt caught Susanne's eye and winked.

Muriel picked up a picture of her, Catherine, Ben and Esther playing bridge on an outdoor deck. "Who took this one?"

"I did." Lilia chuckled. "The image is a little out of focus, but I really liked it."

Muriel kissed her granddaughter's cheek. "It brings back so many wonderful memories, sweetheart. Thank you for framing it."

Lilia patted an empty space on the mantel. "The new family photo can go here. But you don't have to put it there. Maybe you'd like it in your bedroom or somewhere else."

Muriel studied the mantel for a few moments and began rearranging frames, placing her gift in the middle. She fretted over the layout until she achieved a balance that pleased her. She backed up to survey the result. "How's that?"

"I love the new look," Catherine said. "It's a snapshot of your life, Muri."

Lilia bounced from foot to foot. "I want to show you something else, Gran. Follow me." She motioned toward the hallway. "We had another picture framed." She stood in front of Muriel's photo wall. "This one's more formal, so we hung it here."

Muriel soaked in a picture of the Bennett women standing in front of the lake, arms wrapped around one another. "It's lovely, too. Thank you for doing this for me." Muriel hugged Lilia and Matt.

Susanne raised her gifts. "Shall I open mine now?"

Lilia nodded eagerly and touched the larger of the two. "Please open that one first."

Susanne carefully unwrapped the gift. She held two framed photos that duplicated Muriel's and hugged them to her chest. "I love 'em, Lil." She spoke to Matthew. "Thanks for capturing such wonderful images for us. And for printing them quickly so I could take them home tonight."

Matt tipped his head toward Lilia. "Her idea."

Susanne gently rubbed Lilia's back, then casually opened her second package. Upon seeing the framed photo, her chin dropped. She turned toward Lilia. "How…how did you…"

Lilia could hardly contain her excitement. "Gran and I loved hearing your Vietnam stories. Especially ones about Quang." She touched the photo and grinned. "I used your phone to forward that image to me when you weren't looking."

Susanne playfully tapped Lilia's nose with her finger, then focused on the photograph. Dave Simms had taken the image soon after the factory contract was signed, and he had emailed it to her as a reminder of the historic moment. Susanne stood next to Quang with a conservative business smile, and he wore his famous jack-o'-lantern grin. She towered next to him by five inches, but they were equals in things that mattered. The photograph brought back many memories.

Susanne hugged Lilia, not releasing her for a long time. "You truly surprised me with this one, Lil. You have no idea how much…"

"Gran and I are proud of you, Mom. You made that factory deal happen. It's a big accomplishment."

Catherine caught Matt's eye and motioned toward the door. "Matthew and I are leaving now so the three of you can say your goodbyes." Catherine hugged Susanne and whispered in her ear. "I'll keep an eye on your mom." She turned and spoke to Muriel and Lilia. "Let me know if you need anything."

Matt cleared his throat. "Congratulations on that contract, Ms. Bennett. Have a safe trip home." He nodded to Muriel, then mouthed "See you later" to Lilia before following Catherine out the door.

Susanne stared at her Vietnam photo, becoming lost in thought as she slumped on the couch. She had ridden an emotional roller coaster the past few weeks, finding unexpected twists and turns around every corner. Receiving the picture as a framed gift had truly surprised her, and she needed a minute to sort through her feelings and thoughts.

"Mom?" Lilia walked over and stood in front of her. "Are you all right?"

She gazed up, her eyes filled with a watery glow. "This'll sound so juvenile, but you've never acknowledged my work before." She dried her eyes. "Your gift means so much to me."

Lilia smiled warmly. "Just 'cause I don't say it, doesn't mean I don't think it." She sat down and rested her head against Susanne's shoulder. "I hope you continue sharing work stories with me. I like it."

Susanne embraced her daughter. "I can do that."

Muriel spoke to Susanne. "I know you need to leave soon, but may we sit together outside one more time? Just for a little while."

"Of course, Mom." Susanne stood and brought Lilia up with her, sliding an arm around her waist as Muriel led them to the redwood deck.

The Bennett women sat contentedly together in three chairs facing the lake to share their last moments together. The pine trees reflected in the water as a cool breeze repositioned clouds overhead. Muriel often found goodbyes difficult, but not today. Her family filled her heart in wondrous new ways, and no distance could alter the indelible love they shared with one another. She had discovered immense joy by embracing their differences, knowing invisible threads of forgiveness, honesty, and trust had created an indestructible bond between them. That connection provided enough strength to sustain her for whatever lay ahead.

Acknowledgments

Writing is a mostly solitary sport, but launching a novel into the world takes a team. It's time to formally thank the individuals who contributed to this creative journey. My deepest gratitude goes to my husband, Andy, for believing in me. He reads every scene and offers valuable feedback in encouraging ways. I never take his unwavering support for granted.

Mary introduced me to the poet, Rumi. His inspirational words shaped my thinking as I plotted this story. May her brother rest in peace, and be further remembered by the publishing of this novel.

Gary helped breathe life into Lilia's character by helping me understand the unique characteristics and challenges of a gifted child. I'll always treasure our evening discussions on the backyard deck of his & Janet's beautiful home in Washington.

Kay has my gratitude for introducing me to her friend, Kathy, who opened my eyes to the everyday world of professional musicians. Since my knowledge of music is miniscule, I couldn't have created Lilia's world without her unique perspective.

Without knowing it, Virginia gave me one of Muriel's best lines while driving us home from Filoli. You keep talking and I'll keep listening. Deal?

Thanks to Margie for describing her pneumothorax experience so I could impose the condition on dear, unsuspecting Muriel. I gave that character some of Margie's feistiness, too.

Jan influenced Muriel's character in subtle ways. I'm in awe of her courage and positive attitude in the face of adversity. Her smile brightens a room.

I am grateful to Christy P. for mailing the lyrics of Tom Hunter's song "Lines on your face" to me. Tom's words helped define Muriel, especially the mirror reflection scene at the end. I'm so glad we met in Sedona and shared a table at Garlands. Lucky me.

Adam helped me think like a guy. Without knowing it, he served as inspiration for Matt's character in several ways. I especially appreciated his one-liner. The phrase was perfect.

Thanks to Nhut for helping me create the character, Quang. If anyone wants to tour Vietnam, let me know. I have your guide.

What would I ever do without, Debbi? Having a best friend who is a teacher and an avid reader to review and improve the manuscript is manna from heaven. She hosts entertaining book signing parties, too. I can't wait until she and I go on another adventure together. She inspires my imagination by taking me to places I normally wouldn't visit.

I'm grateful to Shawn for her friendship, and for being an early reader. She painted my manuscript red, helping to make the final product so much better. Her long list of insights and observations guided my rewrite in a major way, and she contributed to the back cover. She's a talented woman who steered me through some dark and stormy waters.

Thanks to Sandra for being an early reader. Her editorial insight—especially surrounding the plot—made a difference. I appreciated her fact checking skills.

My daughters, Kimberly and Kristy, found time in their busy schedules to critique the manuscript. They never hold back from their momma.

A novel requires an enticing cover, and the following people helped bring this one to life. Debora is a gifted artist.

She somehow managed to extract an image from my mind and turn it into an exquisite watercolor that perfectly captured the spirit of this story. Dave scanned the painting for Rita so she could shape it into the cover. Thanks to Tom and Nancy for inviting me to their Florence, Oregon vacation home, which became the setting for Muriel's residence. Rob's and Cyndi's east coast lake pictures shaped the art in surprising ways.

Last but not least, thanks to Carol for her excellent structure, editing, and formatting expertise once again. She always keeps me honest and pushes me to do better (Susanne thanks her immensely). She is a fabulous literary partner, and I hope we continue to put many books out into the world together.

With my acknowledgments now expressed, please know that any shortcomings in this novel are entirely mine.

Author's Note

Thanks for reading *The Bennett Women*. Will you please take a few minutes to review the novel on Amazon and/or Goodreads? Your word-of-mouth referrals are very much appreciated.

If you're curious about how Matt and Lilia's relationship evolves, you'll love my next novel, *The Things We Don't Say*, winner of an indieBRAG award. Kirkus Reviews calls it *"A poignant romance that explores the complexities of a long-distance relationship."*

To learn more, visit www.robertacarr.com.

Available on Amazon

www.ingramcontent.com/pod-product-compliance
Lightning Source LLC
Chambersburg PA
CBHW032148190626
46814CB00005BA/1895